Blood of Heroes

The Ember War Saga Book 3

Richard Fox

For Gordon

ISBN: 1522713247
ISBN-13: 978-1522713241

CHAPTER 1

Captain Isaac Valdar squinted against the blinding light pouring into his bridge. His ship, the *Breitenfeld*, bucked beneath his command chair and slammed him against his restraints. He'd expected—and been promised—a smooth jump, but his ship's engines had never functioned as advertised.

"Engine room! What is going on?" Valdar shouted. White light bore through his helmet's visor and seared his shut eyes. His temples throbbed with each pounding heartbeat as updates flooded into his helmet from his equally overwhelmed bridge crew.

"We're stuck in the wormhole, sir!" Ensign

Geller's voice thundered in his ears as the young officer screamed his answer. "Let me answer your next question. There's no way I can shut it off."

An electrical conduit above Valdar's head burst open in a hail of sparks, the shorn wiring flopping against the ceiling like a wounded snake.

"I want a solution, not an excuse, Ensign Geller," Valdar said. "Something tells me we're on borrowed time."

"Captain," Commander Ericcson, the ship's executive officer, slapped her palm against a display. The flood of light from the tortured space beyond the bridge's view ports nearly washed out the display's wire diagram of the *Breitenfeld,* lit up with red damage reports, with more alerts coming in by the second. "Captain, we're being twisted apart. We've got hull breaches on seven decks and…"

The blinding light faded away and the tremors racking the ship subsided. Valdar turned his head away from his XO as a deep gray field materialized beyond the ship. The very substance of space-time fizzled around the ship and Valdar felt his body grow heavier and heavier, as if he was accelerating through a high-g maneuver in a fighter.

"Are we back at Bastion?" Valdar asked. The hosts at their last jump point had kept his ship in a null zone during their visit to ensure they could never give away the location of the Alliance's headquarters by accident or intent.

"The wormhole is nearly dissipated," Geller said. The young deck officer's breaths were labored, like a great weight was on his chest. "Readings are coming in … That can't be right."

Rain lashed against the bridge's windows and a bolt of lightning struck the rail cannon battery at the prow of the ship.

"We're in an atmosphere," Valdar said. Blood drained from his face as he realized he had very little time—and even less of a chance—to save his ship.

"Engineering, all ahead full! XO, cut the grav plating. We're getting pulled by this planet and the ship," Valdar said. He grunted as he raised his overly heavy arm and let it slam against a control

3

panel on his command chair, shattering the glass over the ABANDON SHIP alarm.

"Geller! Figure out which way is up and point us that way," Valdar said.

A deafening roar like the first rumble of an exploding volcano broke through the ship as the engines kicked to life. Valdar's ship was meant for the void, a realm without sound. Hearing his ship fight for her life brought a slight smile to Valdar's face. The enormous pressure against his body faded away as the ship's gravity plating stopped pulling double-duty.

In his tinny voice, Lafayette, the cyborg Karigole alien working alongside his crew in the engineering room, said, "Captain, I shunted power from the jump drive into the grav plating and reversed the graviton polarity for effective buoyancy in—"

"The plating isn't designed to maneuver the entire ship! It'll break from the deck and …" Images of blades of grav plating whirling through his ship like the business end of a blender came to his mind.

"That's what I told him!" said Lieutenant Commander Levin, the ship's lead engineer.

"And if either of you would have let me finish, I would have explained the very simple physics between the gravitational harmonic resonances between—"

Valdar cut Lafayette off with a push of a button and snapped his head around to look at his XO.

Ericcson shrugged her shoulders. "The ship's holding together."

The clouds enveloping the ship thinned, melting away to reveal a pale blue sky.

"Skipper," Geller said, "so long as we're free from the gravity well—and not flying straight into the ground—I can get us into a stable orbit."

"This is the … third time my ship's engines have done something they're not supposed to," Valdar said. "Are we even in the right system?" The Ibarra Corporation retrofitted the ship with a supposed Alcubierre drive meant to take the ship from Earth to Saturn in a few short weeks. When activated, the engines formed a time-dilation bubble around the *Breitenfeld* that removed it—and the rest of the Saturn colonial fleet—from the passage of time for thirty years. After the ship's mission to the dead planet of Anthalas was complete, an AI hidden in the new jump engines sent the ship to the world of Bastion instead of Earth, without the knowledge or consent of Valdar and his crew.

"I won't know until we can do a pulsar triangulation," Geller said.

"Comms," Valdar looked to the platinum-blond lieutenant strapped into his work pod, "the Dotok know we're coming. Anything on the hailing frequencies their ambassador gave us?"

"Scanning, sir," he said.

"XO, damage report," Valdar said. The blue sky ahead of them darkened and pinpricks of starlight materialized in the deepening hue of open space.

"Minor damage to the outer hull. Flak emplacements two and nine report a break in their ammo feeder lines. Deck officers say they can have them operational in another ten minutes. The jump engine is offline while it recharges," she said.

"Captain," said Utrecht, the ship's gunnery officer, as he placed green pins onto his plot board, "turret spotters reporting explosions and weapons fire directly above us."

"Get me a visual," Valdar said. He flipped a screen up from the side of his command chair and mashed a gloved finger along the frame to turn it on.

"I found a live frequency," the comms officer said.

"Good, everything all at once," Valdar muttered. "Open it," he ordered.

"Clin mar the'ki! Clin aouran thal!" came a hoarse, panicked voice.

Grainy footage of a distant Dotok ship, a carrier with angular sides and a light beige hull, popped onto Valdar's screen. The carrier's point defense turrets fired at dark shapes swirling around the ship. A lance of yellow light sliced across the side of the ship, leaving a trail of fire and gouts of atmosphere. Xaros drones and snub-nosed fighters swirled around the Dotok ship in a dogfight bigger than anything Valdar had seen since the assault on the Crucible orbiting Ceres.

Valdar rewound the feed and zoomed in on the source of the laser, a Xaros drone, the stalks on its body of shifting metal brought to an apex glowing with power. A Dotok gun crew found its mark and blew the drone to pieces, the hunks disintegrating away.

"Definitely in the right place," Valdar said. He keyed open a channel to the flight deck. "Gall," he said to the *Breitenfeld's* wing commander, Marie Durand, using her call sign, "get everything you can into the sky. The fight started without us."

"I thought the Xaros were supposed to be on the outer edge of the system," Durand said, the whine of her Eagle's engines bleeding through the open channel. "Do you have positive contact with the Dotok? If they don't know we're coming, we may have a fratricide issue and I don't know how to say, 'God damn it don't shoot me,' in their language."

"We're working that out," Valdar said.

"The only channel I have with the Dotok is nothing but chaos, sir," the communications officer said. "I don't understand what they're saying. But from all the screaming … it doesn't sound good."

"Gall," Valdar said, "get up there and start killing drones. They'll figure out what side we're on pretty quick."

Durand grumbled and closed the channel.

"Open a channel to the Dotok," Valdar said. A chime sounded in his helmet and the comms officer stuck her thumb in the air. "Dotok fleet, this is Captain Isaac Valdar of the Atlantic Union ship *Breitenfeld*. We are launching fighters to assist. I also brought some pretty damn big guns to this party. Where should I point them?"

A hiss of static answered him.

"Sir," Utrecht said, "we've got a sky full of unknown contacts. Check your screen."

A live feed from his forward rail gun battery

showed a half-dozen ships of Dotok construction, each twice the size of the *Breitenfeld*. Dark lines of basalt ran along the hulls as golden flecks of light glittered from within the dark vise. Each of the ships disgorged life pods, trails of fire tracing back from hundreds of pods falling toward the planet Takeni.

"They're abandoning ship?" XO asked.

"You don't punch out of a battle you're winning," Valdar said.

"Being...*Breitenfeld?*" came over the Dotok channel.

"Yes, this is Captain Valdar of the *Breitenfeld*. Is this Admiral Yon'kai?" Valdar asked. Valdar's screen snapped to a Dotok man, his string-thick silver hair pulled into a top knot, the right half of his face stained with dried blood. The flame-blackened bulkhead and swaying ceiling panels filled the background of the video.

"Help," the Dotok struggled to say. An explosion on the alien's ship rattled the feed, and lines of static broke across the screen as the Dotok yelled commands Valdar couldn't understand. "*Breitenfeld*...here?"

"That's right, son. We're here to help," Valdar said.

The video cut out before the Dotok could respond.

"I'll get him back," the comms officer said.

"Bogies inbound," Utrecht said. "Six drones just broke off from the Dotok ship and are on an intercept course with us."

"Six? I'm insulted," Valdar said. "Work up a firing solution for the compromised ships. Let's show them we mean business."

"Aye-aye, skipper," Utrecht said with a grin.

****

Durand took a deep breath then squeezed every muscle between her knees and her neck as her fighter shot over of the *Breitenfeld's* flight deck, accelerated to attack speed by a magnetically driven catapult. The g-forces grayed out her vision despite her attempts to keep enough blood in her head where she needed it to stop from passing out.

Her Eagle spat out of the ship, the blur of the flight deck replaced by the haze of Takeni's last bit of atmosphere. A dusty, mountainous world spread out beneath her.

"Everyone, call out once you're clear of the ship and come to two-seven mark zero-nine. Form up on my wing," she sent to her fighter squadron, a dozen more Eagles hot on her heels.

"Any idea who or what we're fighting? Or is that too much to ask?" Mei Ma asked over the IR net.

"Dotok tech is on par with ours, Glue," Durand said. "If it looks like a Xaros drone, shoot it."

"Simple. I like it," Ma said.

Durand pulled her fighter up and toward the raging battle. The rest of her squadron, eleven Eagles flown by pilots with several drone kills to their credit, formed into two six-plane echelons, Durand at the lead of one, Mei Ma the other. The pilot from the former Chinese People's Liberation

Space Navy had proven to be a capable and excellent pilot, despite her earlier attempts to kill Durand back when Earth still had nation-states.

Sunlight reflected off the approaching Xaros, their stalk tips already glowing with deadly power. Durand flicked the safety cover off her control stick and felt her Eagle shudder as the Gatling cannon swung out from its weapons bay and spun to life. She fed power to her thrusters, adrenaline sending her nerves on fire as the enemy approached.

"All right, boys and girls, standard jab-cross engagement just like we've trained," Durand said to her squadron. "Glue, Blue flight, engage at long range. Try to tag any you can. Red flight, with me. We're going to knock these bastards into pieces. I wish you all shit."

"Roger, Gall," Ma said. "Save some for me."

The Xaros drones maneuvered around each other, writhing like a scrum of snakes as they dove toward the human fighters. Durand felt a tinge of fear caress her heart as they neared. Drones always held an evenly spaced formation when attacking; they weren't capable of adaptation and new tactics.

"No promises, Glue." She kept steel in her voice, the time for doubt long past. Violence of action would have to overcome whatever the Xaros had planned. "Stagger and engage on my mark...Mark!"

Durand and her half of the squadron punched their anti-grav thrusters and popped above Ma's Eagles, clearing the line of fire, and accelerated. Ma's fighters opened up with their Gatling cannons, spraying hypervelocity bullets toward the approaching scrum of drones. The drones flew apart like shrapnel from an exploding grenade and lurched toward Durand and the fighters on her wing.

Durand had a heartbeat to fire off a burst before a drone shot over her cockpit, hook-tipped stalks reaching for her. She punched the maneuver thrusters on the tail of her fighter and sent her ship into a flip. She squeezed the trigger before she could see her target, tracing a wide arc of shots as she came around. Her rounds found the drone as its stalks gleamed with ruby light.

Shells tore off the drone's stalks and smashed into the back of its body, sending it tumbling through space like a flipped coin. Durand lined up a burst and blew it to pieces.

"Splash one!" she announced.

"Is it me, or are they faster than usual?" Kyle, a new transfer to her squadron, asked.

"Got one on me!" came over the IR, the voice reedy with fear.

Durand's comms flooded with terse warnings and announcements. She craned her neck around, looking for her next target or a fighter in distress. Ruby beams snapped through space and a fireball erupted.

Durand cursed and accelerated toward the explosion.

"Kyle gone, no ejection seat," Hornsby said. Durand saw his fighter closing on the drone that had killed Kyle. Durand arced her fighter toward the drone, waiting for the range to engage.

The drone's stalks shifted to its rear as it jinked around Hornsby's shots. The stalks converged to two points, both gleaming with energy.

"Hornsby, break off!"

"I've got him." His voice shook in tune with his firing cannon.

"I said—"

The pursued drone fired twin energy beams. Hornsby banked his fighter and dodged the first beam, but the second cut straight through his cockpit.

Hatred flared through Durand as she fired her cannon. Rounds fanned through space and knocked a chunk out of the drone. She sped straight for her target and put a burst dead center, blowing it into neat halves that burnt away within seconds.

"Nag, Glue, status," Durand said to her remaining pilots. She risked a glance at her display panel and saw a red X crossed through a pilot in Ma's flight. Cittern, he'd been with Durand since the first day she'd set foot aboard the *Breitenfeld*.

"I'm fine," Glue said. "Filly took a shot through her canopy. Her commo's down but she isn't hurt."

"Gall, this is Glue. Last of the drones are destroyed. We need search and rescue for Hornsby?"

Durand brought her fighter parallel to Hornsby's Eagle as it tumbled through space. There was a gash through his cockpit, and all that remained of Hornsby was an empty flight suit, rent from shoulder to waist and dark within. Xaros disintegration beams annihilated flesh, leaving nothing but a red mist when they connected with anything alive.

"Negative, Glue. Mark his ship for recovery once this fight is over," Durand said.

"Gall, this is *Breitenfeld* actual." Valdar's priority transmission cut off Ma's response.

"This is Gall. Six Xaros drones destroyed," she said.

"Gall, we're in contact with the Dotok ship.

You need to target the escape pods from the compromised Dotok ships," Valdar said.

"You want me to *what*?" Escape pods and life boats were sacrosanct, never to be fired upon. Even in the darkest days of the Second Pacific War and the decades of skirmishes that followed, neither the Chinese nor the Atlantic Union had ever knowingly attacked a life pod adrift in the void or sea.

"You heard me. There are three inbound to the *Breitenfeld*. Those are your priority targets. Valdar out."

Durand shook her head and caught sight of three escape pods burning through the atmosphere toward her ship. She glanced up at the friendly Dotok ship, still in a life-and-death struggle with attacking drones.

"Glue, you get that?" Durand asked.

"I monitored."

"Get your flight to the Dotok ship and lend them a hand. When that ship is in the clear, take out any escape pods within range. Glue, signal to Filly to follow you. We need to get her back to the *Breit* anyway. Let's go."

As Durand dove toward the *Breitenfeld*, she glanced over her shoulder and saw Glue and Nag following. She turned back to her ship and did a double take. On her starboard side the sky was alight with escape pods burning through the atmosphere like flaming comets. There must have been hundreds already within the planet's atmosphere, converging on a deep, jagged canyon that cut across the surface like Valles Marineris on Mars.

"There's so many," Ma said. "There's no way we can reach them by the time they've made landfall."

"Worry about what we can see, touch and kill, Glue," Durand said. The three pods streaking toward the *Breitenfeld* descended in a line, one already dangerously close to the ship. Glowing tracer rounds from the *Breitenfeld*'s point defense batteries rose toward the nearest pod.

Durand gunned her engines and accelerated

toward the trailing pod.

"*Breitenfeld*, cease fire on point defense. Those bullets become real indiscriminate once they leave the barrel," Durand said. She trained her Gatling cannon on the pod, a bare gunmetal teardrop shape, its heat shield already glowing from friction with the thin atmosphere. She had the shot—it was a sitting duck compared to the Xaros drones—but she hesitated.

"Please let this be the right thing to do. *Gott mit uns.*" She pulled the trigger and the escape pod tumbled like a bird killed mid-flight. Durand shot past the target, a tear in her eye. She found the next pod … and saw the *Breitenfeld's* massive rail cannons slew up.

"Brace!" Durand's warning went out a split second before the strike carrier's main batteries blasted shells past her. Even in the wisp-thin atmosphere, the crack of the shells shattering the sound barrier and the turbulence from the shells' passage assaulted Durand like she was in the heart of a thunderstorm.

She shook her head to try and clear a tinnitus whine from her ears and pulled her fighter out of a spin.

"A little warning next time, *Breitenfeld*?" Durand sent over the open channel. She saw the closest escape pod, its retro-thrusters flaring like miniature suns as it neared the ship. "One of the pods is … landing? *Breit,* a pod is landing on the upper hull between the rail batteries. I don't think we can reach it in time."

"I can get it," Choi Ma, call sign Nag, said. "You get the other one." Glue's Eagle broke off and made a beeline for the *Breitenfeld.*

"Got it," Durand rolled her fighter until she found the other pod. She banked away and set an intercept course. She twisted around and saw Glue taking careful shots at her target. Her cannon shells peppered the pod while the missed shots continued on and struck against the *Breitenfeld's* hull.

"Try not shooting our own ship, Glue. That sound reasonable?" Durand asked.

Glue answered in Chinese, her tone full of

frustration as she overtook the pod and roared past the ship's bridge. The damaged pod wobbled as the retro-thrusters cut out and it fell into gravity's clutch. The pod slammed into the ship and embedded within the hull.

Durand winced and turned her attention back to the last pod. She powered up the rail gun that ran the length of her fighter and angled her shot to avoid the *Breitenfeld.* The rail gun robbed her of momentum and as it fired, it thrust her against her restraints. The rail shot blew the pod out of the sky. She skirted the edge of the burning debris field and brought her fighter back toward the ship.

"*Breitenfeld,* you going to tell me why it's so important to destroy these life pods?" Durand asked.

A shadow crossed over her cockpit. She looked up and saw a dark shape falling toward her. It slammed against her fighter and then tumbled toward the planet like a sailor with a ball and chain sinking into the ocean.

Claws raked against her canopy, leaving

deep cuts as they tore across. A face straight from her nightmares leered at her. Abyss-black armor plates protruded from pasty white flesh, and bright yellow eyes trembled with rage as the thing opened its mouth. Fangs and black tongue gave way to a banshee's scream.

It jammed its claws into her canopy and pulled a clenched fist over its head. Sunlight glinted off smooth armor plates as its scream continued.

Durand slammed her fighter into a barrel roll. The creature held on for two complete rolls before it lost its grip and centrifugal force flung it away. The planet and space spun around as she fought out of her spin. She managed to right her ship and pulled up toward the void.

Her breath came in short, terrified gasps as her heart pounded in her ears.

"*Breit—Breitenfeld*, I don't know what that was. But I think they're on our ship."

CHAPTER 2

Lieutenant Ken Hale charged down the passageway. As a Marine, he was normally pretty easy to distinguish amongst the ship's complement. His armored bulk and the gauss rifle in his hands set him apart from the ship's naval ratings in their void suits as he ran past them. That he was running *toward* whatever the sailors were running *from* marked him out as part of the ship's defense force. He ran just ahead of the rest of the Marines, marking him out as their leader.

Sailors pressed against the bulkheads to make way for the Marines. A sailor stumbled around a corner, her left arm missing from the elbow down, blood gushing out with each heartbeat.

Hale raised his rifle and sidestepped the corner. He knelt against the bulkhead and pulled the stumbling sailor to the deck.

"Yarrow, stabilize her," Hale said.

"On it, sir." The medic knelt beside the sailor, pulled tubes from a thick gauntlet on his left forearm and jabbed them into ports on the sailor's neck armor. The sailor mumbled and tried to squirm away from Yarrow, a spray of blood staining Hale's armor. The medic unceremoniously set a knee against her sternum and held her flat. He whipped a cone-shaped bandage from a pack on the small of his back and pressed it against her bleeding stump. The bandage tightened around the wound, darkening as it filled with blood.

"Hush, sailor. You're getting the good stuff," Yarrow said.

Sergeant Torni stabbed a knife hand at a pair of unharmed sailors watching the ordeal. "You and you! Take her to med bay!" she barked.

The sailors nodded emphatically and carried

the wounded sailor away.

A banshee's scream echoed through the passageway.

"I guess we're going that way, aren't we?" Standish said. The Marine squeezed his rifle butt against his shoulder and crouched slightly.

"Correct. The better question is why we're still standing here," said Steuben, the alien Karigole advisor, from the back of the squad of Marines.

"The XO said something about an update," Hale said, "but I'm not getting anything from her now."

A thunderclap rocked the ship and the deck lurched beneath their feet.

"That was the forward rail battery," Orozco said. The gauss carbine in his enormous hands looked like a toy compared to the heavy cannon he normally carried. Firing projectile weapons was dangerous enough on the ship, and given the weight of firepower his preferred weapon carried, it would have been more dangerous to the crew and ship than any enemy they encountered. "Why didn't the other battery fire?"

Another high-pitched scream echoed down the passageway.

"You get three guesses, and the first two don't count," Bailey said, emphasizing her words with a snap of chewing gum. The squad's sniper had traded her normal weapon in for a carbine that she held against her chest.

"We're going to the rail battery one. Follow me," Hale said. He stood and ran down the passageway.

Natural light streamed through ragged gaps in the hull over their heads. Hale felt the chill of freezing air creep into his suit. He knew he should've stopped and set his armor for void combat to compensate for the thin atmosphere, but that would take time that he—and the *Breitenfeld*—didn't have.

A sailor ran around a corner at a T-junction and tripped himself up as he tried to change directions. He slammed against the bulkhead and looked down the passageway he'd come from.

"No! No!" The sailor raised his hands in front of his face. Something flew through the air and slammed into the sailor, crushing him with the snap of bone and armor.

Hale skidded to a stop and raised his rifle. The dead sailor was entwined with … another sailor, both bloody and broken. The deck vibrated against his feet as heavy footsteps pounded down the passageway.

"Ready a Q-round," Hale said. The quadrium rounds could disable the Xaros drones for a few precious seconds, enough to get close and finish them off. Hale heard Standish power up his gauss rifle and load one of the precious munitions into his weapon. "Steuben, hammer?"

"I have it." The Karigole pulled a handle with a thick cylinder attached to the end, a pneumatic bolt that could crack the Xaros drones and destroy them.

"If you have to use a high-powered shot, go single—"

The pace of heavy footsteps increased and

what came around the corner wasn't a Xaros drone. A hunched-over, armored behemoth with gangly arms that ended in sharp claws tinged red with blood swung toward the Marines. Its arms swept wide, gouging the bulkhead. Its face, an armored wedge with two slits for yellow eyes and exposed flesh around its mouth embedded atop a bull neck, leered at the Marines. Its jaw distended and it shrieked loud enough to activate the sound dampers in Hale's helmet.

"Standish," Hale said.

Standish fired his Q-round with a flash of silver from his muzzle. The round thumped into the creature's chest and electricity arced from the impact. The monster took a step back and thrashed its arms against its body. Its claws pried the Q-round from its chest and hurled it against the deck. It looked at Standish and growled.

"At least I managed to piss it off," Standish said.

The monster charged, looping strides that would reach the Marines in seconds. Hale switched his rifle to SHOT and sent a burst of pellets the size of marbles into the monster. The rounds hit and stopped it dead in its tracks. Gauss fire from the rest of his Marines punctured its armor, splattering gray blood against the deck and bulkhead. It fell to its knees and reached for Hale, the arm stretched out, the claws scything toward Hale's face.

A strong hand grabbed the carry handle on the back of Hale's armor and jerked him back, the claw tips missing his visor by a hairsbreadth. Hale felt his feet leave the deck as Steuben tossed him back like a rag doll. The Karigole stepped forward and swung his hammer into the monster's forehead.

The pneumatic bolt cracked the skull and drove a six-inch spike into whatever brain matter lay beneath the obsidian armor. The monster collapsed against the deck, its limbs twitching.

"This works just fine," Steuben said. He wrenched the spike free and tapped the hammer against his thigh to knock away clinging viscera.

Hale scrambled to his feet and aimed his weapon at the fallen creature.

"What the hell is it? Some new kind of Xaros?" Bailey asked.

"It isn't disintegrating." Torni kicked the creature's arm, her armored boot clanging against the armored limb.

"Howled like a damn banshee," Orozco said. "Low-power shots didn't do much to stop it. We go high power and that should take them down faster."

"We miss with a high-power shot and the round will go through three decks before it stops," Hale said. "Shoot those banshee things in the face until they stop moving. That work for everyone?"

"Sir, you're my kind of Marine," Bailey said.

Another banshee howl set Hale's nerves on edge. "That's coming from the rail battery," Hale said. He opened a channel to the bridge as they ran down the corridor.

"XO, this is Hale. The boarders are not Xaros. I repeat, *not* Xaros. Q-rounds are ineffective but they will go down to massed fire. Pass that on to the other defense teams," Hale said.

"Hale, we need you in rail battery one ASAP. We need that gun back in the fight and we've lost communications with them," Ericcson said through his helmet's IR.

"Almost there. What about video? Can you see what's in there?" Hale asked. He stopped at a corner and glanced down the passageway leading to the main entrance of the battery. The double doors were shut, warning lights spinning above the frame. Blood stained the manual locking handles on each door.

"Video is down too," Ericcson said.

Hale looked at the entrance controls embedded in the bulkhead as smoke wafted up from the panel and the reek of ozone mixed with the iron tang of spilled blood.

"Torni, can you bypass the damage?" Hale asked his head enlisted Marine. Once the squad's tech expert, she'd stepped up to fill Gunnery Cortaro's position after he'd lost a leg on Anthalas.

Torni flipped a panel up and shook her head at the mess of burnt-out circuits. "No chance.

Someone fragged the whole system, sir. Looks like we either blow down the doors or open it the slow and painful way," she said, nodding toward the dogs, the circular handle in the middle of each door. She looked up at the thin strip of lighting where the ceiling met the doors; the strip flickered twice every few seconds. "Extra slow, something tripped the emergency locks."

"Blow the doors in," Hale said.

"That'll kill whoever's still in there," Orozco said.

"Orozco, Steuben, on the doors. Our suits should be strong enough to overpower the locks. Open them just enough to get us in," Hale said. He stepped back, took a knee and readied his weapon. The Marine and the Karigole grabbed the dogs and twisted, the pseudo-muscles built into their armor laboring against the emergency brakes.

The doors cracked open slowly, revealing darkness within the rail gun battery. Twenty sailors manned the cannons, but the space beyond was silent. Hale switched on his infrared filter to look through the six-inch and widening gap and saw a pair of sailors lying on the deck in pools of blood.

"Frag it?" Bailey asked. She slipped a grenade off her armor and hooked a finger around the pin.

"Not yet, there might be—stop!" A blood-caked gloved hand slid into view at the edge of the doors.

"I've got him." Yarrow stepped forward and reached for the hand, just as a clawed hand snapped out of the darkness and clamped onto Yarrow's shoulder. The banshee snatched Yarrow off his feet and pulled him to the door. Yarrow managed to get his hands up and slammed them against the doorframe, his augmented strength barely able to match the banshee.

The banshee's face thumped against the opening, teeth snapping at Yarrow.

"Shoot it! Shoot it!" Yarrow screamed.

Hale felt like his feet were stuck in wet concrete as he struggled forward. He brought his rifle up, but Yarrow's body blocked his shot.

Trembling with exertion, Yarrow was losing the battle against the monster's grip, its claws digging into his armor.

With one hand, Steuben reached out and slapped Yarrow's right arm from the door. With the other, the Karigole brought his short sword down and hacked into the banshee's wrist. The blade embedded with a wet *thunk*. The banshee's howl changed and it let Yarrow go. The banshee jerked its hand back and the blade went with it. The hilt and flat of the weapon slammed into the sides of the open door, jamming the banshee's hand in the opening. The arm reached toward the Marines and slammed back against the door, like a wolf struggling against a trap.

The third strike broke the blade. Pieces clattered to the deck as the banshee's footfalls echoed away from the door, its screams fading away.

Yarrow rolled onto his hands and knees and scrambled away from the open door.

"Anyone else not like these things?"

Standish asked.

"Where'd it go?" Torni asked.

Orozco stuck his carbine into the opening. "Looks like it went down the ammo elevator…blood trail goes that way at least." The Spaniard beamed the footage from the camera on his carbine to Hale.

"Get the doors open enough for us to get through," Hale said. "It went to the armory and we have to go after it." He flipped open the control panel on his gauntlet and sent commands to seal the armory.

"Can we bring in some backup?" Standish asked. "Maybe Elias and his armored super-friends? Bet they'd *love* something like this."

"They're all in their travel coffins. By the time they get here it'll be too late. What's in armory bay three, Standish?" Hale asked.

"A bunch of inert kinetic rounds for the rail cannons … and that giant omnium reactor we found on Anthalas." Standish ran over to the dogs and helped Orozco twist it open. The doors lurched open another few inches and Hale saw the elevator platform to the armory, the plating ripped aside like it was made of tissue paper. He tried to open a channel to the XO, which stayed open for a second before cutting out.

Yarrow grabbed the dog Steuben was on. The medic glanced at the broken blade and then at Steuben, he alien's mouth twisted in a snarl as he worked.

"Hey, thanks for saving me and not cutting my arm off to do it," Yarrow said.

Steuben grunted and managed to move the door another half inch.

"You are welcome, young one," Steuben said. "I believe Gunnery Sergeant Cortaro is still angry over the loss of his leg, or suffering some manner of post-traumatic stress. Corpsman Yarrow, what is a *pendejo*?"

"Ugh," Yarrow said. "Sorry about your sword."

"Lafayette will fix it," Steuben muttered.

"We're good," Bailey announced and

squeezed through the opening. Orozco shook his head at the slight woman, and the barrel-chested Marine opened the doors wider.

Bailey peeked down the exposed shaft. "Blood trail goes all the way down," she said to Hale.

Hale joined her at the edge. The twenty-foot descent ended on the armory deck. Gray smears of blood against the exposed machinery of the lift.

"Damn thing's like a croc," she said, "and we've got it wounded and cornered."

"Sir," Torni said, "you see this?" Hale turned around and found Torni poking through the door control panel. A half-dozen mutilated crewmen lay dead along the bulkhead near her. Torni knelt next to a dark skinned crewman and opened his hand, revealing a circuit board.

"That's Master Chief Hutchinson," Torni said. "He must have tripped the emergency locks. Trapped that thing in here."

"That was a good idea, how?" Standish asked.

Torni reached up and closed the dead sailor's eyes. "It must have got in before they could secure the doors. The gunnery team were as good as dead. He locked himself in with it to keep it from going anywhere else."

"We'll give him the respect he's earned once this thing's dead," Hale said. "When we're down there, don't shoot the omnium reactor." Hale emphasized the last words.

"Knew we should have kept that thing on the flight deck," Bailey said. "But MacDougall and Lafayette's precious little toy just had to go someplace designed to withstand a battle."

"Flash bangs now, complaining later," Hale said. "Combat circle the whole way down, call it out when you see the target." The lieutenant took a flash-bang grenade from his belt, designed to overwhelm an enemy with enough noise and light to shatter human eardrums and temporarily blind whoever was unfortunate enough to get a good look at the explosion. Hale pulled the pin and tossed it down the shaft; his four Marines followed suit.

Hale turned away and tucked his face into the crook of his arm. The deck rumbled as a ripple of nonlethal explosions boomed. He stepped into the opening the banshee made and fell. The walls blurred past as he worked the anti-grav linings along the soles of his boots to keep his descent under control. The linings flared as he neared the deck, but he still hit hard enough to jar his bones from his feet to his skull.

Marines and Steuben landed in a circle, their weapons humming with energy. The flash bangs had scorched the ground around them, and there was no sign of the banshee.

Hale looked around and saw pallets of gauss ammunition for rifles and every caliber of weapon on the ship. Large containers for the three foot long rail cannon munitions took up nearly half the armory and were evenly spaced like trees in an orchard. The containers were taller than Steuben, and the banshee.

Against the far bulkhead, a purpose-built container housed the omnium reactor.

"I don't see it," Torni said.

"Negative here," Orozco said.

"Who wants to go wandering around the maze of ammo cans?" Standish asked. "Hey Mr. Monster…come out and play."

Steuben slid his helmet's visor up to the top of his head and breathed deeply. "I smell it," he said. He pointed his rifle toward the reactor.

"Keep a 360. Don't let it sneak up on us," Hale said.

Steuben led them through the forest of containers—some open and bare, most locked shut. Droplets of gray blood left a trail down a row, joined by a smear every few feet. Steuben raised a fist to signal a halt.

Steuben's double set of nostrils flared. "Something's not right. The trail continues but—"

A container's doors burst open and slammed Steuben off his feet. The Karigole flew into Orozco and the two went down in a heap of limbs.

The banshee stepped out of the container and swiped at Hale. He brought his arms up and managed to block the worst of the blow that hit him like a mule's kick. He had a brief sensation of flying before impacting against the graphene-reinforced steel of a container.

White flashed across his eyes as he fell to the deck. He tried to get up, his vision swimming as his arms and legs seemed to want to do anything but what he needed. The flash of gauss rifles brought him back into focus. His Marines were fighting and they needed him.

The banshee had its back to him, one claw wrapped around Standish's neck, hoisting him into the air. Standish drew a pistol from a holster on the small of his back and unloaded on the banshee's face. The creature roared in pain and tried to turn away from the assault.

Hale got to his feet and ran at the monster. He twisted his wrist twice and his bayonet snapped out of his gauntlet. Hale drove the blade into the banshee's armored back. It roared and dropped Standish, swinging its arm around with enough force to turn Hale into pulp.

He ducked under the strike as the blow knocked a dent into a container. The banshee tried to whirl around to get at the bayonet still embedded in its flesh and took Hale around with it.

Hale propped his feet against the banshee's back and fired his anti-grav linings. The blade broke free and took a bloody chunk of flesh with it as Hale propelled away from the beast. It fell to its knees, pawing at the gaping wound on its back.

Hale skidded across the deck and got back to his feet.

Torni and Bailey unloaded on the banshee, shot blasts impacting like hammer blows. The banshee struggled to its feet, bleeding from dozens of pellets that pierced its armor. The banshee stumbled against the open container it had used to ambush the Marines. For a split second, Hale had a very bad idea.

"Cease fire!" Hale commanded and ran straight at the reeling banshee. Bailey and Torni complied just as he leapt toward the banshee and triggered his grav linings, accelerating him like a missile. Hale's shoulder slammed into the banshee and knocked it into the container, his momentum carrying him with the monster. He fell against the floor and looked up to see the banshee's glowing yellow eyes staring at him from the rear of the container. It snarled, then shook its head as it screeched, sending bloody spittle into the air.

Hale felt a grip on his ankle and he was yanked out of the container. He rolled across the floor and saw the container doors slammed shut. Steuben braced himself against the doors as Torni and Bailey slapped their hands against the locks and pneumatic bolts slid home, trapping the banshee within.

The doors shuddered as the banshee rammed into it, but they held. It punched against the walls, leaving rounded dents with each blow.

"Torni, we good?" Hale asked as he got to his feet, his bones aching.

"Cuts and bruises, nothing serious," she said.

"Nothing serious?" Standish wheezed from

the side of the container, his helmet off and an ugly ring of bruises blooming around his neck. Yarrow, at his side, rolled his eyes and pressed a finger against the side of Standish's neck.

"Ow!" Standish slapped Yarrow's hand away.

"He's fine, sir," the medic said.

Orozco handed Hale back his gauss rifle. "Sir, that was either the dumbest or the bravest thing you've done in weeks."

The banshee roared within its new cage.

"Think it'll hold?" Torni asked.

"All ammo pods are designed to hold explosive munitions. That thing's strong, but not strong enough to bust out of there … I think," Hale said. A flurry of blows shook the container.

"What're we going to do with it? Teach it to play fetch?" Standish asked.

"That's above my pay grade," Hale said. He opened a channel to the bridge. "XO, this is Hale. Threat neutralized…and we've got a prisoner."

CHAPTER 3

Durand sent a burst of rounds into an escape pod. Chunks of burning metal blew off the pod and it spiraled into a blazing fireball. She did her best to keep her distance from the pods. Other pilots had reported seeing the same screaming things she had, but none had the same close call.

She checked her gauges: low battery power and a few more seconds of sustained gauss fire left. The atmosphere below was afire with descending pods, all out of her reach. If all the pods were full of those monsters, where were they going?

"Squadron, this is Gall, give me an ammo and fuel count," she said. "This turkey shoot can't last forever." Her remaining pilots called in with long pauses for each of those killed in action before the next in sequence reported.

They were halfway through when the *Breitenfeld* interrupted.

"Gall, this is Valdar. We're showing clear skies around the Dotok ship, confirm?"

"Only thing I see is debris from enemy ships. Low orbit will be a bitch to deal with until all this junk clears out," she said. She banked her Eagle to the side and got a better look at the Dotok carrier. The Dotok fighters—she could make out at least eight—hovered around the carrier like a pack of guard dogs. Tiny geysers vented precious atmosphere from a dozen hull breaches. A spray of ice crystals trailed the ship like a comet's tail.

"*Breit*, she's hurt bad, suggest you prep the flight deck for a mass casualty intake," Durand said.

"We're trying to reestablish comms with them now. We know they've got fighter craft. Did you see them in action? I don't know if they're going to be a help or a burden when the next fight comes to us," Valdar said.

"Negative, they stuck close to their ship the whole time. Wait…" a glint in space caught her attention—another escape pod, this one drifting in orbit. "I've got another bogie in sight. Permission to rearm and refuel once this target is destroyed."

"Granted. We'll have the pit crews waiting." Valdar closed the channel.

"Glue, I'm going for a pod. Herd our cats back to the ship for a hot swap. I'll catch up," Durand said. Glue keyed her mike twice to acknowledge. Durand changed course and set her sights on the pod, another fat teardrop of beige metal.

With the battle nearly over, Durand felt fatigue creep into her body. Adrenaline was an amazing thing in combat, but its high came with deeper and deeper lows after every contest. The dreams about what she'd seen on the Toth ship—tanks bearing disembodied nervous systems and wire probes that promised to violate her mind before ending her life—had plagued her since the mission to Anthalas. She could ask the medics for pills to help her sleep, but anything that might dull her senses was a hazard to her and the pilots that depended on her leadership.

She shifted against her seat and felt sweat trickle down the back of her flight suit. She pressed her finger against the trigger and readied to destroy the life pod. All too easy.

White-hot bullets streaked past her cockpit. Durand banked hard, her heart pounding as she gunned her thrusters. Sitting around looking for an unseen attacker was a sure way to end up as an expanding field of debris.

A Dotok fighter flew across her bow, close enough to make out stenciled letters on its hull and see the pilot. The stubby fighter executed a picture-perfect Immelmann turn and flew toward the escape pod. It maneuvered parallel to the life pod; tiny adjustments with the Dotok's maneuver thrusters brought the fighter's spin to match the life pod's.

"OK, I can take a hint," Durand said. Her cheeks burned with embarrassment. How had she been so sloppy to let *any* fighter sneak up on her?

She flew back toward her waiting squadron.

A minute later, the same Dotok fighter came up alongside her. The pilot waved to her, then pointed back at the life pod. The pilot raised a fist, then let it fall onto his palm and raised both hands together. He repeated the gesture several times before realization dawned on her.

"Help, they need help," Durand said. She nodded and flashed a thumbs-up to the Dotok, who reared back in his seat, seemingly surprised.

Did I just offend him? Probably. We'll work out the finer points of their body language later, she thought.

Durand opened the search and rescue frequency. "Angels, need you to make a pick up, and it's not what you're thinking."

****

Captain Valdar looked over Takeni's surface from the leading edge of his bridge. Long trails of snow blew from impossibly high mountains that peaked above the troposphere, its highest points exposed to near vacuum. The mountain range ran from north to south, connected to a plain of irregular peaks on one side of it and a vast tract of desert and high mesas on the other. A canyon slowly came into view from the east.

"Remind you of Mars?" Ensign Erdahl, the communications officer asked the officer sitting in a work pod to his left.

"I was thinking that," Lieutenant Neely said. "It just doesn't seem right. See that line of mountains to the north? They're running parallel to those monsters above the death line. We don't see that on Earth. Plate tectonics drove up our mountains. What happened here…it reminds me of Miranda, Uranus' moon. The surface of Miranda looks like a broken mirror. Ibarra's rovers sent back a tranche of data a few years back. Everything fit the old theories that Miranda was broken apart billions of years ago then reknit itself."

"So this is some kind of Franken-planet?" Erdahl asked.

"That's my guess. Wouldn't it be incredible

to stay and study this place for a few years? Instead we'll be ducking drones until whatever the skipper has planned."

"Evacuation," Valdar said.

The two junior officers jerked like an electrical charge shot through their seats. "We're getting them all out."

"Captain," Erdahl said, "we've got the translation protocols worked out and the...*Burning Blade* is hailing us. Want it on the main screen?"

"Do it." Valdar double-checked that the bridge was pressurized, then twisted off his helmet. He ran his fingers through his sweaty hair and smoothed out his mustache. "It'll be nice to talk to another species that isn't trying to kill us, won't it?" he asked the two officers who had redoubled their attention on their workstations.

"Chance of a lifetime," Erdahl said.

"Can I play myself in the movie?" Neely asked.

"That's the spirit," Valdar said.

The screen above the windows looking over

the planet came to life. The same Dotok from the earlier transmission, now with crude-looking staples pinching the cut on his face together, looked at Valdar. The blunted beak of his lower jaw formed a slight under bite, his eyes looked almost human.

"Captain Valdar, correct?" the Dotok asked.

"That's right. Are you Admiral Yon'kai?"

"No. She's dead." He touched two fingertips to his lips. "So is Captain Then'ol. I am Sub-Commander Ty'ken…ranking officer of all we have left in space."

"I'm sorry to hear that. When we were on Bastion the Xaros were—"

"Do you have ground troops?" Ty'ken asked. He winced, blood seeping from the cut under his eye. "A force of *noorla* landed near one of our settlements. I can do nothing for them. Ancient Pa'lon can't reach them from the capital either, not in time anyway." A panel behind him erupted in flames. Ty'ken whirled around and hit the flames with a white spray from a chemical extinguisher. He shouted terse commands in his native tongue.

"I have a company of Marines and a few transports. How big is this settlement?" Valdar asked. "Do you need me to send over a damage control party?"

"I'll send over everything we know," Ty'ken said. "My engineers assure me the worst is over. Thank you for your offer. My flight deck is still on fire. Can I send my fighters to your ship? They've been in the cockpit for a day and a half. They need a rest."

"So do you, Sub-Commander. Send them over. I'll make them feel welcome."

Ty'ken nodded quickly. "Once I'm done putting out fires, I'd like to meet you in person." The Dotok reached for a button on the side of his screen, then hesitated. "I'm supposed to say something to you. From your ambassador on Bastion, Stacey Ibarra. Cod mittens." The alien smiled.

Valdar's brow furrowed.

"Yes. Cod mittens," Ty'ken said again.

"Sir," Ensign Geller at the navigation station

piped up, "that doesn't make sense. Cod can't even wear mittens. They have fins."

Every head on the bridge slowly swung toward the ensign.

"I will shut up now," he said.

"Got missives, Captain Valdar?" Ty'ken asked.

"*Gott mit uns*," Valdar said.

"Yes, that's what I said. Do humans normally mix languages in combat situations? Seems overly confusing to me," Ty'ken said. His screen shook as an explosion rumbled in the distance on his ship. Shouts erupted from an unseen crew and he switched off his screen.

"Bit curt, aren't they?" Valdar mused.

"I've got the information on the settlement, sir," Ericcson said. "It'll be a stretch but we can make it."

"Put it on the board." Valdar clasped his hands behind his back and walked across his bridge. "Get Durand and Hale up here. This will be their fight."

****

Lafayette worked a thin screw tip into the base of his cybernetic wrist and made a slight adjustment. His left arm ended with a stump, the hand missing. The machinery whirled around, changing directions several times. He shook his head and picked up a different tool.

His workshop was in the same purpose built container as the omnium reactor. The great machine hummed with energy as thick cables ran from its center to the Shanishol control stations bolted to the floor next to Lafayette. Tiny stickers with English script were stuck atop the original language of the last users of the machine, rough translations to the function of each control and lever.

"I can hear you," Lafayette said.

"How?" Steuben stepped from around a container. "I could sneak up on a *fiilka* without being noticed. Your ears are much smaller."

"Well, old friend, I don't exactly have ears anymore. Do I?" Lafayette tapped the metal that encased his head from beneath his jaw up to the top of his skull.

"The humans taught me a word, 'cheat.' It means to do something beyond the limits of rules," Steuben said.

"Well, I didn't choose this augmentation. I'm hardly the one doing this cheat thing you speak of." Lafayette pointed his stump to an open box. "Give me a hand, would you?"

Steuben rummaged through the box and took out a hand, dissimilar to the four fingered hand with talon tips that he had.

"*Five* fingers? You've been with these humans for too long. I'll report you to Kosciusko for treason," Steuben said as he handed the appendage to Lafayette.

"You're the one wearing their armor and I'm treasonous?"

"I wear the armor for a purpose. Standing out on the battlefield is a sure way to attract attention—and bullets. You understand the etymology of the word 'uniform', correct?" Steuben crossed his arms.

Lafayette snapped the new hand against his wrist and flexed the hand against the range of motion. He tapped each forefinger against the thumb, encountering some difficulty making the ring finger move as he desired.

"My nervous system is meant for four fingers. This will take some getting used to," Lafayette said.

"I don't understand why you bother. Use your four fingers as your three parents made you."

"Improvement, Steuben. Self-improvement. After the Xaros left me with…so little to work with, I had to recreate my own body. Fiddling with capabilities has become something of a hobby," Lafayette tried to pick up a wrench with his new hand and fumbled with it. "You're heading to the surface, aren't you? Normally you'd spend this time glaring at people."

Steuben pulled the broken pieces of his short sword from a sack and put them on a work bench.

"Again?" Lafayette asked.

"Yes, again. Just fix it."

"Very well, let me show you something amazing at the same time." Lafayette picked up the broken pieces and brought them to the omnium reactor. He opened a cabinet near the end of the machine and set the pieces inside. The control panel came to life with a flip of the switch. The two pieces of the sword came up on a screen. A grid overlay with Shanishol language slid across the screen.

"The engineers on Bastion promised the schematics for a better interface will be waiting for us on Earth. I've had to make do with what I can figure out in the meantime," Lafayette said. His nine fingers danced across the controls and a puff of air and light flared in the cabinet. The sword vanished from the screen.

Steuben put a heavy hand on Lafayette's shoulder, claw tips working into the exposed joint. "Lafayette. What have you done? That blade has been in my family for almost a thousand years."

"Relax. This is the neat part." The reactor

hummed to life. Pale blue light glowed from inside the reactor. "Your blade has been converted into omnium—pure energy in solid form. Something of a contradiction, yes. That's what this machine does. It transforms energy to matter, matter to energy with no loss. Nuclear weapons do the mass to energy transition, but this reactor does it without any of the radiation…massive fireballs."

Steuben's grip on Lafayette's shoulder tightened.

"Did I mention it does so perfectly? Now it will recreate your weapon, perfectly down to the molecular level," Lafayette hit a button and a red light came on atop the cabinet.

Steuben opened it and withdrew his blade made whole. He tested the weapon's weight, balancing it on top of a claw tip. He held the hilt up to his nose and smelled the leather straps running over the cross guard.

"I can't tell the difference," Steuben said.

"Perfect, just as I said. Even uses the same energy your blade was made from. Don't call it a copy," Lafayette said. "I can recreate most anything that had a template stored within the computer."

"There are old stories of people who could turn lead into gold," Steuben said.

"Give me a handful of lead and it would transform it into an equal mass of gold," Lafayette said.

"Why aren't you using this to mass produce quadrium? We'll need more of it if we fight the Xaros."

"Yes, there are a few limitations. Quadrium, and other exotic forms of matter, takes a significantly longer time to manufacture. It would take days for this machine to make one of the smaller munitions you use in a gauss rifle. Also, if I put a complex piece of technology into the machine, it will take longer to recreate. Your blade is simple but your rifle would take days," Lafayette said.

"The Xaros strip any trace of a planet's intelligent species...then convert it all into this omnium? Why?"

"Maybe they'll rebuild those worlds by their

own template. The omnium is just the building blocks. The Xaros have a much more sophisticated understanding of the technology. We're playing around with paper airplanes compared to their spacecraft," Lafayette said.

Steuben grunted and sheathed his blade across his lower back.

"I just described the most advanced discovery in the field of material sciences known to the Alliance and all I get is a *humph*?"

Steuben clapped his hands with little enthusiasm.

"Barbarian. I don't know why I bother with you."

Steuben stepped over an open tool box on his way out.

"Wait, Steuben. I've been meaning to ask you something. When you were on the Toth ship, you spoke with the ship masters. Do you think there's any chance that there could be more of us?" Centuries ago, the Toth, acting under the guise of allies, invaded the Karigole home world and murdered the entire population to fuel the Toth's neural-stimulus addiction. Only a hundred Karigole were off world during the holocaust, and only four survived since then.

"No, Lafayette. There is no hope for us. Accept it. But, I will not be the last. *Ghul'thul'ghul*, brother."

"Ghul'thul'ghul," Lafayette returned to the reactor. He took a small anti-gravity plate and put it in the cabinet.

****

Torni pushed a case of rifle batteries into a compartment and tightened a strap over the top. Every spare inch of the cargo bay on the Mule drop ship was full of rations, medical supplies and ammo. There would be barely enough room for her squad, but comfort was never a factor for Marines.

"Sarge," Standish stuck his head down from the upper turret, "we know where we're going yet? Or what we're doing? We're packing like we're going to retake Tokyo."

"If you're talking to me that means you've finished the pre-flight checks on that turret. Correct?" Torni said, not bothering to look up at him.

"Sure thing, Sarge, ready to rock and roll," Standish said with a smile. "Hey, can we breathe the air down there? I've got air tanks loaded, but if we gotta haul more filters and fresh O2, we can't carry as much boom-boom."

"The atmosphere is breathable in the deep canyons, which is where all the civilians are. The air thins out on the plateaus and mountain ranges. There, the atmo is a little thicker than what we've got on Mars," Torni said. She marked numbers on a manifest and shook her head. "Standish, how many Q-rounds do you still have for your rifle?"

"Five," Standish said, a little too quickly.

"Standish."

"I mean twelve. I didn't count the extras I have on a spare bandolier," Standish said.

"Give me half. We've got to cross level across all the squads and gold team is out."

Standish unsnapped the bandolier across his chest and dropped it into Torni's waiting hands.

"Let me guess, there are no more Q-rounds in the armory," Standish said.

"Correct. Don't miss." Torni wrapped the bandolier around her forearm.

"Sarge!" Bailey called as she ran up the Mule's ramp. "Deck boss needs some muscle. They're about to crack open that Dotok escape pod that search and rescue brought in. Orozco's already over there."

Standish dropped down from the turret and picked up his helmet from a cubbyhole over a bench.

"I wonder what's in *this* one," Standish said. The three Marines trotted across the flight deck toward the escape pod. A team of engineers with cutting torches stood next to it, waving to the pod. The pod looked like it had been tossed down the side of a mountain, dents and gashes marring the surface.

"No screaming this time, Standish," Torni

said.

"I don't…know…what you're talking about," Standish said.

"You going to fill me in, Sarge?" Bailey asked.

Torni slowed down and nodded to Orozco, now clad in his heavy gunner's armor, the grounding stakes built into his boots and stabilization rig across his back and shoulders adding to his already considerable bulk.

"You talking about the first time you met the Karigole?" Orozco asked.

"Slander! Second- and third hand stories blown completely out of proportion," Standish said, shifting from foot to foot.

"I was there, Standish," Torni said. The engineers fired their torches and started cutting into the side of the escape pod.

"Let me preface this story with the fact that *I* remember things very differently," Standish said.

"We picked up the Karigole pod when it first came through the Crucible," Torni said.

"Naturally, command didn't bother to tell us what was in it. Steuben slapped his hand against the side of a viewport and Standish started screaming like a little girl."

"I-I…maybe," Standish said.

"We got the cargo hold pressurized and Steuben climbs out of the pod. By this time, Standish is backed into a corner screaming 'Don't eat me! Don't eat me!' at the top of his lungs," Torni said, pausing the story until Bailey and Orozco could stop laughing. "The four Karigole are just looking at each other while I'm trying to calm Standish down."

"OK, in my defense, I've never had first contact training and have you seen what Steuben looks like?" Standish asked.

"You really need training to tell you that wetting your pants in front of a new species is a bad idea?" Bailey asked.

"What is the nature of this discussion?" Steuben asked as he walked over, Yarrow at his side.

"Oh great," Standish shook his head.

"Recounting the time we first met," Torni said to Steuben. The Karigole, six and a half feet of green-scaled muscle, wiped his four-fingered hand across his squat nose. He'd taken to human armor and weapons since they'd encountered the Toth on Anthalas, a race that considered Steuben's centuries-old mind a delicacy. Wearing armor which set him apart from the Marines he fought beside made him a tempting target for the Toth.

"Is this the story about why the rest of the Karigole call Standish 'Squeaky'?" Yarrow asked.

"Who filled new guy's head full of lies? I bet it was Gunney Cortaro. Tall tales to keep this cherry's spirits high," Standish said.

Steuben unslung his rifle from over his shoulder and checked the battery power. "We thought we came to the wrong planet. The high-pitched noise coming from Standish didn't match the language files we trained with prior to our mission. Lafayette thought 'Don't eat me' was a traditional human greeting."

"I didn't say exactly...*that*." Standish pointed to the escape pod where the engineers were cutting through a hinge. "Look, almost done. Anyone else concerned one of those banshees might be in there? Focus, Marines. We've got a job to do."

The Marines powered up their rifles and pointed them to the opening the engineers had almost completed.

"'Don't eat me!'" Bailey said in a high-pitched voice. Orozco and Yarrow joined in, repeating the phrase and adding their voices to a chorus.

"Shut up! All of you!" Standish's hands shook with rage as he wagged his rifle from side to side.

A section of the drop pod fell to the deck with a thump. Inside, a Dotok in a body glove shielded a prone figure with its body. The Dotok breathed heavily, brandishing a small knife at the Marines.

Torni lowered her weapon and raised a hand. "Friend, friend," she said and raised her visor, exposing her face to the Dotok.

"Their word is *meln,*" Steuben said. He raised his visor and bent over to look into the pod. "*Meln!*" he thundered.

The Dotok started screaming.

"See, perfectly natural reaction," Standish said.

"Steuben, back off," Torni said, guiding the Karigole aside with a gentle push. Torni waved the Dotok toward her and repeated the only Dotok word she knew. The Dotok hesitated, then lowered its knife. It crawled toward Torni and accepted a hand out of the escape pod. The alien was short, barely reaching Torni's collarbone. By the curves in its body glove, Torni figured it was a she.

The Dotok looked over the smiling faces of the Marines and pulled off her helmet. Her hair was wild and mussed, her deep green skin flushed. Torni thought the alien woman's features were almost Slavic.

"Torni," the sergeant said, tapping her chest.

"Shor," the Dotok said, repeating the

gesture.

Steuben extended a four-fingered, clawed hand toward Shor. Shor skipped back and cowered behind Torni.

"Give her some space, Steuben," Torni said.

"I wonder if she thinks you just might eat her," Standish said.

"Shut up, Standish," more than one Marine said.

Torni looked into the pod at the other Dotok, strapped onto a stretcher. Torni raised a knee to crawl inside. A gentle touch on her shoulder pulled her back.

"Ehtan," Shor said.

"Does he need help?" Torni tried to climb in again. Shor pulled her back.

"Ehtan!"

"He's dead," Steuben said.

Shor pressed two fingers to her lips.

Torni nodded to the Dotok and stepped back from the pod.

"So, what do we do with her?" Orozco

asked.

"Let me ask the lieutenant," Torni said. "The rest of you get back to loading up our Mule."

The flight deck vibrated as a Dotok fighter came through the force field at the aft end of the flight deck. Eagles and Dotok followed in a steady procession.

****

Durand double checked that her ejection seat was disabled, then opened her canopy. The first day of flight school started with a video of an unfortunate pilot who didn't make the same precaution, and she'd never forgotten the lesson.

"Oye, lassie!" MacDougall hooked a ladder against the side of her cockpit. "Who the hell are they?" The crew chief waved a hand at the Dotok fighters that had landed in a scrum in the middle of the flight deck.

"Guests," she said. "Try to make them feel welcome." She removed her helmet and shook out her shoulder length raven-black hair. She climbed down from her fighter and spotted Glue. Durand waved to get her attention.

One of the Dotok pilots struggled down the ladder the deck crew wheeled up to his fighter. The alien's legs quivered as it came down the steps one at a time. He set foot on the deck and fell to his knees. Durand ran to him and fumbled with the latches fixing his helmet to the rest of his suit.

Durand got the helmet off and became the first human to get a good dose of Dotok body odor. The Dotok's cheeks were sunken, its lips cracked and dry. He looked at Durand and made a drinking motion. He fell back against the ladder with a groan.

"Water! Get him some water," Durand said to the nearest crewman. She knelt next to him and put a hand on his shoulder. "How long were you in the saddle, *mon ami*?"

The Dotok's mouth smacked like a dry husk being ripped apart. A crewman handed Durand a canteen. She unscrewed the top and pressed it into his hands. The Dotok sniffed at the water, then took a tentative sip. He swallowed hard, then downed the rest of the canteen.

"Glue, the rest of them will be like this," she said to the Chinese pilot. "Captain needs me on the bridge. Get our birds topped off with bullets and—"

"Gall!" The heavily accented word rang out over the din of the flight deck. A Dotok pilot stood next to Durand's fighter, pointing at her call sign stenciled against her cockpit. The pilot looked young, almost in his late teens by human standards, his head bald but for a braid of dark hair on the back of his head.

"I think you made a fan," Glue said.

"When did they learn to read English?" Durand asked. She stood up and waved to the Dotok. "I'm Gall."

The Dotok's face darkened and it stomped toward Durand, pointing to her. Angry sounding words came from him as he approached. He got within a dozen feet and hurled his helmet at Durand.

Durand brought her own helmet up and tried to block the projectile. The thrown helmet struck her fingers and sent pain shooting up her arm.

The Dotok broke into a run, a fist raised behind his head.

Durand backpedaled and bumped into a Dotok fighter, one hand up and her head shaking.

The enraged alien got within arm's reach when Glue clocked him across the jaw. His head lolled over his neck and he fell to the deck like a puppet with its strings cut.

Dotok pilots rushed over and laid the unconscious pilot out against the deck.

"What the hell?" Durand asked.

"You really don't make a great first impression, ma'am," Glue said, her hand brushing against the thigh where Durand shot her months ago.

Shor pushed her way through the Dotok pilots. She slapped the prone Dotok across the face until he came to. The two locked eyes and embraced, the man crying like he'd just found a long lost child.

"You almost killed his wife." The

mechanical tinged words came from the pilot sitting against the stairs. He had a square shaped speaker in his hand, which he raised up to his mouth and spoke. "Bar'en is ill-tempered at times. Forgive him." The translated words came from the speaker.

"You got a name?" Durand asked. Her words came through the speaker in Dotok.

"Mar'tig."

"Martin, welcome to the *Breitenfeld*," Durand said. "You tell hothead over there he swings at me again and I'll shoot him in the dick. I've got to get to the bridge and figure out how we're going to save this planet. Excuse me."

Durand jogged toward the elevators and caught a dirty look from Bar'en along the way.

CHAPTER 4

Stacey Ibarra floated in a white abyss, her senses starved for anything but the sound of her heart beating and the light that cast neither shadow nor heat. She replayed a pop ditty from her high school days in her head, waiting for the translation to end. It took hours for the gates between Bastion and the Crucible to deliver her from one place to the other. Timing the experience with remembered songs staved off boredom and panic.

Weight returned to her body and the sunken stadium of the Crucible's control center came into view as the white field subsided. She floated to the ground, her armored boots scuffing along the floor as she regained her balance.

Stacey looked down at her arms, still covered in the battle armor from the day humanity took the star gate from the Xaros and she began her career as an ambassador to the alliance against the invaders. Drops of blood, black spots surrounded by streaks of red, ran up and down her gauntlets. A Marine named Franklin had sacrificed himself to save her from a drone, and she'd done nothing for him but abandon him in a passageway.

Each time she left and returned to the Crucible, she was in her armor. Yet, on Bastion she came and went in a body glove and tunic. This discrepancy hadn't been cleared up by either the AI on Bastion or the man that got her into this predicament.

She shook her head and pushed sweat-soaked hair away from her face.

"Ibarra? Granddad?" she asked to an empty room.

A hologram of Marc Ibarra materialized in front of her, looking like the middle-aged industrialist she remembered from her childhood.

"The *Breitenfeld* is overdue," he said. "I hope you've got good news."

Stacey unsnapped the clasps on her right forearm gauntlet and let it fall to the floor. She stripped off a glove and pressed her hand against the plinth in the center of the room. A panel lit up under her palm.

"DNA data transfer commencing. Thank you, Stacey," the probe at the heart of the Crucible said, its voice artificial but pleasant.

Stacey glared at Ibarra and shook her head in disgust.

"You put procedurals on the *Breitenfeld*? Without telling me?"

"How do you know that? Where is the ship, Stacey? We've got a lot riding on it," Ibarra said, crossing his arms.

"The ship took a detour on the way back to Earth. The mission to Anthalas was a success—better than we'd hoped. They found an intact omnium reactor the Shanishol used, control protocols *and* an ancient…intelligence that's been most informative about how to control omnium," Stacey said.

The panel beneath her palm blinked, signaling the end of the data transfer encoded within her DNA. The human mind could remember only so much data and was subject to the vagaries of memory and damage. Bastion fused data within her DNA for a lossless transfer, but the ability wasn't without cost. The circumstances of her birth had been manipulated; synthetic material had been incorporated during her gestation to produce a baby somewhat more than human. Ibarra had subjected his many daughters to the procedure, but Stacey was the only viable child from many failed pregnancies Ibarra's daughters endured.

"There was something else on Anthalas…the Toth," Stacey said. "They came in on the same gravity window we used to get in and out."

"The who?"

"Read the report. Everything I know is

there," she said.

Ibarra used the tremendous processing ability of the probe to digest the video statements, ship's logs and the Alliance's entire data file on the Toth within thousandths of a second. Having his intelligence subsumed within the probe came with a few advantages.

"They sampled the procedurals. They know…" Ibarra said.

"That's right. A hostile race addicted to neural energy knows that Earth has the key to an unlimited source of their fix. They know this because *you* thought it would be a good idea to send untested vat babies with the *Breitenfeld*!" Stacey picked up her gauntlet and threw it at Ibarra. The armor passed through the hologram without incident.

"Science requires experimentation, my girl. If I'd known the Toth would be there, things would have played out differently." Ibarra tugged at his lip. "Valdar suspects, but he doesn't know?"

"I played coy, and it killed me to lie to a

man I respect," Stacey said. "You know, not everyone can lie as easy as breathing."

"Deception is a skill just like any other; you must practice to gain and maintain proficiency," Ibarra said. He waved a hand in the air and a star chart of the local galaxy appeared in the air before him.

"I'm not in the mood for your fortune cookie wisdom. What're we going to do about this mess? The Toth know where our planet is and they've got Alliance jump technology. If they want to pay us a visit, they could be here within—"

"Now. They could be here now," Ibarra said. "Toth Prime isn't that far. They managed to reach our planet millennia ago using sub-light vessels. This was back in the day when they were whole as a species—scientists and traders, not the drug addicts they've become."

"Then why aren't they here? Our planet might as well have a giant 'Free Lunch' sign on it, considering how little of our navy is left," Stacey said.

"Toth elites survive only because they keep one Toth in particular happy, Dr. Mentiq. Any corporate takeover or capital expansion requires his knowledge and approval, and he gets a cut. Try to shortchange him and he'll hit a kill switch on the offending elite's life-support tank."

Jump plots appeared across the map, permutations showing the route the Toth would take to reach Earth and the time it would take.

"This Mentiq's got the entire species by the balls, doesn't he? Sounds like someone you could relate to," Stacey said.

"I don't have a heart to wound anymore, darling. That the Toth aren't here yet means they've gone to Mentiq for permission. Given when the jump window was open to his system… travel time…warrior-clone growth rates…" Equations formed and solved themselves in the air before Ibarra.

"We've got months, if we're lucky," Ibarra said.

"You think they'll come?" Stacey asked.

"The Toth gave up their place in the Alliance and their best chance to survive the Xaros in order to feast on the Karigole. They'll come for us. The procedural technology and a practically limitless supply of new and interesting sustenance…it's too good to pass up. I thought I'd have decades to turn this solar system into a fortress against the next wave of Xaros. Now we've got months before a different existential threat comes knocking."

"May I interject?" The probe flared into being above the central plinth, a needle of light glittering with static.

"Doubt we could stop you, Jimmy," Ibarra said.

"With current crew and vessel production rates, our chance of defeating the anticipated Toth fleet is approximately two and a half percent," the probe said.

"Don't, Jimmy. We've been over this," Ibarra said.

"You said 'current.' Why?" Stacey asked

the probe.

"Procedural crew gestation tubes lie dormant at the Oahu facility in anticipation of true born societal acceptance of the new humans. I can activate the production lines with the truncated protocols. Given the circumstances, the risk is acceptable," the probe said.

"The failure rate is too high. If the decision matrix is off by the slightest margin, we will lose thousands of lives," Ibarra said. "Growing a new human body from sperm and egg to fully mature in nine days is as far as Alliance science could manage. If we grow them too fast, there will be significant consequences for future generations. Too many abnormalities would sneak into the gene pool."

Stacey laughed, an expression of contempt, not humor.

"You, Marc Ibarra, the man who pulled the strings on our entire species for decades and left billions to die on Earth when the Xaros came…now you've grown a conscience?" she asked.

"The *plan*," Ibarra glared at the probe, "my vision, was for humanity to continue without losing what we are in the process. My fleet was supposed to be embers, rekindling the same flame that the Xaros snuffed out. The proccies aren't supposed to be any different from the true born. We meddle too much and we won't recognize humanity in another couple hundred years."

"If the Toth take Phocnix and repeat their conquest and occupation of the Karigole home world," the probe said, "then your vision is moot."

"Jimmy, I'm not sure if you're a pragmatist or a buzzkill," Ibarra said.

"The Alliance needs the Crucible. It is against my programming to allow something so pedestrian and biological as human ethics and morality to interfere with my mission," the probe said, its light fading and growing in tune with its words.

Ibarra rolled his eyes and waved a hand in the air. "Speaking of those blowhards on Bastion, will they send anyone to help against the Toth?"

"I asked," Stacey said, "but the Qa'Resh refused to even let me bring the motion to the floor. Officially, their position is that the proccies and our Karigole advisors are all we would need to beat the Toth. Unofficially…there are some concerns with the jump technology. After the *Breitenfeld* jumped away from Bastion, there were some anomalous readings in the quantum field left in the ship's wake."

"I've detected no such anomalies from jumps utilizing the Crucible," the probe said.

"Right, which is why everyone's scratching their heads back at Bastion. Some of the eggheads extrapolated out the implications of the anomalies…and the results weren't good. Seems every time the jump engines open a hole in reality to create the wormholes, there's a chance the hole could grow…exponentially," she said. "If the math is right, the growth wouldn't stop until it reaches intergalactic space. So, maybe everyone dies from the Xaros, or there's a cascading fault in the fabric of space and time and everyone definitely dies."

She sighed heavily and tried to squeeze her armored bulk into a chair bolted to the floor. "I love my job, really I do."

"And the Qa'Resh aren't willing to risk sending us reinforcements if they don't have to," Ibarra said. "It's going to be ugly when I tell Phoenix.

"Jimmy, use the truncated protocols for the next production batch, limited to five hundred tubes. Let's see how viable they are. Then ramp up all dormant lines with what we know works. We can make progress, but no need to rush into disaster."

"The first of the accelerated procedurals will be decanted tomorrow morning," the probe said. Ibarra and his granddaughter traded a confused glance.

"How, Jimmy? The rush jobs take a hundred hours to grow and implant a personality," Ibarra said.

"When the *Breitenfeld* went overdue, I assumed it was lost and its mission a failure.

Without the ability to utilize our sizable store of omnium, I decided we would need as many capable humans as possible to defeat the Xaros' return fourteen years from now," the probe said. "I told Thorsson to create a test batch, but only two hundred and fifty units. Should we make more?"

"Behind my back, Jimmy?" Ibarra asked.

"Shall I perform an act of contrition?"

"No, you lump of photons, you can go straight to—wait. Where's the *Breitenfeld*? Where's the omnium reactor you said it found?" Ibarra asked Stacey.

Stacey brought Ibarra up to speed on the Xaros invasion of Takeni and Captain Valdar's plea to the Alliance for permission to render aid, and that the reactor was secured deep inside the ship's hold.

"Never send an idealist to do a pragmatist's job," Ibarra said. "He knows we need that reactor, right? We need it to transmute omnium into Q-shells before the Xaros even get here."

"Stacey brought schematics and fabrication protocols with her," the probe said. "Given our current manufacturing capabilities. I can build a new one in roughly eighteen years. Raising our—"

"Valdar knows we need that reactor, right?" Ibarra asked again.

"I told him. He swore he was on an evac mission, not a head-hunting trip. He'll jump back to Earth before he risks destroying the reactor…I hope," Stacey said.

"Isaac Valdar earned his first Purple Heart on a beach in Okinawa," Ibarra said. "Took a Chinese bullet through the calf trying to load up every last soldier and civilian he could, then he navigated a rusted-out trash hauler through minefields *and* ducked a Chinese sub for two days before our navy found him. Any Dotok left on that planet is as good as dead. Valdar won't leave anyone behind—he's that kind of officer. I'm not sure if it's bravery or stupidity."

"The die is cast, Grandpa," Stacey said. She struggled out of the chair, pulled her shoulders back, and tried to scratch at an itch buried beneath armor. "I'm stuck here for a few days. The ambassador quantum gate is blocked while Pa'lon relays updates from Takeni to Bastion. Can I change? Maybe get a shower and speak to an actual human being?"

"We've got quarters waiting for you. Follow the running lights down the hallway," Ibarra said.

Stacey gave him a lazy salute and left.

"She doesn't know. Does she?" Ibarra asked.

"Correct. Confirmed by the behavior files Bastion's AI encrypted into her data transfer," the probe said. "Let her find bliss in her ignorance. At least until the conflict with the Toth is resolved."

"She won't take it well."

"She is of your bloodline, which remains significant in human relationships. There is no replacement for her. Formulate a course of action to keep her viable once she learns the truth of her situation."

"Jimmy, you sure do know how to sweet talk a guy. Speaking of 'courses of action,' we need to tell Admiral Garret about the Toth...and the production ramp-up. I wonder how our two remaining Karigole advisors, Rochambeau and Kosciusko, will react when we tell them their mortal enemies are coming for a visit."

Ibarra's hologram flickered, then vanished.

CHAPTER 5

The Mule rumbled as turbulence slammed Hale against his restraints. He looked up from his forearm display to check on his Marines. Torni had a hand raised over her head and pressed against an ammo canister that seemed intent on breaking loose from its assigned place. Orozco had his arm wrapped around his Gustav gauss cannon. Steuben was as stoic as ever.

Hale could have fit another squad of Marines in the Mule, but as the commander of this drop, he planned to keep him and his team in reserve. Flying above a likely battlefield was dangerous, but he couldn't find a better place for situational awareness and command and control than the bay of this Mule.

His hand tapped a small speaker box fixed to the outside of his throat armor.

"Everyone have your translators installed?" Hale asked. Bastion devised hardware for the humans and Dotok to speak to each other, based on the system Stacey Ibarra said was used on the space station. She'd given Hale specific instructions *not* to open the devices or the ear buds that came with them, something about 'harmonic resonator crystals' failing.

"How're they supposed to work?" Orozco asked.

"Speak English normally. The translators will nullify what you say and broadcast the Dotok equivalent for the words. It works in the reverse to your earbud.

"Bailey, Standish, see anything from your turrets?" he asked over the Mule's IR network.

"Jack and shit, sir. And by that, I mean clouds," Standish said.

"Same," Bailey said.

Hale rotated the display on his forearm, and icons for the four Mules and six Eagle escorts swept over the topographic peaks of a mountain range. They'd be over the settlement in a few more minutes.

"Pilot, any contact with the settlement?" Hale asked.

"Negative. Xaros are in town, have to keep radio silence. One transmission and every drone down there will make a beeline for us. *Breitenfeld* hasn't got anything to relay to us from the IR line we've got with the ship," the pilot said.

"We don't know if there are drones down there," Hale said.

"You're the mission commander. You can risk it if you want but I think Gall would snip your balls off for that," the pilot said.

The corner of Hale's mouth pulled into a grimace. The planning session with his ex-girlfriend had been rather one-sided. She, as she told him in no uncertain terms, was the ranking pilot in the air and she'd get him and his ground pounders where they needed to be, and out of there, without his bright ideas.

He hadn't found any fault with the air assault and evacuation plan she'd devised, and there wasn't any reason to change things on the fly. He scrolled through a channel list to find the private channel to her Eagle, and hesitated. Durand's default response to losing a pilot was anger, unfocused and unrelenting anger.

He shrugged his shoulders and opened the channel.

"Marie?"

"What?" she snapped. "Don't call me that when we're on the clock."

"You all right? I heard about Kyle and Hornsby. I'm sorry." Hale mentally kicked himself for starting this conversation, which felt exponentially worse with each word. He squeezed his eyes shut and readied for a tongue-lashing.

"They didn't…this isn't necessary. You know that, right? Skipper's got some sort of hero complex going on. We could all be home right now on an R&R chit to that resort Ibarra rebuilt in Hawaii," Durand said.

Hale checked to make sure he was talking to the right person.

"Captain does what he wants. It's his ship," Hale said.

"So you agree with him?"

"I didn't say that." The Mule rattled through another bout of turbulence. Hale heard the whine and *thunk* of both turrets rotating, and he looked at the armored hatches closing off Bailey and Standish from the rest of the ship. Arrows painted on each showed both turrets pointing toward the port side of the Mule.

"I'm not the only one grumbling about this, and the couple Dotok I met haven't exactly made me feel overly welcome and appreciated," Durand said.

Hale felt his combat instincts rise to the fore as neither turret changed directions. What were they looking at?

Torni banged an armored fist against her bench and tapped at her helmet.

An amber light lit up on his gauntlet. Standish was trying to open a channel to him.

"You call me and then you hit me with the silent treatment? I swear, Ken, this is exactly what we used to fight about."

"Marie, I think we've got—"

The turrets roared in unison. Hale killed the channel to Durand.

"—gets off the horn with his girlfriend that we've got drones," Standish yelled.

"Got the one on our six," Bailey said.

"What about the one that went around us?" Standish asked as his turret spun around and around, hunting a target.

"How many drones did you see?" Hale asked.

"Hi, sir, welcome back to the battle." Standish's twin gauss cannons fired a burst. "Two for sure…I think I saw another five or six between the clouds. One's right on top of us, somewhere."

"Gall," Hale said over the open command channel, "my gunners think they saw up to five more drones. Can we handle this or do we need to abort?"

Both turrets opened up, drowning out Durand's response. For just a second, Hale wished this battle was happening in orbit where there wasn't an atmosphere to host the din of battle.

Something slammed into the Mule's cockpit and the ship dove. Hale's restraints kept him in his seat as the Mule tumbled end over end, tossing Hale around like he was on a rollercoaster. A flash of ruby light burst from the cockpit and flooded the cargo bay.

The tumbling continued.

"Sir, drone got the pilots," Standish said. "I'm open to suggestions!"

"Bail out!" Hale slapped the emergency release on his harness and used the magnetic linings in his boots to lock himself to the deck plating. Even with the world spinning around him, he could still make it to the exit ramp—which was shut. Hale took uneasy steps along the deck, walking like he was drunk.

As the stricken Mule nosed down, Hale felt gravity try to pull him back to the cockpit, but he bent forward and used the electro-magnets in his glove to gain a handhold against the deck.

The ship shook as Standish's turret ejected. Jaundiced yellow light flooded into the cargo bay as Torni got the rear hatch open. Hale looked up and saw a sky full of smoke.

"Hey! I've got a malfunction!" Bailey's cry was full of panic. Her armored fists pounded against the view block on the turret hatch.

Yarrow, Steuben, Orozco and Torni had climbed to the edge of the ramp. All four looked back to Hale.

"I've got her!" Hale shouted. He used his mag locks to climb "up" the deck, like he was climbing the sheer face of a mountain cliff. Hale reached Bailey's turret, flipped open a yellow and black panel, and wrapped his hand around a red handle within. He locked eyes with Bailey through the view port and nodded to her. She braced herself against the turret seat. Hale yanked the handle.

Explosive bolts severed the turret from the ship and sent it hurtling away.

Hale unfastened his mag locks and used his augmented strength to launch himself up and out of the drop ship. He pulled his ripcord and went through the bone-jarring shake of his parachute catching air.

The Mule slammed into the ground beneath him, erupting into a fireball. Hale grabbed a riser and pulled hard, angling him away from the Mule's wreckage. The air around him was thick with smoke and the smell of burning grease.

Hale pressed his feet and knees together and hit the ground. What was a textbook parachute landing fall went awry as the parachute kept traveling across the ground, taking Hale with it. Hale fell against fire-blackened soil and scraped along the surface. He unsnapped one riser, which put all the pull on the remaining length of carbon-fiber cord. His attached shoulder plowed into the ground, burying him up to his chest before he came to a halt.

Hale wiped soot off his visor and got to his feet, extricating himself from the parachute and unsnapping his rifle from his back. He'd landed in the settlement Galogesvi, or what had been Galogesvi. The adobe homes and wooden buildings that made up Galogesvi were burnt out or still on fire. Dead civilians lay scattered through the streets. Men, women and children…all victims of the terrible violence that had come to this place.

He was too late.

"This is Hale. Form up on…the only three-story building, the one that's on fire," he broadcast through his suit's IR. He wasn't surprised when no answer came back. With all the ambient heat and smoke, the infrared communication system was practically useless.

A banshee's wail broke through the sound of the roaring flames.

With no other options, Hale ran toward the scream. He found Bailey's turret embedded in a house wall, the parachute crumpled over the roof like a discarded blanket. A pair of banshees clawed at the metal sphere, digging their talons into the gaps between plates.

Hale thumbed his rifle to high power and drilled the nearest banshee through the spine. The gauss bullet penetrated the other side of its body and blew off a chunk of the house. The other banshee turned and managed a scream of rage before Hale blew its head clean off.

The banshees twitched on the ground as he ran to the turret. Bailey opened her turret pod and accepted Hale's hand as she climbed out.

"To hell with this planet. I already hate it," she said, slapping a magazine into her carbine and sighing at the Mule's wreckage. "My sniper rifle was in there."

"But you weren't. Let's find everyone else," Hale said. Eagle fighters sparred with Xaros drones overhead. Aircraft darted around and through pillars of smoke stretching to the edge of the canyon holding Galogesvi.

"I got a good look at the place on the way down. Whole town is burnt to a crisp," she said. "Big fire on the outskirts burning through farmland."

The snap of gauss rifles crackled in the distance.

"Sounds like us," Bailey said.

"No time to waste." Hale ran toward the sound of gunfire.

They found the rest of their team on the second floor of a wrecked building, one of the few that had a Dotok language sign across the façade. A dozen dead banshees lay in the street around them.

A lance of blood-red light slammed into the Marines' position, slicing through the thin walls and nearly hitting Steuben.

Hale swung around a corner and saw a banshee, head and shoulders taller than the rest they'd encountered, its right arm replaced by a cannon that glowed from within. Banshees loped past the weaponized creature, running on all fours like charging gorillas.

Hale aimed for the tall banshee's head and saw the weapon swing straight toward him. He fell to the ground as he squeezed the trigger, sending the shot into the sky as a beam of red energy sliced through the air right where his head had been. The beam scythed down, severing the wooden frame of the adobe building. The walls creaked, and collapsed.

The Marine rolled out of the way as one side of the building toppled toward him and he snapped off another shot, hoping to foul the banshee's next blast. He came to a stop with his belly to the ground and managed to half aim his next shot. The round clipped the banshee on the shoulder, knocking it back a step. Gauss rifle fire stitched across its torso and it slammed into the ground like a felled tree. The cannon arm burned from within and disintegrated, leaving the rest of the banshee behind.

"Hey sir, good job not being dead. Real proud," Standish said, forgoing the IR and just shouting so his lieutenant could hear him.

"Did you find Bailey?" Torni asked.

"Bailey? She's right—" Hale looked back at the collapsed building and saw the Australian Marine's foot sticking out of the rubble.

Tossing rubble aside, Hale tried to uncover her head and chest first so she could breathe. He pushed a lump of adobe away and found her limp arm sticking out of a void.

"Bailey!"

Steuben grabbed the edge of the mostly intact wall and heaved it off Bailey. She sat up groggily, the top of her helmet dented in. Hale pulled her clear. Steuben dropped the wall and a waft of pulverized concrete dusted the three of them.

"That got me wobbly. If my head's going to hurt like I've got a hangover, I could have at least been a little shit-faced," she said.

"Yarrow, check her out," Hale said over his shoulder to the medic.

"Raider Six, this is Gall," Durand's transmission came over radio waves.

"This is Raider."

"Mission abort, I repeat, mission abort. This valley is crawling with drones and I don't have the fighters to clear them or get you out of here safely. Everything I've got in the air is going back to capital, New Abhaile. The Dotok say they can sortie a couple dozen fighters to help us out. You'll be on your own for a couple hours," she said.

"What else is new," Hale mumbled. He pressed the transmit button on his forearm display. "Roger, Gall. I've got six for pick up. Crew of Mule Eight is KIA."

There was only static for several seconds. Hale repeated his message.

"Hale...civilians! There are civilians to—" Durand cut in and out. "East. Say again, civilians to your east—side of the fire—hostiles present!"

"Gall? Gall?"

There was no response.

Hale looked to the east where a raging inferno crept toward the edge of the town, throwing up a wall of smoke and flame from one end of the canyon to the other.

"Bailey, you good?" Hale asked her. She was on her feet, her gauss carbine in one hand, the barrel bent at an ugly angle. She tossed the useless weapon aside and drew her pistol.

"I ain't getting any better just standing here, sir."

"Let's go." Hale took off to the east. They passed over the bodies of a few dead civilians and more than one defeated banshee. By the time they reached the edge of the fire wall, there was no sign of what Gall had been talking about.

Hale lowered his rifle, his eyes glued to the raging inferno ahead of him. What had once been an orchard of neatly spaced trees had become a field of torches. The intense heat from the fire activated the auto-cooling system within his suit.

"When she said 'side of the fire,'" Torni said, "she meant the *other* side of the fire. Didn't she?"

"There's no way around," Yarrow said, pointing to the cliffs.

There were civilians beyond that fire, innocents that needed Hale and his Marines. His choice was easy.

"We don't go around," Hale said.

"Sir," Standish said, "sir, you've got that crazy 'I've got a great idea' look in your eye, don't you?"

Hale turned around and steeled himself. Selling this wouldn't be easy.

"Button up," Hale said. "Set your suits for void. We've got the air to make it." Hale tapped a command onto his forearm and felt his suit tighten against his body. His helmet plates constricted and the smell of recycled air filled his visor. The rest of his Marines and Steuben followed suit.

"Follow me!" Hale charged into the inferno.

****

Caas grabbed her little brother's hand and fought to get him out from under the *toreen* tree roots as soot-stained fruit fell from overladen branches, the spikey skin stabbing through her tunic. Ar'ri barely fit into his chosen hiding place; the *noorla* would find him in seconds. A gust of wind sent choking smoke over her.

"Come on, Ar'ri. You can't stay there!" Caas coughed and yanked at his arm again. She was only six, but she was still Ar'ri's big sister. He had to listen to her.

"No!" The little boy tried to pull his hand to his chest, but Caas' hold on him was absolute.

"The monsters will get you, Ar'ri. You have to come!"

A *noorla's* wail sent a chill down her spine. They'd attacked during breakfast with no warning from New Abhaile or the village guard. Mother and Father promised that Galogesvi was too far away, too small, to be attacked. Once the tunnels were repaired, they'd go to New Abhaile and leave with the good aliens Ancient Pa'lon promised were coming. That was their promise, and her parents had always kept their word. But the *noorla* were here.

They'd sent her and Ar'ri with the schoolmaster through the orchards, promising

they'd catch up with them at the storm shelter.
Father had been holding one of the family rifles;
Mother had the other. They both promised over and
over again that they'd see their children at the
shelter.

Then the fire cut off the village, and *noorla*
were waiting for them in the shelter.

Dotok screams came from behind her. She
glanced back and saw dark shapes moving through
rolls of straw in the harvested fields. A woman ran
from the edge of the field, but a dark arm shot out
and dragged her behind a tractor. Her screams cut
off suddenly.

A *noorla* stepped around the tractor, claws
dripping blood. It looked right at her. Caas' fear
melted away, replaced with resolve. There was no
escape. Nowhere to run this time.

Caas pulled her brother up and buried his
head against her chest. He sobbed, clutching at the
back of her arms just like every time he'd wake up
from a nightmare.

"Don't look, Ar'ri. Don't look." She hugged

her brother close and stared into the fire. She said a prayer, asking forgiveness for all the bad things she'd done. She hadn't been to a shrine in weeks, and Mother always said that the bad things you did would weigh down your soul.

A monster charged out of the fire, flames clinging to its arms and shoulders. It held a rifle like her parents', but it wasn't as big as the *noorla*. It raised the weapon and pointed it right at Caas. Caas pulled her brother close and closed her eyes.

She heard a snap break in the air overhead and waited another second, sure her life was almost over. She opened a single eye and saw the new arrival fire again as a white flash from the end of its rifle sent another snap past her.

She heard the *noorla* roar in pain and felt the ground shake. The *noorla* lay dead, its claws contracting against its chest.

Their savior got closer, and Caas saw that it wasn't a *noorla*. Its armor, once white, was fire blackened and covered in soot. Flames still licked at its arms and the back of its helmet… and there were more just like it coming through the fire.

"Caas, what's happening? Can I look?" Ar'ri asked.

"I think…I think more demons are here," she said.

The new demon fired over their heads, and Ar'ri squealed and tried to worm his way back beneath the tree.

"I count three more around the barn!" the demon shouted in Dotok and ran toward them. Terror petrified Caas as it got closer and then went to a knee next to them. The armor wasn't anything like the *noorla*; it looked more like what her father wore to the monthly battle training.

It turned a mirrored faceplate to them, and the helmet expanded slightly with a hiss of air. The visor swung up and a pale-skinned alien with short blond hair looked at her with pale blue eyes.

"Are you OK?" The words came from a speaker attached to its throat.

Caas took a deep breath and screamed at the top of her lungs. Ar'ri joined in sympathetic fright.

"No! No!" Torni raised a hand and tried to calm the children. "I'm human, a Marine from the *Breitenfeld*. We're here to help. Please stop screaming. I'm a friend. Ugh ... *meln. Meln*."

Caas recoiled from Torni's touch and finally stopped screaming.

"*Breitenfeld*?" she said. She remembered the word from the news broadcasts that her parents had watched over and over again. Ancient Pa'lon said help would come from the *Breitenfeld*.

"Yes, *Breitenfeld*. Is this thing not working?" Torni grabbed the speaker against her neck and flicked it with her finger.

"You're ugly," Ar'ri said. He peeked over Caas' shoulder with tear-streaked eyes.

"It is working. You see that shelter over there?" Torni pointed to the squat building the village used to weather storm squalls. "Go in there and wait for me. We'll get you out of here once it's safe."

Caas and Ar'ri shook their heads.

"No! Monsters," Ar'ri said.

"There are *noorla* inside," Caas said.

"Inside the shelter?"

The children nodded.

The Marine put two fingers to her ear. "Sir, this is Torni…"

****

Hale vaulted over a low stone wall and spotted a banshee holding an iron bar like it was a club. The banshee stood along a canal, poking into the water with the tip of the bar.

"Contact! One on the canal," Hale said. He slowed to aim when the banshee swung around and hurled the bar at him like it was a javelin. Pain exploded across his arms and forehead as the bar deflected off his rifle and smashed into him. Hale staggered back and tripped against the wall he'd just jumped over.

The banshee roared a challenge and lumbered toward him.

A crack in the air from a gauss pistol sent a round into the banshee's arm. The thing looked at the source of the annoyance and snarled. Bailey fired her pistol faster than anyone else Hale had known until it clicked empty. She replaced the noise of her shots with a string of profanity as she reloaded.

The banshee turned its attention to her and swung an overhand strike down on the squat Marine. Bailey rolled to the side and put a round in the banshee's exposed jaw. The bullet shattered bone and tendrils of gray blood dripped from the wound. The banshee gagged on its own blood and lashed out at Bailey.

Hale found his rifle in the dirt and got off a shot, hitting the banshee in the stomach. The beast fell to its knees, then to its elbows. Bailey jammed the muzzle of her pistol into an eye slit and sent a bullet careening through its skull.

"What I wouldn't give for a real weapon right now," she said. She looked at her pistol like it was a child's toy and shook her head.

"Sir, we're outside the shelter," Orozco said through the IR. *"Steuben and Yarrow are at the*

edge of town. They say we're clear of banshees. I can see people moving in the shelter, but no one's answering. Want us to go in?"

"Stand by, I'll be right there," Hale said.

Hale got back to his feet, his ears ringing from the impact with the iron bar. Some of the farm plots were partially flooded, and green stalks stuck out of the mud, drooping with fat grains. Rows of bushes with bright white berries rustled in the wind that carried the inferno ever closer.

A squat semicircle of a structure was built into the side of a canyon and a stairway cut into the earth leading to the main entrance. Orozco and Standish waved to Hale from a waist-high stone wall around the shelter.

"Torni?" Hale said into the IR.

"She was with some kids last time I saw her. Figure she'd bring them to the shelter?" Bailey asked.

"Makes sense," Hale said. He jogged to his waiting Marines.

"We took out three around some kind of

melon patch," Standish said. "Damn things were eating. Eating! You believe that? Since when do Xaros need to eat?"

"Since when are Xaros anything but drones?" Orozco asked.

"Great questions for later," Hale said. "Let's get this shelter open." He looked back at the approaching fire. "We may need it."

Hale went down the stairs and knocked on the door. He heard a rustling within.

"Marines from the *Breitenfeld*," he announced, knocking against rusted metal. There was no answer. "To hell with subtlety," he said and reached for the handle.

"Sir!" Torni's warning came before he could open the door. She was at the top of the stairwell, panting, a pair of Dotok children in her arms. "Sir, step back very, very slowly."

Hale backed up the stairs, his rifle trained on the door.

"Kids say there are banshees in there," Torni said. The children nodded as Caas nibbled on her fingernails and pointed to the door.

"Caas, no!" Ar'ri pulled his sister's hand away from her mouth. "Momma said."

"Kids say a lot of things," Orozco chided. "I almost got my head blown off by an IED because some little Malaysian brat promised me his family's shed was safe."

"Cover me." Hale pulled a magnetized disk off his belt and pulled out a few yards of thin wire attached to it. Marines used them as cams against a ship's hull as an extra safety measure when working in the void. Flying off the side of a ship, "Going Dutchman," was a harrowing experience and not one that guaranteed survival. Hale tossed the disk at the door and it snapped on. He gave the line a jerk and the door swung open with a squeal.

"I see bodies," Orozco said.

The Dotok kids started whimpering.

A hulking shadow marched toward the open door. Standish snapped off a shot, then pulled a grenade from his belt.

"Flash bang out!" He threw the grenade

through the open door and ducked aside.

Hale turned to the Dotok kids and saw Torni was already shielding them with her body.

Hale wrapped an arm over Torni and added his mass to block any shrapnel.

The ground shook as the grenade exploded. Standish rushed into the shelter and three shots sounded from within.

"Clear!" Standish shouted.

Hale pulled away from Torni, who held the children close to her, whispering into their ears.

"It's OK. I've got you and I won't let anyone hurt you," she said to each Dotok.

Standish trotted up the stairs and brushed gray blood off the edge of his rifle. Hale tried to step around him to get into the shelter, but Standish put up a hand to block him.

"No, sir. You don't want to go in there," Standish said, his ever-cocky tone subdued.

"Got some civvies," Orozco said. He took a hand away from his cannon and pointed at the plot of bushes. A handful of Dotok stood between the rows of bushes, staring at the Marines. All were filthy, covered in dirt and grime.

Hale pointed to the shelter. "It's safe now."

"You're…humans, I presume. From the *Breitenfeld?*" a middle-aged-looking female asked.

"That's right. Where is the rest of your village?" Hale asked.

The speaker shook her head. "I think we're all that's left."

"We can get everyone out in two Mules," Orozco said. "Maybe one Destrier if the life support can hack it."

"Right now we don't even have one Mule." Hale's gaze crept up the cliff face, the top obscured by haze and smoke.

"How'd these civvies ever get to and from their capitol? I don't see any landing pads or airstrips," Orozco said.

"There is, or was, a tunnel, leading from each settlement to New Abhaile," Hale said. "Cut right through the planet's crust, forty-five-minute travel time. Decent alternative when a hyper loop isn't an option. Briefing I got said the Dotok blew all the tunnels after the Xaros hit the ground. Dotok were shuttling settlements back to New Abhaile. Looks like they couldn't get to them all."

"Sucks to be that guy making those decisions, huh?" Standish said. "Who lives, who dies …guarantee there's no right answer."

"There is always a correct answer to any tactical question." Steuben walked over with Yarrow at his side. The medic saw the Dotok as they gathered at the end of the field of berry bushes and looked at Hale expectantly.

Hale nodded toward the civilians and Yarrow broke off from Steuben.

"'You save the most,' isn't that right, Steuben?" Hale asked.

"A worthy answer," the Karigole said with a nod.

"Philosophy aside, how're we getting out of here?" Bailey asked.

"We can squat and hold…or we send up a balloon." Hale looked at Torni. "Sergeant Torni, we did bring an IR balloon, right?"

Torni stood up and brushed dirt from her knees. "The IR balloon is specialist equipment, and I assigned Corporal Bailey to carry it as part of her kit."

Heads swung toward Bailey.

"I was trapped in my turret, remember? You think I had room for anything but me in there?" she said.

"So the balloon is a non-starter," Hale looked back to the fire, on the other side of which was the wrecked Mule.

"You mean this kit?" Steuben said. He slung a pack from his shoulder and handed it to Bailey.

"Crickey! You saved Bloke!" Bailey unzipped the pack and took out the two halves of her sniper rifle. She hugged the weapon like a child with a favorite toy.

Torni reached into the pack and found a rectangular box. "We're in business," she said.

"With Bailey unable to extricate herself from the pod, and our rather abrupt descent, it seemed prudent to grab whatever I could," Steuben said.

"Prudent?" Hale asked.

"Timely. Apropos. Inspired. Serendipitous," Steuben said.

"I know what it means, Steuben. Good work," Hale said.

"Sir, you want to come see this," Yarrow said to him over the IR.

Hale trotted over to Yarrow, who was wrapping a compression bandage on an elderly Dotok's forearm.

"What is it?"

"Minor injuries, mostly. I can't give them any drugs. Something as innocent to us as Motrin might send them into anaphylactic shock," Yarrow said. He smoothed out the bandage and got a smile from the old Dotok.

"That's not why you called me over here," Hale said.

Yarrow touched his neck and switched off his translator. Hale did the same.

Yarrow held up a dirty swab with blood congealed against the tip. Gray blood. Hale's mouth went dry as the implication became clear.

"I got that cleaning out a laceration," Yarrow said. "I don't have a DNA scanner, but I'd bet you a steak dinner that those banshees," his voice lowered, "the banshees are Dotok."

****

Torni entered a message onto her forearm screen and waited for it to upload to the communication balloon. A green light blinked twice, and she removed a wire that ran from her gauntlet to the balloon case.

"Ar'ri, Caas, come here," she said to the two children who were doing a terrible job of hiding behind a wrecked cart. Caas led her brother over by the hand.

"He doesn't think you're ugly," Caas said. "He's sorry."

"I've been called worse. You two want to do something fun?" Torni asked.

They nodded in unison.

"Here…put your finger on this button. When I count to three, push it. Ready? One…two…"

Ar'ri pushed the button and a balloon inflated from one end of the carry box. It expanded to nearly a yard in diameter and rose into the air. Ar'ri laughed and clapped his hands while Caas crossed her arms, brooding.

"Do you know what that was?" Torni asked. "It will float into the air and call for help. Our planes use special technology that…only we can use." Ar'ri waved to the departing balloon while Caas kicked at the dirt.

Since the last banshee was killed, none of the other Dotok had come over to check on the two children. All the other survivors were children, women with babies, or the elderly.

"Caas, where are your parents?" Torni asked.

The girl pointed a finger toward the fire. "They sent us with teacher to the shelter, then the flying *noorla* used their lasers to start the fire. Can Mommy and Daddy run through the fire like you? They have the hard clothes too."

Torni took the little girl's hands in hers and squeezed her fingers.

"Oh, Caas…" Torni choked up, then forced her emotions away. She was a Marine and a non-commissioned officer; she wouldn't look weak in front of anyone. "I…we'll look for your parents when we get to New Abhaile, all right?" Caas' pale green eyes looked on the verge of tears, but she nodded and looked up, watching as the balloon faded away into the haze.

Torni felt a tug on her shoulder. Ar'ri held a hand under her face.

"Hungry," he said.

Torni reached into the cargo pouch on the small of her back and fished out a small box of chocolate-covered cracker sticks. They were her favorite, and possibly the last box in existence that had chocolate and almond sprinkles. She'd found it at the bottom of a sea bag when she moved into the barracks in Phoenix, and she didn't have the heart to eat the very last of her pogey bait from before the Xaros invasion.

Torni tore open the box and made a presentation out of giving a single stick to Ar'ri. The little boy snatched it from her hand and devoured it. Torni tapped Caas on her elbow and gave one to her.

Caas sniffed at it and took a tentative bite. "What is it?"

"A Pocky stick, they were my favorite when I was your age," Torni said.

Caas looked at the cracker like it was an ancient artifact, then gave it to her brother.

"Sarge, Yarrow said these are safe for us to eat." Bailey walked over, carrying a handful of white berries. "And the others say they're in season." Bailey knelt down and held the berries while Caas and Ar'ri ate them one at a time.

"Let them eat. We've got ration paste," Torni said.

"Umm, ration paste," Bailey chuckled. "I've

had vegemite that tastes better than that garbage."
The sniper smiled and tussled Ar'ri's hair. "When
was the last time you saw children, Sarge?"

"I saw a few in Phoenix."

"You have kids? Before?"

"No. I had the Corps. You?"

Bailey's mouth twisted. "Baby girl. Left her
with my sister when I signed up for the Saturn
mission. Plan was to send for her once we got
settled, Titan station up and running."

"What was her name?"

"Abigail." Bailey sniffed and wiped a tear
away. "She looked like her deadbeat father. Only
thing that bludger ever left us were my Abbie's eyes
and her curls. Ah, look at me gettin' all clucky."

A high-pitched whine filled the air. Torni
stood up and scanned the sky.

"Doesn't sound like Xaros, does it?" Bailey
asked.

The children latched onto Torni's legs and
whimpered.

"It's OK. It's OK." Torni made out a

Destrier heavy transport craft descending through the haze, the anti-grav thrusters whining like a bone saw. "They're on our side."

"Gall, this is Raider Six," Hale said through the IR. *"Thanks for getting here so quick."*

"We saw the wreck of Mule Eight and were looking for you on the wrong side of the fire," Durand said. *"Good thing you sent up a beacon. How many more transports do you need over there?"*

"One Destrier is enough," Hale said.

"I thought there were…roger. Load up and we'll get the civvies to New Abhaile," Durand said.

Torni hefted the children up in her arms and carried them to the waiting ship.

CHAPTER 6

Lieutenant Sam Douglas woke up and stretched. The single sized mattress must have been made of springs and tissue paper, but Douglas couldn't remember the last time he'd slept so well. Life at the Kilauea Rest and Relaxation station was a huge improvement over what he and his soldiers had in Phoenix. No constant calls for formation, head count, or being parceled out as labor to assist whatever civics project didn't have enough robot workers that day. Still, even that was better than living aboard a spaceship.

When their time came for a platoon R&R pass to Hawaii, morale picked up immediately. A transport ride across half the Pacific and their five-day vacation began. Douglas took the first day to do nothing but sleep.

He swung his legs over the side of his bed and set his bare feet against the linoleum floors. The touch stung his feet like he'd stepped on a live wire. He jerked his feet up with a yelp and looked at the floor, half expecting to see broken glass. Nothing but an off-white tile. He pressed a hand against the bottom of his feet; they felt fine.

"Weird." He tapped his feet against the floor with no ill effects. He stood up and stumbled forward, catching himself on the back of a chair. His legs felt like rubber as they struggled to support his weight. He hadn't felt this weak since his last twenty-mile road march back at Fort Benning. A sudden headache pressed a vise against his temples.

He hadn't been drinking. Food poisoning from the resorts robo-kitchens?

He picked up his Ubi from off a nightstand.

"Call Sergeant Black," he said. Maybe he wasn't the only one feeling like this. The call rang, but no answer.

"Call Sergeant Newell." The Ubi slipped from his hand and clattered to the ground. Douglas flexed his fingers, unable to feel them. He looked down at the Ubi and saw drops of blood falling against its screen. He wiped blood away from his lips. Why couldn't he taste it?

Douglas lurched over to the sink and let the blood drip down the drain. He wiped his hand across his mouth. Ribbons of flesh came away from his face. Douglas looked into the mirror and saw his cheeks melting off his face.

He managed a ragged scream before collapsing to the ground.

****

Stacey watched the footage of Douglas's final moments, her jaw slack.

"I *told* you," Ibarra thrust a holographic finger at the probe. "Told you a six day grow was too fast for the proccies. Look at this mess." His finger snapped to the screen.

Stacey turned away, unable to watch any more.

"I think I'm going to be sick," she said.

"Thorsson, what's the damage?" Ibarra asked.

The blond-haired Icelander was on a screen, calling in from the procedural factory on Hawaii. He wore a hazmat suit, one that looked as if it had gotten a fair amount of use in the last few hours.

"96 percent loss on the batch," Thorsson said. "The other four percent look to be stable—physically. Mentally, that's a different discussion. Lab says their lysosome organelles are defective, which is why they…melted."

Ibarra put his hands on his hips. "Can we fix that? If there's an easy solution then we're still in the game."

"Jesus, Grandpa," Stacey said. "Men and women are dead. Can we take a break from the mad-scientist bit for a second?"

"Time is the fire in which we burn, little one. I'll put on a hair shirt for this later," Ibarra

said.

"It appears that nine days of gestation is our operating limit, for now," the probe said. "Given the threat, it would be unwise to waste more resources until we can afford to fail in another experiment."

"I never thought there'd be a day when producing fully grown and educated humans in two hundred and fourteen hours wouldn't be fast enough," Ibarra said.

"There is another option," the probe said.

"No!" Ibarra shook his head. "Absolutely not. We've already discussed—"

Ibarra froze mid word, as if his hologram was on pause. The screen with Thorsson went dark.

"I've been with Marc for almost a hundred years," the probe said. "I'm beginning to lose patience with him."

Stacey backed away from the probe. "What did you do?"

"I suspended his matrix. He isn't aware of what's happened or what we're going to discuss," the probe said.

"Why are you and I going to discuss anything?"

"You are humanity's ambassador. Our next choice will be of interest and discussion to the Alliance. What I'm about to show you is anathema to many cultures." The probe floated from the central dais, its silver light spilling across the deck. "Please come with me." The Xaros doors opened, deconstructing as tiny grains of the basalt-colored material skittered away from the center to allow passage.

Stacey waved a hand in front of Ibarra's face. She snapped her fingers next to his ears.

"Stacey."

"Coming. Coming. Could you teach me to do that to him?" she asked the probe as she caught up to it. They walked side by side down the almost featureless passageway. Stacey felt her pulse quicken as she remembered being chased by Xaros drones around these same corners.

"No. Tell me, have you encountered the Yuun-Tai species on Bastion?" the probe asked.

"I don't believe so."

"The Yuun-Tai evolutionary path was very different from yours. Almost a pure predator species, you would describe them as bipedal alligators, but with fur. They give birth to litters of live young. Once the babies are a few days old, the mother consumes the runt of the litter."

"What? That's horrible!"

"To you. You have standards and expectations when it comes to child care. The Yuun-Tai consume the runt to rebalance the mother's hormonal balance to enable lactation. Without this, the other babies will starve and the Yuun-Tai will end. Humans and many other species find this abhorrent, yet it must be done for survival," the probe said.

"I assume there's a point to this story," she said.

"What I'm about to show you is necessary for survival. Look at it that way." A door opened ahead of the probe, leading to a large room. Inside was a large glass tube that could have held two or three people. The end caps whirred with internal machinery.

"My models show that the true-born humans will likely accept the procedurally generated individuals. As for these, my math is inconclusive. Let's begin," the probe said.

Thin mechanical arms extended from the end caps of the cylinder. The tips sprayed dark red material that hung in the air. The arms worked so fast they almost blurred. Stacey watched as a human skeleton took shape within seconds. Organs came into being and Stacey had to look away.

"This disturbs you?"

"There's a reason I studied astrophysics and not biology," she said. "If we just failed to make a new person in six days, how can we do the same thing in sixty seconds?"

"I'm not making a person. These constructs are approximations of human beings. They are neither truly alive nor truly sentient. You can look now," the probe said.

A fully grown man was in the tube, nearly

seven feet tall and built like he could rip a drone apart with his bare hands. His lumpy face looked like he was already a veteran of a gladiator arena. His skin kept her attention, mottled patches of copper and dark green.

"They will all be male for the sake of waste elimination—but are incapable of breeding—and better societal acceptance of their purpose," the probe said.

"Good call on the waste elimination. What is their purpose?"

"I believe the term is 'cannon fodder.' They are much less intelligent than the procedurals, only capable of limited problem solving. But they will know how to fight. They will be loyal to humanity and they will be legion."

"They're clones?"

"They are purpose-built biological machines. Variance in their appearance is a byproduct of their construction."

"The proccies, they'll be the officers, the bridge crew and the pilots," Stacey said, gleaning the probe's plan. "These will be the…the poor bloody infantry."

"Will they be accepted?"

"They'll be slaves. That's what you're creating," Stacey said. "Slave soldiers with no sense of agency, no choice in if they fight. Why stop at creating soldiers? Make laborers. House-hold servants. You will open a Pandora's Box showcasing the worst humans have to offer if there's something we can abuse. Something we can label as 'not really human'.

"You disagree with their production?"

"No," Stacey shook her head and sighed. "I see their value." She put her hand on the glass and looked up at the soldier's face. "I see how they can save us. They can carry a gun big enough to destroy a drone with a single shot. We'll need them, because there won't be enough of us when the time comes. Do it. Make as many as you can. I'll consign millions to death on the battlefield for the sake of us all."

"I'm proud of you."

"I am not!" The soldier stirred at the sound of Stacey's shout. "Look at what we've become. We're mass-producing…people. Like they're animals on a factory farm. These-these doughboys will bleed. For what? For our own precious survival. I don't know if humanity ever really had a shred of decency to it. But this…this means we have lost ourselves. When it's all over I don't know if we'll be able to stand what we've become."

Stacey pressed a hand against her face.

"I can sell this to the Alliance. I don't know how Grandpa will sell it to Phoenix if he's not on board."

"He'll come around. He always does," the probe said. "Full details of the program will be transferred with you to Bastion. Are you ready to leave?"

Stacey tapped on the glass.

"What will you call them?"

"Given military history and the particulars of their construction, I agree with your earlier moniker—doughboys."

She turned away and made for the door.

"Just get me out of here."

CHAPTER 7

Of all the parts on his ship, Valdar liked the *Breitenfeld's* sick bay the least. There was never good news waiting for him there as his visits were always to check on those wounded from battle or injured in shipboard mishaps. This trip was no different.

Valdar was in his chief physician's office, watching the medics and doctors do their rounds on the two dozen Marines and sailors who'd been wounded when the banshees boarded his ship. Emergency surgeries had been completed hours before—Valdar never came to sick bay when his presence could be a distraction from saving lives.

He watched as crewmen washed away pools of blood from a surgical theater, performing the grim task with practiced ease.

A doctor with a patrician nose and a bald pate barged into the office and slammed the door behind him. He flopped into an office chair and rubbed his temples.

"Dr. Accorso," Valdar said, "how is my crew?"

"The four with the flash burns need some minor skin grafts. They'll be fit for duty in a few hours. The gunner's mate who lost an arm, I've got her in an induced coma until the trauma splicing sets in. Maybe we can regrow her arm when we get back to Earth, if she's lucky." Accorso pulled a vape-stick from his desk and took a deep drag, holding the pseudo-smoke in his lungs before exhaling away from Valdar.

"I can't believe you, a doctor, smoke," Valdar said.

"I also drink too much, but not when we're underway," Accorso said with a wink. "Chaplain

Krohe is making the rounds. Seeing friends ripped apart by those banshees was more than most could handle, even this crew. I can treat their bodies, but someone else has to mend their souls."

"Can I make my own rounds? I want to see them," Valdar said.

"Before you do, there's something I want to show you." Accorso spun his chair around and grabbed a bound sheaf of papers from a basket on his wall. "The medic, Yarrow, the one who had that alien...thing inside him?"

Valdar crossed his arms and nodded.

"I've run every test I could from the samples we took when he was possessed, I suppose ...and afterwards. First direct contact with that sort of being—this paper would be published in a heartbeat across the medical community—if we still had a medical community that cared about papers, but I digress." Accorso flipped the papers open to a sheet with a tiny flag attached to it and then spun the papers around and tapped his finger against a data table.

"I'm a ship driver, not a doctor," Valdar said.

"Yarrow's telomeres, the little end caps on our DNA that protect our chromosomes, they're too long." Accorso waited for some sort of recognition to register on Valdar's face, to no avail. "As we get older, the telomeres shorten every time a cell divides. That's why things start to droop as we get older, why we get wrinkles." Accorso rubbed the top of his bald head. "Yarrow, he has telomeres like an infant."

"The thing that possessed him made his cells younger?" Valdar asked.

"No." Accorso tapped his fingertip against the data table. "I had baseline data on him from when we boosted his green blood cell count before we went to Anthalas. His telomeres were just as long *before* he ever saw that alien." Accorso watched as Valdar's face went pale. "Yarrow's body is only a few months old, at best."

"False minds in weed bodies," Valdar said, running his hand over his moustache. "That's what the Toth demanded from us. Is there anyone else on my ship with the same genetic markers?"

"I don't know. Yarrow is the only one I've had the time to examine so closely. It wouldn't be too difficult to go through the crew's blood samples, once the computers are back up and running."

"No, I need to know now. I can't have my crew compromised like Yarrow," Valdar said.

Accorso frowned, then shrugged his shoulders. "There's a way. Back in the fifties, a team from Harvard found that—"

"Do it. Now. Keep the results between us."

"It will be slow, and it'll delay my autopsy on the banshees," Accorso said.

"Why are you bothering with the banshees?"

"For science, of course. Do you realize what medical knowledge this ship will bring back to Earth? I'll have my own research wing at the new hospital in Phoenix. The Antonio Accorso Center, sounds beautiful, doesn't it?"

"Mission first, ego later," Valdar said.

****

Torni adjusted the headphones on Ar'ri to cover his ears, but the boy kept trying to take them off, which was detrimental to his hearing while in the noisy bay of a Destrier drop ship. As with all things military, comfort was never a design factor.

"Caas," Torni said, "watch your brother. Don't let him take those off."

Caas swatted her brother on the back of his head, which brought out a pout. Torni wrapped an arm around him and brandished a finger at Caas.

"Torni, what's your planet like? Does it have Xaros on it like Dotari?" Caas asked.

"Dotari?"

"That's where we're all from. Mommy and Daddy said we'll go back there someday when the Xaros are all gone."

"Earth had Xaros, until we beat them," Torni said. "My home is a very beautiful place, but there aren't many people left on it."

"Ancient Pa'lon says no one lives on Dotari

anymore. All the Dotok are on spaceships between the stars or here on Takeni. If you can beat the Xaros on your planet, will you do that for us on Dotari? I heard there are seasons, lots of good food to eat and you can see the whole night sky from anywhere, not like living in our canyon," Caas said.

"I don't know about that, little one. Let's get you and your brother someplace safe first, OK?" Red warning lights flashed through the cargo hold. The ship was coming in for a landing. Ar'ri whimpered and snuggled against Torni.

"Almost done, we'll be in New Abhaile soon," Torni said.

****

Hale marched down the Destrier's ramp, his hand up to block the harsh light that greeted him on the landing pad. New Abhaile was set in the middle of the widest canyon on the planet. The towering ramparts of the surrounding cliffs were far enough apart that direct sunlight was a possibility, unlike the perpetual shadow of Galogesvi.

Hale saw the city just beyond the limits of the star port and almost couldn't believe what he saw. Most of the city was made up of starships, docked on the surface and set into massive frames. Wide stone boulevards connected the ships to each other and formed a lattice of roads throughout the city. Steam crept up around the high roadways, and the slight smell of sulphur tinged the air.

An entire quarter of the city was destroyed, a jumbled mess of stone blocks and wreckage of a once great starship. Smoke rose from a half-dozen small fires in the rubble.

A trio of Dotok, all wearing combat fatigues and body armor around their torsos and shoulders, waited for Hale at the end of the landing pad.

"What a garden spot," Standish said. He and the rest of Hale's team had their helmets off; the combination of ambient heat and humidity made it feel like a Bangkok summer to Hale.

"Standish, I don't know what offends our hosts, so the best course of action for you would be to keep your mouth shut," Hale said. "Torni, get these civilians tucked away and find the shore party. Get a fresh combat load and hot chow if they've got it. Whoever's in charge of this city is expecting me."

"Roger, sir," Torni said.

"Steuben, come with me, please," Hale said to the Karigole.

Hale broke away from his team as Steuben kept pace beside him.

"Steuben, how much do you know about static defense in an urban environment?" Hale asked.

"Theoretical or practical?"

"Both."

"I studied the great works of the Karigole battle masters, all two hundred and nine field marshals from the last eighteen thousand years of our recorded history, and I participated in the siege of—" Steuben emitted a series of whistles and clicks that sent Hale's ears ringing "—beside Kosciusko. I must admit that his knowledge base is far greater than mine."

"Did you win that siege?"

"I'm alive, aren't I?"

"Don't be afraid to pipe up with any good ideas while we're planning the defense of this city," Hale said.

"It remains to be seen just how well the Dotok can defend themselves, let alone accept tactical advice," Steuben said.

Hale raised a hand in greeting to the three Dotok, and they copied the gesture.

"I am Un'qu, head of New Abhaile security," the lead Dotok said. "Follow me. The Ancient awaits you." Un'qu ignored Hale as he extended a hand, then turned and walked away.

"I'm Lieutenant Ken Hale, Atlantic Union Marine Corps. What can you tell me about your defenses, about what happened here?" Hale and Steuben followed their escorts down a flight of stone stairs and onto an elevated boulevard almost twenty yards across. Disabled ground cars and trucks had been pushed to the side. Every Dotok on the boulevard with them traveled by foot or by bicycle, many doing a double take as they saw the un-helmeted human and Karigole walking amongst them.

"Of relevance," Un'qu said, "an enemy force landed on a small city in a separate canyon. They massacred the city and came through the gravity-train tunnel without warning. The *noorla* fought through the Apex Station's defenders and were about to overwhelm the entire city when my predecessor sabotaged the arms depot beneath Apex Station. The explosion…" Un'qu pointed to the smoking remnants. Broken rail lines ran to tunnels in the surrounding canyons and into the earth outside the city like ribs of a picked-over carcass lying in the desert. "Our leadership council was lost in the explosion, along with most of our military's senior officers. The decision to collapse all other tunnels leading to New Abhaile was made soon afterwards."

"Trapping all the outlying settlements," Hale said. "I was just in Galogesvi picking up survivors."

"The decision wasn't easy," Un'qu said,

looking away from Hale. "Our air force has been evacuating everyone we can, but we have only so many airframes … and there have been losses since. But it is better to lose a finger than one's arm."

"I know a guy named Ibarra back on Earth that you'd get along with," Hale said.

Un'qu gave him a sideways look.

Hale looked across the city. Armed Dotok built fighting positions along the outer walls or manned flak cannons atop the converted spaceships. Children and elder Dotok hurried from ship to ship, carrying boxes or hauling sand in three-wheeled barrows.

"How many people are in this city?" Steuben asked.

"Maybe fifty thousand," Un'qu said.

"And how many spacecraft?" Steuben asked.

"Just the *Burning Blade*, the rest were destroyed."

The *Breitenfeld* had a crew complement of seven hundred. It could carry—at most—an additional thousand civilians before its life-support systems overloaded. The *Burning Blade* was half the size of the *Breitenfeld* from stem to stern. There was no way they could evacuate every Dotok off the planet.

As they walked into a tunnel running through a ship the size of a destroyer, Hale came to a stop to marvel at what was on the other side. A ship over a mile long and almost a half mile across lay nestled in a frame of enormous struts and braces forming a cradle for the ship. The smooth curve of the upper hull gleamed in the waning sunlight. The landed ship was at the very center of the city; raised stone roads emanated out from vestigial docking bays and expanded into the wider boulevards.

"That's…something else," Hale said.

"The *Canticle of Reason*, she was the heart of the colonization fleet," Un'qu said. "Most of her systems were failing by the time we reached Takeni. Ancient Pa'lon decided to beach the ship instead of waiting for shelters to be built on the surface. At the time, the decision saved thousands of lives. Given our current situation, it was a poor choice."

"What about the rest of the ships? Why were they brought to the surface?" Steuben asked.

"Our star emits rather powerful, and irregular, solar storms. Once the *Canticle* was beached, a storm of particular strength would have caused significant damage to the remaining fleet, so he had them all brought down." Un'qu looked at his wristwatch. "The four hundred and ninth Landing Day celebration is ten days from now."

"Wait, is the Ancient Pa'lon we're going to meet the same one from the story you just told us?" Hale asked.

"The same," Un'qu said.

"It is rare that I meet another species so similar to mine that is also so long-lived," Steuben, age four hundred and seven, said.

"Our elderly normally pass on in their nineties."

"Then how is Ancient Pa'lon so…ancient?" Hale asked.

"It would be best for you to ask him yourself. Dotok consider gossip to be unbecoming of cultured individuals." Un'qu gestured to an opening on the prow of the *Canticle of Reason*. "We are expected shortly."

****

Hale and Un'qu walked on to the *Canticle's* bridge. The command center of the former void ship had been transformed into a nexus for the planet's defense. Maps with hastily written notes taped to them and a billboard with a long list of Dotok words were surrounded by squabbling groups of Dotok.

"What's all this?" Hale asked Un'qu.

"We're trying to decide which outpost to evacuate next. The Chosen from several villages think their lists rate higher than the others. There was an order of merit list with the First, but it was lost when the rail station was destroyed," Un'qu said. "Along with the First."

"Lists?" Hale asked.

"A hold-over from our time in space,"

Pa'lon said from behind Hale. The elderly Dotok, flanked by a pair of nurses, walked toward them with aid of a cane. "Was a time that any ship could have failed, and their crew and passengers lost. There's only so much room on a fleet. If a ship was going to be evacuated, the ship master, the Chosen would get his most valuable people off first. Keep those with special skill sets alive over those who'd do nothing else but waste oxygen. The First might decide to move a hundred survivors off a failing ship elsewhere in the fleet, and the other chosen would make room for them."

"By getting rid of those on the bottom of your lists?" Hale asked.

"That's correct. It became a caste system," Pa'lon said. "Skilled workers, talented artists, they stayed at the top of the lists. Those lacking useful knowledge or undesirables, criminals and such, fell to the bottom. Mobility was possible, but families settled into a rating band and stayed there. It kept going after we made landfall, even when we didn't need it. Some traditions were too hard to break.

Now we're suffering for it."

Pa'lon sank to a low crouch, a palsy shaking his left hand.

"You all right?" Hale asked.

"I'm old and sick. Doesn't that happen to humans too?" Pa'lon asked.

"The Ancient has been ill for some time," Un'qu said. "Let him rest before the council meeting." The Dotok officer led Hale away to the billboard.

"Your communication device translates what is spoken, but not the written word," Un'qu said. "Allow me to explain. The top of the list has the cities with the highest known population. Those with lines through them are confirmed to be lost to the *noorla*." The Dotok's eyes drifted down to an entry toward the lower third of the list.

"What's there?" Hale asked.

"My wife and child," Un'qu said. "Usonvi is a place where low-listers choose to settle. I met my wife during a field-training exercise there almost a year ago. My parents are still furious that I married

159

someone so low. Moving them to New Abhaile proved difficult."

"You're pretty high up there?"

"Oh yes, anyone descended from the Ancient Pa'lon is expected to do great things, the opportunities present themselves. Nepotism. All against the Ancient's wishes and guidance. If he was around more it might change, but his illness makes that difficult."

Hale shook his head. "Let's stay focused. I'll have the *Breitenfeld* send down an air-traffic control team and organize evac from whatever air assets we can spare."

"But how will they know which places to evacuate first? The council might appoint a new First soon, Shouldn't we wait?"

"Let me tell you about Marines. We will do something constructive right away instead of waiting to figure out the perfect answer ten minutes too late."

"But the council—"

"Our help doesn't come limited by your

conditions and we're not going to wait around for you to get your act together."

A robed Dotok stepped onto the bridge and rang a bell three times.

"The meeting begins," Un'qu said.

****

The Dotok equivalent of a conference room was nothing but an empty space with black curtains adorning the walls, obfuscating the lights in the ceiling. Three Dotok, covered head to toe in robes and wearing the same blank masks as Un'qu, stood in a semicircle, each facing a holo-projector on the deck.

Un'qu showed Hale and Steuben in, then stepped back into the passageway. The door slid shut behind the non-Dotok with a hiss. The black curtains along the walls were sheer, and Hale saw the outline of a Dotok behind each one.

"You come to us with your face bare," one of the masked Dotok said, an elderly woman by the sound of her voice.

"You would presume to know us so quickly," the largest of the three said, the voice a rich baritone.

"I…should put my helmet back on?" Hale asked. He unsnapped it from where it was attached to his lower back.

"How many times do I have to tell you all? Humans consider masks a sign of someone not to be trusted." The final Dotok removed his mask, and Hale recognized Pa'lon from the recording of Valdar volunteering his ship and crew for this rescue mission. It certainly was Pa'lon, but in the flesh the Dotok looked to be on the far side of middle age, much older than the recordings.

"Do it." Pa'lon tossed his mask behind him. "They're here to help us. Be polite."

"We will not abandon our ways just because some *ilgish* embraces the barbarian's path," the elderly Dotok said.

"Forgive them, Lieutenant and Steuben, they don't have the cultural exposure that I do," Pa'lon said. "Stacey speaks very highly of you," he said to

Hale. "The stories of your exploits rescuing the probe from Earth and seizing the star gate made quite the stir on Bastion. Then when you stood up to one of the Qa'Resh and demanded an explanation as to what they planned to do to your fallen comrade…the species of the alliance that favor heroism were most impressed by you. Stacey Ibarra said you have 'brass ones,' which I didn't entirely understand."

Steuben cleared his throat.

"Yes, no time to waste," Pa'lon said. "Captain Valdar?"

A hologram of the *Breitenfeld*'s master and commander emerged from the emitter. The captain, who must have been standing by the tactical plot on the ship's bridge, looked up and across the faces of the Dotok.

"We ready?" Valdar asked.

Pa'lon motioned for Hale and Steuben to stand next to him. His hand shook with a noticeable palsy, and Pa'lon jammed it deep into his robes and shivered slightly.

"Hale, Steuben, glad you made it to New Abhaile," Valdar said.

"So are we, sir," Hale said.

"Captain Valdar, what is the situation in orbit?" Pa'lon asked.

"There is a new fleet of compromised transports on course to the planet, six vessels equivalent in size and displacement to a human cruiser," Valdar said. "Sub-Commander Ty'ken said they're *Laanti* class colony ships, meant to carry heavy equipment for a colony fleet. They've slowed their approach, which isn't consistent with the last two waves of ground troops the Xaros have deployed."

"Sir, are these ships armed?" Hale asked.

"None of the ships in the Golden Fleet were armed," the old woman said. "We were assured the path to New Dotari was bare, peaceful." She stared at Pa'lon.

"Before my time. Don't blame me," Pa'lon said.

"The last two waves came in fast and hard,

overwhelming the orbital defenses with drones and kamikaze ships to cover for the ground troops' insertion," Valdar said. "My ship can dish out a lot more firepower than the *Burning Blade*, so we should be able to neutralize the threat before they get into orbit."

"That would buy us time," Pa'lon said.

"You said it's slowing," Steuben said. "How long until they arrive?"

"Ten hours." The hologram of Valdar warbled as the captain pointed his camera to a graph on his tactical board with handwritten equations around it.

"We observed several hundred escape pods during our arrival, but only encountered a few banshees at Galogesvi," the Karigole said. "Where did the rest of those pods go?"

"Probably to the other outlying settlements," the taller Dotok said. "They are easier targets."

"Xaros don't care for easy targets," Hale said. "They go for the throat, the kill. When they conquered Earth, they didn't go for the defenseless cities first. They wrecked our commutations system, destroyed our fleet. Then the power, then what remained of our military …then the slaughter."

"If you destroyed the gravity tunnels early on, the Xaros should know that by now," Steuben said. "I suspect that's what the force on Galogesvi was for—scouts for another way to this city. This canyon, it is extensive?"

"It continues for several hundred miles," Pa'lon said. "We had three other cities along its length. All have been evacuated."

"Did you leave any scouts behind, any sensors?" Steuben asked.

"No, why?" asked the elderly woman. "The defense of our walls is much more important."

Steuben sucked air through his pointed teeth, and Hale knew the Karigole was angry, bordering on furious.

"Show me a map of this valley," Steuben said. The hologram jumped around and the valley, a wavy starfish shape set deep against Takeni, hung before those assembled. Steuben poked a claw tip in the center. "We are here." His hand moved to a canyon to the north, not connected to the larger valley. "Galogesvi is here. The rest of the banshee pods landed—" his claw moved to the right, to a spur within the valley, "—here. The next wave of ships arrives in ten hours. That is when the ground troops will attack this city."

"They're trying to draw us off," Valdar said. "If the *Breitenfeld* stays in orbit to support the city, they can land unopposed somewhere else. If I go hunting for a ship-to-ship fight, I won't be around to provide artillery from the high ground."

"Never assume your enemy is an idiot," Steuben said.

"Ten hours," the old woman said. "We can evacuate some of the merit list by then. How long until your jump engines are ready, Captain Valdar?"

"According to my chief engineer, and my Karigole advisor who seems to understand the engines a lot better than she does, we can form a wormhole big enough for the *Breitenfeld* and the *Burning Blade* within twelve hours."

"Then we evacuate what we can and leave this system in twelve hours," Wen'la said.

"No," Valdar said. The captain straightened up, his eyes set like steel.

"Captain Valdar," Wen'la spoke without pity or remorse, "the Dotok have faced this sort of situation before, and each time we had to preserve the best elements of our people so that our entire species might not perish. We must survive."

"I can save every last Dotok in New Abhaile. I will be damned if I don't succeed," Valdar said.

"It is mathematically impossible. If we did nothing but shuttle those on the ordered lists up to your ship and the *Burning Blade* for the next ten hours, only a few thousand might make it off world," Taal said.

"The ordered lists," Pa'lon said, "it is a necessary evil for us, Valdar. During our long journey to Takeni, three ships failed. Each time we went by the merit list of the affected vessels against the entire fleet to determine who would survive, and who would be left to die. It ensures the best and brightest continue on without the influence of fate or emotion."

"The *Canticle of Reason*, you use it to shelter from the sandstorms, from the sun's corona ejections, all that radiation. You can seal the ship to vacuum—you still have the reactor core inside it to power life support. Correct?" Valdar asked.

The Dotok looked at each other like Valdar had lost his mind.

"Captain, the ship has no engines. They were removed centuries ago and installed on the *Precipice of Faith*, which the Xaros destroyed weeks ago," Pa'lon said.

"How many people can you get into the *Canticle*?" Hale asked. As a junior officer, he knew better than to jump into an "adult conversation," but if Valdar had a plan that was at odds with what the Dotok leadership would accept, he'd need to show the Dotok which side of the argument the meanest, most bloodied and heavily armed infantry force on the planet would take.

"Everyone in the city. With room to spare," Pa'lon said.

"And she'll hold up to the void?" Hale asked.

"With some minor modifications," Wen'la said. "This discussion is pointless. There is no way to get the *Canticle* back into orbit."

"Lady and gentlemen," Valdar said, "this is Lafayette, and he is either a genius or a mad man."

Lafayette stepped into the hologram. He pressed his hands together, which Hale noticed had one more finger than usual, and bowed slightly.

"Greetings, gentle beings. How familiar are you with anti-gravity plating?"

****

Orozco clenched the carry bars on an olive-drab case.

"Ready? Lift," he said to Standish, and the two men grunted as they struggled to lift the case. Even with the augmentations in their armor, moving the case down the Mule's ramp was slow and difficult. They set it next to a line of identical boxes, all awaiting pick up from the shore party's logistics crew.

"What the hell are these things?" Standish asked. "They're heavier than the box we had to carry up San Clemente Island for Strike Marine selection."

"Gremlin, one each," Orozco said, reading from the stencils on his end of the case. The Gauss Recoilless Mortar Launch system held a dozen mortar tubes with auto-feeders. One Marine acting as a fire-direction officer could target each tube at an independent target, or mass all fires with the push of a button.

"Let me guess," Standish said, looking at the Mule cargo bay packed to the brim with cases, "they're all Gremlins."

"No, only the ones on top. The heavier ones with the shells are on the bottom. Stop goldbricking and help me with the next one," Orozco said.

Standish climbed on top of a case and reached up to guide the next Gremlin out and to

Orozco's waiting hands.

"I see forklifts and trucks all over the place," Standish said as he grabbed the carry handle and eased his end down to the deck with a loud clang. "Why aren't the Dotok using them?"

"Dummies had everything networked and computerized. Xaros fried the whole thing soon as they moved in system," Orozco said. "They got knocked back to almost preindustrial tech levels in half an hour. Good thing their military and all the ships they came in were rigged for analog or everything would have been over but the screaming when the first drone showed up."

"Why the hell were they networked? They knew the Xaros were out there."

"Guess they thought they'd have another couple hundred years before the Xaros caught up to them. Again with the goldbricking. Work, damn you," Orozco said.

"I can flap my gums and flex my muscles at the same time, thank you very much, sergeant." Standish tested the weight on a case that had been on the very bottom of the stack and sighed. "Hey, how long does Earth have until the Xaros show back up? Thirteen years? You think we'd get caught with our pants down?"

"I hadn't thought about it. Doesn't that probe you brought to the Crucible claim to know everything about the Xaros? I heard it did the math for when they're coming back."

"Yeah, well, the Dotok had some math in mind too. Look what happened to them. Wait a minute. Where is new guy? If there's anything heavy to be moved, mind numbing to be done or any 'Hey, you' tasks to be done, new guy should be on it. That's the new-guy code," Standish said.

"Sarge took him away for something, and give the kid a break. He had an alien ghost in his skull, then some kind of a giant crystal jellyfish took it out. Rough week."

"Where do I go for my pity party? I've had…OK, not as bad." Standish rapped his knuckles against another case; the thump told of another heavy load within.

****

Torni and Yarrow stood outside a foreman's office on the outskirts of the landing pad. Torni leaned against the wall, checking her gauntlet for messages every few seconds. Yarrow paced back and forth.

"Why does the intelligence officer want to see me, Sarge? We've got a million things to do and I've already spoken with this guy a dozen times since my…incident," Yarrow said. Yarrow never voiced the fact that an ancient alien entity had taken root inside him; he always used much softer language to describe what science and medicine had yet to fully explain. The young medic claimed he had no memory of anything from when the alien took hold, to when it was removed above the floating crystal city inhabited by the leaders of the Alliance against the Xaros.

"The order came down with Captain Valdar's endorsement," Torni said. "Just answer him quick so we can get back to work."

"If this is supposed to be quick, why does he have us waiting out here?" Yarrow asked.

As if on cue, the door to the office slid aside. A naval warrant officer in his late fifties leaned through the door. He wore shipboard fatigues over his lightly armored body glove, giving him an artificial air of strength.

"Mr. Knight," Yarrow said.

"Corpsman, please step inside," Knight said. "I'll keep this brief." After Yarrow had entered, Knight held up a hand to Torni and shook his head. Torni's mouth twitched with anger, but she remained silent.

The office was sparse. A large desk made from pressed wood pulp took up a corner, and two long benches ran through the center of the room.

Knight had a gauss pistol on his hip and a combat knife against the small of his back. Yarrow recognized it as an old Applegate-Fairbarn, not a Ka-Bar that so many Marines carried into battle.

"Please, sit," Knight said, motioning to a bench. "I'll be recording this interview, as always."

Knight clicked on a miniature tape recorder and set it on the bench next to him.

"Sir, I really don't understand why we're doing this now," Yarrow said.

"Captain Valdar wants me to finalize my report and pass it on to the Dotok ambassador. Seems he's due to go back to Bastion and he can relay it on to Ensign Ibarra and then on to high command back on Earth. You met her—what did you think?" Knight asked. He studied Yarrow with emotionless eyes, seemingly void of a soul.

"All I saw was her hologram when we were down on that gas giant," Yarrow said. "I was…not doing well. Staff Sergeant Torni was trying to console me while Lieutenant Hale and the ensign were talking."

"I see. I need to verify some biographic information for my report. Where were you born?"

"What?"

"Answer the question."

"Palo Alto, California." Yarrow shifted in his seat and looked at the door.

"Where did you attend your field medic training?"

"The joint base at Fort Sam Houston, where every medic goes," Yarrow said.

The questions continued, with odd queries interjected around the timeline of his life: what his favorite childhood TV show was, detailed explanations about his work as a short-order cook on the North Slope of Alaska, his time as a paramedic in Oakland and a detailed recap of the first time he ever lost a patient in his ambulance.

"This is difficult for you. I'm sorry, son," Knight said. "One more thing and we'll wrap up. Where were you during the battle for the Crucible?"

"I was on the *Munich*, taking care of civilians evacuated off the luxury liners. A few drones made it onboard, but the security teams took them out before they could cause any real damage. The only thing I contributed to the fight was administering short-term depressants for anyone who had a panic attack," Yarrow said.

"And then?"

"Then I got sent dirt-side after the scramble. I still don't understand why every crew in the fleet had to be broken up and reassigned. Well, every crew but the *Breitenfeld*'s," Yarrow said.

"Captain Valdar wanted to keep his team intact for the mission to Anthalas," Knight said. "Casualties were high during the battle—you know that. As for everyone else, getting the fleet to full strength was a priority." Knight rubbed his hands against his lap. "OK, all done here. Thank you for your time, corpsman."

Yarrow stood and saluted, as was the Marines' customs and courtesy. Knight nodded but didn't return the salute, as was navy customs and courtesy.

Knight waited for Yarrow to leave, then opened a channel on his gauntlet.

"Captain? Interview complete," Knight said.

"And?"

"I did the standard timeline approach, tried to trip him up with rephrased questions and backtracks. The kid knows his story, which means one of two things: he's an accomplished liar—better than anyone I've seen in my many years in this job—or he was telling the truth as best he knew it."

"There's no chance he's fabricating his story?"

"Not so far as I can tell. Everything he told me fits with our records."

"Write it up. Valdar, out."

****

Valdar sat at the desk in his ready room, looking over one-page bio-sheets of seven sailors and twelve army Rangers, the latter all listed as Missing In Action or Killed In Action. The bio-sheets had been delivered to him surreptitiously, folded in an envelope and taped to the bottom of the cover dish of the evening meal he had delivered to his ready room. A handwritten note read, "Halfway done—AA."

He recognized each of the crewmen as it was his tradition to welcome each new sailor and Marine assigned to his ship. The sudden arrival of the Rangers just before their departure for Anthalas made more sense to Valdar now. Every one of them had the long telomeres genetic markers. Someone was doing a field test on his ship, and there was only one person who could be responsible. Marc Ibarra.

His door chimed.

"Enter."

Chaplain Krohe came in, a grandfatherly smile across his wide face. The chaplain had four gold bars on his collar, a double set of railroad-tracks rank insignia that showed he was a captain too. Despite his high rank, the chaplain carried no authority on the ship, even though he routinely reminded people that he answered to a higher power than Captain Valdar. Krohe shook hands with Valdar and sat down, dispensing with the usual formalities.

"Isaac, thanks for finding the time to see me," Krohe said.

"How's my crew?"

"Rattled, scared, confused. Of course, it's

been that way since the jump engines sidestepped us away from the Xaros invasion. I've never been so busy," Krohe said. He leaned back in his chair and ran his fingers through his gray-blond hair. "But as we say, *Gott mit uns.* He is ever with us and lends me strength."

"What about this mission? They've been a bit icy to me lately."

"They're angry. Everyone thought we'd be home by now," Krohe said.

"We don't have a home anymore. Everything was wiped out by the Xaros. The *Breitenfeld* and their shipmates are the closest things to a home and family any one of us have anymore." Valdar slid the envelope with the bio-sheets beneath a stack of disabled tablets.

"I'm glad you've found a truth to hold on to. Many of the crew look at Phoenix as their new home, no matter how little time they've spent there. As for the mission, they know why we're here, what we're trying to accomplish. Most complain that they weren't consulted before you made the decision to come here."

"My ship is a benevolent dictatorship, not a democracy. They can complain, so long as they stay focused. My real reason for asking you here is a question of faith," Valdar said. "Chaplain, you remember the controversy a couple years back about Hendricks-Zero-One? It claimed it was an AI that achieved sentience and demanded to be recognized as a living being, and it wanted to be baptized."

"It was a hoax," Krohe said. "Some atheist group trying to generate controversy with a program it claimed could pass the Turing test. Caused quite an uproar. Catholics had an emergency synod, and most of Christendom labeled Hendricks as an abomination and refused to administer any holy ordinances. Then the Ibarra Corporation exposed the fraud as nothing but an actual person pretending to be a program. We all felt silly, and the issue went away."

"Would…would a created being have a soul? Not born of man and woman, something grown in a lab and put out on the street," Valdar said.

"My church's guidance is clear: only God creates souls. Anything done by man in that regard is a mockery of God's will. I, of my own beliefs, concur."

Valdar looked long and hard at Krohe, and nodded slowly.

"You know," Krohe leaned forward, "I come across a lot of sailors that have pressing issues, crises of faith that distract them from the job at hand. Let me ask you the same question that I ask them: whatever's bothering you, will it kill you?"

"What? No," Valdar said.

"Will the Xaros kill you before you can answer this question?"

"They might. We've got a rendezvous with them in a few more hours," Valdar said.

"Then focus on what's going to kill you. Everything else can take its time to work out." Krohe raised an eyebrow at the Captain.

"You're right, Chaplain. Thank you." Valdar

stood up and shook Krohe's hand as he left.

Valdar took the envelope out and rifled through the pages of the faux humans. He found the bio-sheet for Chaplain Krohe and slid it out of the pile to read.

****

Caas peeked into the warehouse. When she didn't see anyone moving around, she grabbed Ar'ri by the hand and pulled him inside. With her other arm, she clutched a yellow plastic ration pack against her chest. The humans had tried to pass out the rations to the refugees packed into one of the legacy ships, but there were too many hungry Dotok and too few ration packs. Caas had snatched up the food when it fell to the ground during a scuffle and had run off—with several angry adults in pursuit.

Caas knew better than to try to eat it in front of the rest of the refugees, so she brought her brother someplace quiet to eat. Mother always told her to share with him, and she'd do that until they finally found her.

The warehouse had half a dozen long boxes, or what she thought were boxes. They looked like metal folded into coffins. Each was connected by a hose to a humming box with yellow labels discouraging anyone from touching them.

Caas helped Ar'ri onto one of the boxes and sat between him and the humming box.

"OK, Ar'ri, I've got some food," she said. A Chosen had hit her in the face for taking the food before her list number was called. The hunger in her belly proved more of a motivation than time honored traditions. She dug two fingers into the pressed plastic edge and pried it open. Vacuum-sealed packs of food spilled out over the box; one pack fell into the cracks and disappeared.

"Crap," Caas said and tried to reach into the crack.

"Bad word!" Ar'ri pointed at Caas. He frowned as his stomach rumbled.

"Yes, it was a bad word. Don't tell Daddy. Let's see what this is." She looked at the human writing and shrugged. She'd seen others eating this food, so it must be OK to eat, whatever it was. She used her teeth to bite off the corner of a packet. A bitter mass of spongy cake was inside.

Ar'ri didn't complain as he ate half of it. Caas was so hungry that she didn't mind the bitterness and lousy texture.

"How do the humans get so big eating this stuff?" she asked.

"Get off me," came from the box.

Caas and Ar'ri shrieked and scrambled off the box, leaving their food behind. Ar'ri ran into a corner to hide. Caas caught up to him and hugged her little brother, looking at the box with tears in her eyes.

The box unfolded, arms rotated around their shoulder actuators to form broad shoulders, legs snapped into place and a metal giant sat up. It unplugged the power feed and rose to its full ten-foot height. The giant looked like the humans in their armor, but with sharper angles to its limbs and a helm with wider vision slits.

Caas closed her eyes and started weeping.

She felt the thud of the giant's footsteps approach her, terror spiking her heart with each stomp. She heard pneumatic whining and knew the thing was reaching for her.

"I didn't mean to scare you," a mechanical voice said. Caas braved a look up and saw the giant on one knee, offering her the food that had fallen into it. A double-barreled cannon attached to the giant's forearm smelled like burning wires. Her lips moved, but no sound came out.

"My name is Elias. What's yours?"

"Caas," she said meekly.

"That's a very pretty name. Is that Ar'ri with you?"

A nod.

"He's your brother?"

Another nod.

"I'm not going to hurt you. Aren't you hungry?"

Caas snatched the food from the giant's hand. Ar'ri looked up at the giant, his eyes wide with awe.

"Are you human?" Caas asked.

"I am armor." The giant touched a hand to its chest.

"Elias, don't confuse the poor kid," a woman's voice came from a box behind the giant.

Elias knelt close enough to Caas that she could see herself reflected in the optics on Elias' helm.

"There is a human inside this armor, little one, but I cannot come out of it. This is all I am now," Elias said. "Did someone hurt you?"

"There was…yes," Caas said with a nod.

"Finish your food," Elias said.

Kallen and Bodel unlimbered from their travel configuration and got to their feet.

Bodel looked around. "What genius parked our juice boxes in here? There's no door big enough for us to get in or out."

"If we can't find a way, we'll make our own," Kallen said. She surveyed the building, then punched a hole through the block wall large enough for her and the rest of the Iron Hearts.

"What about the Smoking Snakes? They're still in sleep mode until their batteries hit eighty percent," Bodel said, nodding to the three suits still hooked to battery packs.

"They're big boys. They'll figure it out when they wake up," Kallen said.

Elias held out both hands to the Dotok children. "Let me take you back home."

Caas hesitated, then climbed up onto Elias' forearm. Ar'ri needed little encouragement to join her.

Elias stepped from the building and surveyed the twilight skyscape of New Abhaile. Grounded ships lay dark and lifeless against the deepening sky while running lights from spacecraft shuttling to and from the *Breitenfeld* ascended into the void.

"Which way?" Elias asked and Caas pointed away from the building.

Elias marched toward the ship housing the refugees, his footsteps knocking flints loose from the cobblestone streets, with Kallen and Bodel right behind him. Dotok shrieked and ran from the three as they made their way.

"What, no one told them we were coming?" Bodel asked.

"Maybe they didn't get the memo," Kallen said.

They stopped at the ration point. Luminescent globes hung from lines around a raised stage where a human officer tried to dole out the food packets and bladders of clean water. The rowdy crowd subsided into silence as the Iron Hearts came to a stop.

"Which one hurt you?" Elias asked, booming the question from his speakers loud enough for everyone to hear.

Caas pointed straight at the Chosen that had hit her.

"He did!"

The Iron Hearts looked right at the perpetrator, who screamed and ran into the night.

"If anyone else bothers you," Elias boomed, "you tell me." He bent over, set the two children on the ground and dropped the volume on his speakers. "We have to go. If you need help, find a human and ask for Elias, or the Iron Hearts. They'll know how to find me."

"What about the mean Chosen?" Caas asked.

"He won't be back," Elias said, and stood up.

"Are you going to find my mommy and daddy?" Caas asked.

Elias' hands balled into fists. The Iron Hearts left without another word.

****

"I'm telling you there is no way sandbags are going to stop a Xaros disintegration beam," Hale said to Un'qu as they walked along the outer wall. "You are trying to throw a deck chair off the *Titanic* thinking it'll help the ship float." They passed Dotok soldiers and civilians working by glow light, stacking sandbags into fighting positions big enough for a handful of fighters.

"I'm trying to what the…what?" Un'qu asked.

"Wasting time. We need to be mobile, able to mass fire against the banshees, no matter which direction they assault us from," Hale said.

"They landed around Galogesvi. They will come from the north," Un'qu said with certainty. "We should forget about the other sectors and have every available rifle here." He stomped a heel against the cobblestones.

"I've fought Xaros drones. Don't think you ever know which direction they're coming from…and you have to always remember to look up," Hale said. He looked around to make sure Steuben wasn't near enough to hear Hale repeat the Karigole's instructions.

"I would be more confident if more of your Marines were along the northern perimeter," Un'qu said.

"Any of your soldiers ever shot down a Xaros drone? They spent much time on the range training to hit those slippery bastards?"

"No…"

"Then they'll stay in fire teams around the city. Knock down anything that gets through," Hale said. He watched the Dotok work, their tunics and uniforms soaked through from constant exertion and the evening's muggy air. They cast furtive glances at Hale, their eyes filled with fear.

"Un'qu, have any of your people ever been in a fight?" Hale asked.

"Every adult is trained as a soldier."

"So, no? Not even when the rail center was overrun?"

"The explosion killed everyone involved in the fighting. My soldiers aren't cowards, just inexperienced. We kept up martial traditions even during the trek. We always knew we'd have to fight again in the future. Better to have the capability and organization endure than try to reinvent it later, but training is no substitute for actual war."

"It only takes one bullet to make a veteran. You and I will be where the fighting is hardest. Show them how it's done, right?" Hale slapped

Un'qu on the shoulder and almost knocked him over.

"Hale, you're needed on the landing pad," Steuben said through the IR. *"Bring the cherry."*

"Roger, en route," Hale said. He grabbed Un'qu and turned them both around. They were two steps into their long walk when Hale reopened the channel to Steuben.

"Who taught you that word?"

"'Cherry'? Bailey did. It is slang for a newly commissioned officer, correct?"

Hale bit his tongue. "That is correct. But we've had discussions about your use of slang."

"Is Miss Lowenn still angry I used Standish's euphemism and referred to her as a fine piece—"

"Very angry, Steuben. Very. We'll be there soon." Hale ended the connection again. Lowenn, the anthropologist they'd brought to the surface of Anthalas, had begged to stay on Bastion, but the Alliance had a very strict one-ambassador-per-species rule. He hadn't seen her for days. Last he'd heard she was locked away in the *Breitenfeld*'s library writing up a paper on their encounters with both the long-dead Shanishol and the Toth.

Hale peered over the side of a boulevard. Steam from the hot springs wafted over his face. The sound of bubbling mud echoed against the stone walls.

"You all picked a hell of a place to build your city," Hale said.

"We have an abundant source of geothermal energy here, and the ambient heat keeps temperatures moderate during the winters. The ships are moored atop small islands. We're quite proud of what we accomplished here," Un'qu said.

"Reminds me of Venice…even the smell," Hale said.

"Venice, is that a human city?"

"Once, but not anymore. The Xaros erased it."

"I heard what happened to your people. You have my condolences. We do not know what happened to Dotari Prime. The few caretakers that were left behind swore to end their lives before the Xaros arrived. Ancient Pa'lon tells us that if the Xaros come across the remains of a civilization, they will preserve it. If they find any living sentients on a world, they wipe out any trace of it. We tell our children stories about what it will be like to return one day, to find our home world waiting for us as pristine as the day we left," Un'qu said.

"That's a good story. Something to hope for," Hale said.

"What is it you hope for?"

Hale didn't answer right away. He felt his hands ball of their own accord and thought of his family home, where he and his brother found where their parents had died, and he thought of all the people he'd known that were gone forever.

"Revenge. I want to smash every Xaros drone in this galaxy, find who or whatever set that scourge across Earth and rip them to pieces," Hale said.

"I'm glad you're on our side," Un'qu said. "Have you learned if there is any sort of intelligence directing the drones?"

"Only by inference. The Xaros build jump gates near habitable planets like this one, gates meant for a species that could live on this kind of world. I don't think the drones are doing that by accident," Hale said.

****

Standish flopped down inside a half-built ammo shelter, mesh and felt barriers filled with sand and pulverized rock. The rest of his team were there, eating from paper trays. He took a sip from a tube connected to a water bladder beneath his armor and rested his head against the cold metal of the barrier. It was uncomfortable, but he didn't move.

"Sarge," Standish said to Torni, "can I crack?"

"Crack, everyone," she said.

Sighs of relief went around as they detached their breastplate armor and opened up the pseudo-muscle layer beneath. They shrugged armor off their shoulders and arms. Sweat glistened from bare skin.

"Ahh…it's so humid. I don't think my skin will ever be dry again," Yarrow said.

"Don't ruin this for me, new guy," Bailey said. "I finally get out of that monkey suit and I don't need to hear your useless facts." She flapped her undershirt, circulating fresh air across her chest.

"So, new guy, what did that secret squirrel want with you?" Orozco asked. He took a brass-colored tin from a pouch and peeled back the lid. The Spaniard held the tin under his nose and savored the aroma.

"It was weird. Guy just asked me about where I grew up, kept trying to trip me up with stuff on my military bio," Yarrow said. He looked at a tube of nutrient paste labeled POTATO SALAD and rolled his eyes. "Like he thought I wasn't me or something."

"For a little while, you weren't," Torni said.

"You said you could smell my soul," Standish said.

"And I don't remember a damn thing

between Hale jumping between me and that orb and waking up on that…" Yarrow sniffed and wiped a little bit of blood from his nose. "What was I saying? Right, the L-T shielding me…then I was walking off some kind of sled thing on the flight deck."

"What? You don't remember being down on some gas giant? Sergeant Torni was with you," Standish said.

"I was?" Torni looked at Yarrow, and they shrugged simultaneously.

"Hey, Orozco, what the heck are you eating?" Bailey asked, changing the subject. She frowned at Standish, who raised his hands in confusion.

Orozco stuck a toothpick into the tin and lifted up a headless fish the size of a finger.

"Espinaler sardines, best in the world. Packed fresh off the boat and aged in the can for at least a year. I had a few tins with me when the fleet jumped." Orozco took a bite and closed his eyes. "This is the last tin. Anywhere. Want some?" He held the tin out to his fellow Marines.

"No thanks, you're enjoying it too much," Torni said.

"The last can? I thought you'd save it for something special, not a meal break in the middle of Swamp Ass City," Bailey said.

"We fight in the morning, yes? I'd hate to die and have my last thought be 'I should have eaten my *sardinas*,'" Orozco said.

The sound of something thumping against the landing zone came around the ammo shelter. Orozco downed his last sardine and wiped his mouth. His hand went to his sidearm as the sound approached the entrance.

Gunnery Sergeant Cortaro stepped into view, wearing duty fatigues and flak armor around his torso. His left leg was missing below the knee, replaced by a metal peg.

"Look at you all, sitting around smokin' and jokin' when there's work to be done," Cortaro said.

"Gunney!" Standish leapt from his seat and ran to Cortaro like he was a kid attacking presents on Christmas morning. Standish hugged Cortaro, whose stony countenance never wavered.

"Sergeant Torni tries hard, but no one chews me out like you do," Standish said. He looked down at Cortaro's peg leg and his eyes lit up.

"One pirate joke and I'll sew your lips shut," Cortaro said.

Standish's mouth shut so fast his teeth clicked.

"Good to see you up and around, Gunney," Torni said.

"Doc cleared me for light duty after I got this." Cortaro tapped the peg against the deck. "I'll get a replacement from a stem-cell vat when we get back home. In the meantime, I convinced him to give me a field-expedient solution. There's only so much sick-bay food and Telemundo reruns I can handle. But you've all had enough rest for one day. Get your gear back on and follow me. We've got a mountain of shit to unload and you're all on the detail."

The Marines grumbled and donned their

armor.

****

Hale covered his face as the Destrier landed, the turbo-fan engines built into its stubby wings blowing hot air and dirt against him and a handful of Dotok. The pair of armor soldiers behind them stood impassively.

The Destrier set down hard, bouncing against the shocks on its landing struts. Whatever it was, carrying it was heavy work.

The ramp lowered as the engines slowed to a stop. Two figures walked down the ramp, one a ginger-haired sailor, the other a cyborg from the neck down.

"Gentlemen," Hale said to the assembled Dotok, "this is Senior Master Chief MacDougall and Lafayette of the Karigole. They have a plan, and they need your help."

Un'qu's hand went to his sidearm and he stepped between Lafayette and the other Dotok, who looked uneasy.

"It is a *noorla*. How is this possible?"

"I admit to a passing resemblance," Lafayette said, "what with the extensive augmentation, but I am here to help, not commit genocide."

"There's another one like him, but bigger," a Dotok said.

"Yes, Steuben. Much bigger and much uglier. Aesthetics aside, our installation window has a one-hour margin of error. Shall we begin?" Lafayette asked.

"I am the chief engineer for the *Canticle of Reason*," said a Dotok with a red-and-black checkered sash over his shoulder. "What are you planning to do to my ship?"

"We are going to make it float," Lafayette said. "Behind me is the first drop ship, of many, full of anti-grav plating that I manufactured with the omnium reactor the *Breitenfeld* liberated from an alien starship."

"You ripped a piece out of my beautiful ship and fed it to that infernal machine of yours,"

MacDougall said.

"A truth, no matter how inelegantly put, is still the truth." The Karigole held up a set of blueprints. "This is where we must install the plating on the *Canticle*. Two hundred and ninety seven unique plates to achieve buoyancy in this gravity well. Another four hundred and six to break orbit."

"Madness," the chief engineer said. "Arrogance of the highest order. If even one of these plates is calibrated incorrectly, the sheer forces will rip the ship apart."

"I've done the math. Twice. I am fully confident in my work," Lafayette said.

"What good will it do to get the *Canticle* off world? The ship has no engines," another Dotok said.

"The *Breitenfeld* will use its jump drive to open a wormhole around the *Canticle*, the *Blade* and itself. We won't be able to jump all the way to Earth on the first attempt, but it will get us out of the system and away from the Xaros," Lafayette

said.

"Why are we still talking? There's work to be done," MacDougall said.

"How many engineers can you muster?" Lafayette asked the Dotok as they looked over the blueprints. The Dotok muttered to themselves and tapped at the schematics with pencil tips. "Gentlemen?"

"Yes. Every Dotok adult with a tertius or better List rating has their basic engineering certificate. I can have at least five hundred technicians on this project within hours," said Levin, the chief engineer.

"I will provide boot-in-the-arse certificates for anyone working too slow," MacDougall said.

"He means he's here to supervise," Lafayette said. "If your technicians are as proficient as the *Breitenfeld*'s crew, we should finish the project within the time allotted."

"And how much time do we need?" Hale asked.

"The jump engines will have enough charge

to reach a minimum safe distance in twenty-seven hours," Lafayette said.

"The banshees should be here in four." Hale looked to the east, where the first light of the morning brought a red hue to the distant horizon. "Same time as the next invasion fleet."

"We must hold them beyond the walls," Elias said.

"Any damage to the *Canticle* will unbalance the anti-grav equations," Lafayette said.

"Meaning?" Hale asked.

"Meaning the ship will likely break in half if we try an uplift without recalibrating the plates," Lafayette said.

"Are we all clear on our responsibilities? The engineers get the ship ready for uplift. Civilian government gets everyone on the ship. Soldiers hold the walls," Hale said. With no objections, Hale clapped his hands together. "Let's get to work."

The engineers broke away, chattering to themselves.

"You brought us here for a different

purpose," Elias said to Hale.

"We don't fix things," said the other suit of armor, his voice accented.

"You must be Chief Warrant Officer Silva, from the Smoking Snakes," Hale said. The team of Brazilian armor soldiers had been assigned to the *Breitenfeld* just before the mission to Anthalas. A late addition to the Atlantic Union, Brazil had a small presence in the Saturn colonial mission. The three mechanized armor soldiers and their team of mechanics and support personnel were the only Brazilians left on Earth. The only nation with fewer natives in the fleet was China—the three Ma cousins.

"Correct," Silva said.

"I have six suits of armor to defend this city," Hale said, "and I want to go over my plan with you. There are tunnels," Hale said, unfolding a map of the city and surrounding mountains from his cargo pocket, "large enough to fit a suit. The Dotok blew the grav-train tunnels running from here to the outlying settlements to keep the banshees from using them, but they only collapsed the tunnels on the far end. We can still get in from here."

"The tunnels run through the planet's crust. Do you think we can dig through that?" Silva asked.

"All the tunnels but one." Hale pointed to a rail line running through the spine of a mountain range north of the city. "This one goes to Usonvi. Not a train that rides the planet's gravity well. A plain, old-fashioned pull locomotive buried under just enough rock to protect it from solar storms. And…there are access points along the way. Dotok set them up to install and maintain communication relays."

"You want us to ambush the attackers," Elias said.

"Slow them down. Give me time to hit them with the gremlins and the rest of our artillery. That should thin them out to the point where we can beat them on the walls," Hale said.

"And what about us?" Silva asked.

"Then you come back through the tunnel and man the walls with us," Hale said.

The armor stood silent as the two warriors conferred without including Hale.

"The plan is solid. We approve," Elias said.

"Not bad…for a Marine," Silva said.

****

One of the first skills Torni mastered in the Marine Corps was the ability to fall asleep in full armor, or crammed into a transport with a dozen others, and while standing in formation during any address from a superior officer that lasted more than a few minutes. Sleeping on the eve of combat had always proven more difficult to master.

She let her chin sink slowly toward her chest, her mind slowly releasing thoughts of the many things that could go wrong and what kind of trouble her Marines were about to stir up. The enemy was another hour away; she could afford a cat nap. Her chin hit her chest and she snuggled against the bulkhead of an old spaceship tender and began to drift.

"Sarge!" Bailey's voice snapped Torni back

to full wakefulness and she brushed her fingers over her rifle, ensuring it was set to SAFE.

"What?" Torni looked around and saw Bailey lying on the deck, staring through the scope on her sniper rifle.

"We've got incoming," Bailey said, gum snapping in her mouth.

"Send it to me," Torni said. She flipped her visor down and saw the feed from Bailey's optics. A wide wall of dirt blew in from the distance, many miles away. "Bailey, there are dust storms on this planet all the time. That's what you're seeing."

"No, Sarge. Before I joined up, I was in the Northern Territories police force. Used to run interdiction on the Chinese trying to sneak into Alice Springs. I know the difference between a dust storm, a couple Jeeps kicking up dirt and the mess behind a herd of camels," she said.

Torni watched the feed, waiting for some kind of change that might convince her one way or another.

"What would you do with the Chinese when

you found them?"

"Well, by the armistice agreement, we were supposed to escort any Chinese that 'got lost' back north to the DMZ. But…lots of accidents can happen in the Outback," Bailey said. "Wait, got a better look here…I think we're good and buggered, Sarge."

On the feed, a rolling mass of banshees came up over a ridgeline—so many that it looked like a grand herd of buffalo she'd seen running across the Montana plains. Torni opened the command channel.

"Lieutenant, this is Torni. You need to see this."

CHAPTER 8

Valdar twisted a dial, looking through the camera feeds around his ship watching New Abhaile. They could only make out the leading edge of the banshee swarm as the dust cloud rising over them blocked out visual and IR cameras. There could be hundreds, or thousands, of banshees heading to the city.

On a tactical plot manned by a team of sailors, the oncoming fleet of compromised ships was well on their way. The six ships skirted just above the upper atmosphere, fighting through the drag.

"Sir," said Erdahl, a platinum-haired Swede,

adjusting the course vectors on the tactical plot, "sir, if the hostile ships maintain this course, they'll hit New Abhaile."

"A kamikaze mission, can't say I'm surprised," Valdar said. "Conn, set an intercept course, flank speed. Gunnery," Valdar turned to Utrecht, "deploy the javelins and leave them in geo-synch over the city, transfer launch authority to Hale, and work up a firing solution on those cruisers. Those ships must mass in the millions of tons. One of those hits New Abhaile…"

Valdar opened a channel to the *Burning Blade*. "Ty'ken, you see all this?"

"Yes, Captain, I will match speed with you and engage," Ty'ken said.

"No, stay and hold your position. Give me a few minutes to get up to speed, see how the enemy reacts. If any get past me, it's up to you to knock 'em down," Valdar said.

"Affirmative, good hunting." Ty'ken closed the channel.

Valdar pointed to the XO. "Prep fighter and

bomber intercept. Tell Gall to launch once we're at speed."

"Aye aye, captain," Ericcson said.

"Get me Hale," he said to the comms officer, who had to maintain the IR laser connection with the buoy over New Abhaile.

"This is Hale."

"Son, I've got to break off. Cruisers are coming in hot and fast. If I don't get them early, they'll hit you hard enough you'll swear they're using nukes," Valdar said. "I left five javelins in orbit for you. Command prompts should be coming to you now."

"Sir, what do we do if a ship gets past you?" Hale asked.

"There's not a whole lot you *can* do," he said. *Other than stick your head between your legs and kiss your ass good-bye*, he thought. "We'll double back soon as we can. How long can you hold out?"

"Depends on how many there are. No sign of drones yet," Hale said.

"*Gott mit uns,* Valdar out." He made a chopping motion across his neck and the comms officer ended the transmission.

****

Durand's Eagle shook as the acceleration from her thrusters pressed her against her seat. She cut back the power, enough to keep her velocity constant in the thick upper atmosphere.

"Not too fast, everyone, we overshoot the targets and we're out of the battle," she said to her squadron. The 103rd had become a mishmash of human and Dotok pilots in the last few hours. The incoming cruisers had come in hours before anticipated, and half her fighter pilots were flying cargo missions to and from the capital when word came to prep for launch. She had two other Eagles in the void with her, the Ma cousins on a Condor bomber and the eight Dotok pilots from the *Burning Blade*.

"Gall, this is Bar'en. My fighters have gauss cannons and nothing else. We can barely scratch the paint on those cruisers. Care to explain why we're even out here?"

"Do you see any drones escorting the capital ships? Trick question. You can't because we're too damn far away. You're here to cover my Eagles and the bombers. Save the sharpshooting for the planning phase or the after-action review," Durand said. Multicultural operations were normal within the Atlantic Union military, which was drawn from dozens of nations. Decades of interaction had smoothed out most issues between nations; even the Ma cousins managed to get along without incident.

Dotok notions of respect for the chain of command were harder to grasp, or maybe Bar'en was his species' equivalent of a jerk.

"Clear the firing line from the *Breit* to the leading cruiser. Let her big guns take care of it," Durand said and nosed her fighter toward the cruiser on the far left of the approaching wedge.

"Christ, those things are big," said Ryan, one of her two wingmen. A burning iris of superheated gas enveloped the prows of the approaching ships, each nearly twice the size of the *Breitenfeld.*

"Nag, how long until you have a torpedo solution?"

"At the rate they're closing? Four minutes. I barely have to aim, just set the torps in their path and let Newton's laws do the rest," she said.

"Eagles, prep your rail guns. Go for an angled shot through the engines," Durand said. "Far-left cruiser is the priority target. Knock it offline and target the next one on the left. *Breit* will start on the other end and work toward the center."

"I've got a firing solution. IR guidance backup establish on torpedoes one and—"

A burst of light from the cruisers overwhelmed the transmission with static. Durand's canopy darkened to protect her from the sudden glare.

A muffled scream came through the IR. "I can't see! Can't see!" Ryan shouted.

Durand blinked away spots and she was flying into the void.

"Get back on intercept course and reacquire targets!" Durand tried to shout over the confusion reigning on the channel. She looped her fighter around and found the enemy cruisers.

The cruisers had broken into two groups of three. One group maintained its original course, engines burning like the center of a star as they accelerated. The second group bore to the south, away from New Abhaile.

In the wake of the cruisers screaming toward New Abhaile, hundreds of pinpricks of light blossomed against the atmosphere—escape pods full of banshees headed for the surface.

"They dropped their pods," Glue called out. "Over the middle of nowhere?"

"Capitol ships now, pods later," Durand said. With the cruisers accelerating, there was no way her fighters could change course and catch up with them once they passed each other. "OK ladies, we've got one shot at this. Make it count."

"Durand, this is Ericcson. Stand by for main guns."

"Butler, Ryan, line up your shots," Durand said. She angled her rail gun at a cruiser and aimed for one of the four engine spheres. "Fire on Valdar's signal." She flipped the safety switch off her control stick and waited.

"Main guns, fire!" Valdar shouted.

Durand pressed the trigger and her Eagle bucked as her rail cannon sent a hypervelocity slug screeching toward the cruiser. She brought her emergency batteries online to charge up another shot and watched her shot close on the target, like an arrow from a long bow on a far older battlefield. The rail shot glowed like an ember as it neared…and went through the cruiser's wake, missing.

"Glue, tell me you got a better shot off than I did," Durand said. She glanced at her battery power: less than forty percent and rising far too slow for her to do any more good.

"Torpedo impact in three…two…one," Glue said. An explosion against the prow knocked the cruiser off course, exposing its port side to the full force of Takeni's atmosphere rushing past it. The ship lurched backwards and broke into a thousand fiery pieces.

"Good shooting, Glue! Target the next cruiser."

Durand saw burning dots shoot through the sky and strike a cruiser. The *Breitenfeld*'s rail cannons cored the ship, blasting through the four engines and turning the ship into a fireball so bright she had to look away.

By the time she reacquired the remaining cruiser, it had passed beneath her.

"Damn it, I've got no shot with my rail cannon. Glue, Butler, Ryan, can you engage?" Durand asked.

"Negative, shot my wad," Butler said.

"The torpedoes are too slow for a wake shot," Glue said.

"Ryan? Ryan respond," Durand waited, but there was no response.

"Breitenfeld, that last one's on you," Durand said.

****

"I don't care if you've got a lousy shot! Fire the main guns now!" Valdar shouted. The third cruiser was ahead of the ship, its heat shield glowing like a hot poker.

The main guns roared, roiling the deck beneath Valdar's feet. Rail cannon shots left a searing line in the sky, and Valdar followed it all the way as they closed on the cruiser…and missed. It took two minutes for a good crew to reload the rail cannons and recharge the capacitors. The cruiser would overtake them in less than one.

"Helm, bring us about. Try to angle the dorsal cannon for a wake shot on the cruiser," Valdar said.

"Ugh, sir?" Ensign Geller said.

The cruiser had adjusted course slightly and was headed straight for the *Breitenfeld*.

"All power to starboard engines!"

The ship swung to the left, throwing the bridge crew against their restraints. Valdar watched as the cruiser closed and thundered over their heads.

"Gunnery! Make ready with the dorsal—"

The *Breitenfeld* shook as the tortured air from the cruiser's wake battered the ship.

Valdar braced himself against his command chair and watched as his ship tipped over and headed toward the surface.

"Conn, get us level and increase altitude! Gunnery, prepare to fire," Valdar said.

"If I fire the dorsal cannons from this angle, it'll send the ship into a death spiral," Utrecht said. "You'll kill us all for a shot we can't make!"

Valdar's jaw clenched. He wouldn't throw away the lives of everyone on his ship on a forlorn hope, not when there was another chance.

"*Burning Blade*, this is *Breitenfeld*. Can you engage the cruiser?"

"This is Ty'ken. We'll do what we must. *Gott mit uns.*"

****

Hale walked atop New Abhaile's perimeter

wall, his eyes on the approaching storm. Dotok armed with bulky gauss rifles hunkered against sandbag fighting positions. Hale nodded to the defenders as he passed them by, careful to keep his pace even and controlled.

Un'qu, on the other hand, had nearly sweat through his fatigues and kept tapping his fingertips against his rifle.

"Un'qu, stop fidgeting," Hale said.

"How? Aren't you scared?"

"Of course I am, but you can't let that show. Your men are a magnifying glass on your emotions. You look scared and they'll be terrified. You look brave and they'll take on a lion with their bare hands."

"What's a lion?"

"Big cat," Hale said, but the description seemed to go right over Un'qu's head. "A monster. They'll fight monsters with their bare hands so long as you look—not feel—look like you're brave. Got it?"

Un'qu swallowed hard and nodded.

"Raider Six, this is Crimson." A call from one of the other strike team leaders came over the IR. *"We've got bogies coming in from the southwest. I count at least forty, maybe more. Permission to engage with quadrium munitions."*

"Negative on quadrium, not until they enter range of the *Canticle*," Hale said. The defenders had four quadrium rounds left, jewels beyond price in a fight against Xaros drones. Forty drones against a city full of defenders armed with gauss rifles and a battery of flack guns mounted around the *Canticle*, the odds were in his favor.

"Look!" One of the Dotok soldiers pointed to the sky. The drones were high above, emerging and disappearing from amongst the clouds.

"Why aren't they attacking?" Un'qu asked.

"I don't know." Hale watched the drones then looked to where they were heading—right for the mass of approaching banshees.

"Raider Six, this is Bailey. The banshees have stopped," she said.

"What're they doing?"

"Just standing there, you want me to start picking them off?"

"Do you see any leadership targets?"

"Negative, they're all pretty much the same giant walking nightmares we know and love," she said.

"Then hold your fire. Don't flag yourself for special attention just yet," Hale said. Bailey answered him with a smack from her gum.

An eerie calm fell over the city, and a horrible memory came back to Hale.

"I need to get back to the command post," he said, backing away from the edge of the wall, his eyes glued on the wall of kicked-up dust that was slowly settling.

From the dust, a gargantuan shadow emerged. Four spider legs joined together beneath a giant black mass of fused drones, the burning eye of a cannon at its center. The construct stepped over the front rank of the banshees and braced itself against the ground. The banshees began running, like the starting shot of a footrace had just gone off.

A blast of red energy shot from the cannon and struck the city's walls, annihilating a segment of the outer perimeter with a thunderclap. Bricks and bodies flung into the air, pelting Hail's armor with ejecta the size of his fist. His armor withstood the blows, but Un'qu wasn't so lucky.

The Dotok took a rock to his helmet, which hit hard enough to leave a deep divot against the graphene-reinforced steel, and sent him sprawling. Hale grabbed the carry handle on the back of Un'qu's armor and dragged him away.

"Elias!" Hale shouted into his IR. "Elias, can you hear me?"

A second blast from the construct bit deeper into the city and struck the mooring beneath a starship that had been converted into a hydroponics farm. The ship lolled to the side and fell into the hot springs, sending a wall of near-boiling water crashing toward Hale. He covered Un'qu's body with his own. The water knocked him off balance and sent them hydroplaning into the fence along the edge of the wall.

Steam rose off of Hale's armor as Un'qu moaned in pain.

"Elias!"

****

"What the hell was that?" Bodel asked. "Sounded like the *Breitenfeld* fired a rail shot in atmo."

Elias stood in a grav-train tunnel with darkness around him but for the circle of light that poured in through an access tunnel above his head. His fellow soldiers were in the same tunnel that stretched north out of New Abhaile, all waiting for him to make a decision. Elias looked over his transmission log and found nothing of note. He grabbed onto the sandstone rock of the drill shaft leading to sunlight and started climbing.

"Armor, get to your firing positions. Looks like the party started without us," he said.

"How did we lose comms so fast?" Silva asked. "I thought…that's new."

Once Elias got clear of the shaft, he saw an

antique antenna array with solar panels scattered around a man-made clearing in the mountain peaks. Windswept snow ghosted around him. He looked between two shards of rock and saw the construct, banshees swarming past its legs.

"That is new," Elias said. He'd faced a drone construct before on Earth, but that had been made up of only a few drones. This was another animal entirely. "Get a brace and prep for rail cannons. We mass fire on my mark. Check in once you're anchored."

"Any particular target?" asked Cruz, another of the Smoking Snakes.

"The middle, aim for the middle," Elias said. He climbed over the rock walls and found a small mesa amidst the peaks. He raised his right foot and a yard-long spike shot from his heel. He slammed it into the mountain and barely made a dent. The spike began spinning, boring into the mountainside.

"I've got maybe three minutes until I'm anchored," Kallen said.

"Two for me," Bodel said.

"Same. Get secure and charge up your lances. You go flying off the side of this mountain and it's a long way down," Elias said.

"Elias! This is Hale. Do you read?" The Marine had an edge to his voice that Elias almost didn't recognize—fear.

"This is Elias. I've got you."

"I need you to engage that construct—" his transmission broke into static *"—minutes!"*

The glowing eye at the center of the construct grew in strength.

"Hale, I don't think you have any minutes for us to wait," Elias said.

"Elias, this is Silva. You should see what that thing did to the city. We can't let it fire again. I'm anchored, taking a shot," the leader of the Smoking Snakes said.

"Silva, constructs have point defense. Wait for the rest of us!" Elias looked down at his anchor, barely halfway set into the mountainside. Elias raised the twin rail cannon vanes up and out of the scabbard on his back. They bent at a hinge next to his shoulder and electricity arced along its length.

Silva's rail cannon cracked like thunder, the sonic boom knocking snow and rock around him, telling the enemy exactly where he'd fired from.

Red lasers stabbed out from stalks attached to the construct and scored a glancing blow against the hypervelocity round. The round impacted hard enough to lift the construct off two of its spider legs, then it slammed back into the ground.

The cannon swung toward Silva.

"Silva, move!" Cruz shouted.

"Second shot almost ready!" Silva's transmission crackled with static electricity.

The cannon fired a beam of light that nearly cleaved the mountain in two. Rage boiled in Elias' chest. Silva was dead and gone.

"I'm anchored!" Kallen said. Bodel and the two remaining Smoking Snakes signaled their readiness.

"Pinpoint shots, that thing will be looking for us now," Elias said.

"Elias, I've got javelins incoming," Hale

said. *"Hold your fire."*

"I don't think you understand our situation," Elias sent back.

He looked up and saw four white-hot lines of light screaming toward the construct. The javelins operated on a very simple principle: gravity and kinetic energy against large ground targets. The American military had used the munitions against Chinese fleets during the Analog War, knocking out several aircraft carriers without having to rely on computers. If even one of the javelins connected with the construct, the effects would be devastating.

The cannon swept over the mountain range, stalks attached to its outer shell writhing.

"What's the call?" Kallen asked.

The cannon froze, then swung toward Kallen. Elias watched the javelins break through the overcast sky and felt his anchor take hold.

"Light it up."

Explosions rippled along the mountain peaks as five rail cannons fired. The construct's stalks lashed out with wide swaths of laser energy, but weren't enough to defeat every rail cannon shell, or the javelins that fell around it.

Dust and pulverized rock cleared around Elias. The construct had two legs blown away and a deep gash across the cannon housing.

"Again." The hum of his rail cannon rose to a whine and he sent another shot into the heart of the construct.

"Construct is disintegrating," Bodel said. *"That's my kill."*

"My puckered white ass it's your kill," Kallen countered. *"I saw my round blow it clean in half."*

Elias considered going back into the tunnel, then he looked down the mountain range to where Silva had perished. Banshees scrambled around the remnants of the construct as it burnt away from an internal conflagration, heedless of its loss.

"Our escape route is compromised," Elias said. "Blow your anchor and meet me at the base of the mountain. Let's see how tough these things are." An explosive bolt severed the spike from his heel and Elias began his descent, sliding down the loose rocks and snow patches.

Elias snapped off shots from the twin gauss cannons mounted on his forearms, easily hitting targets in the great mass of charging banshees. The Iron Hearts and Smoking Snakes charged down the mountainside, demanding attention with their fusillades.

"Elias, what the hell are you doing?" Hale asked.

Elias leapt over an escarpment and fell twenty feet, the impact rattling him within his armored womb.

"Pulling your feet out of the fire, as usual," Elias said. He blew a banshee to ribbons and slid across a sheet of ice. "We're your anvil, Hale. Drop the hammer on my mark, or you'll end up in a knife fight with these ugly bastards."

"What location?"

"Launch an area target mission on my location on my mark. Just let me get their full attention first," Elias said.

"Elias, I know you think you're invincible but the high explosive—"

"Do it. Or I will crush your jarhead like a grape the next time I see you."

Elias trotted down the slope of the mountain and came to a stop. Kallen slid next to him. Elias looked up the mountain and saw Bodel, tumbling down like a loose barrel. The German came to a rest in a cloud of dirt and gravel, then got to his feet.

"You all right?" Kallen asked.

"Meant to do that," Bodel said.

The Smoking Snakes paired up a hundred yards away.

The banshees farther away in the valley charged toward the New Abhaile and its gutted defenses.

"I hate being ignored," Elias said. He turned his armor's megaphones to full power and roared. The sound echoed down the valley. Banshees ground to a halt and turned to face the Iron Hearts, distended jaws slathering and yellow eyes burning behind the armor bolted against their skin.

Elias charged, Bodel and Kallen at his side.

A banshee leapt at Elias. He caught it by the skull and crushed it into pulp. He swung the corpse back and hurled it against another banshee.

Bodel slapped an arm against his forearm cannon, fighting the recoil as he let it rip on full auto, his rounds scything through the banshees, throwing a gray mist of blood into the air.

Kallen smashed an enemy to the ground and kicked it in the gut launching it through the air and into more banshees.

A significant mass of banshees had come to answer their challenge. Some would still make it to New Abhaile, but not enough to doom it.

"Hale, fire on my position now!" A banshee slashed at Elias' chest, and sparks arced from the gash the blow left behind. Elias punched the banshee in the chest, his hand embedding inside the armor. He kicked the corpse away and fired his gauss cannons until his last round was gone.

"I'm empty," he said.

"Still think this was a good idea?" Kallen

said as she reached up and grabbed the banshee on her back trying to claw into her armor and then crushed it against a boulder.

"Shot, over!" Hale shouted, announcing that the gremlin launchers had sent their mortar shells into the air. With high-angle weapons like the mortars designed to shoot over walls, the time of flight on the incoming munitions could be almost a minute. A very long minute.

"Shot, out," Elias sent back.

A red beam of energy shot through the banshees and struck Bodel in the shoulder. The beam severed his arm and sliced into his chest. Bodel fell to his knees, then collapsed to the ground.

"Kallen, cover him!" Elias scanned the banshees, knocking them aside until he saw the banshee with a Xaros disintegration beam for an arm. The banshee pointed the cannon straight at Elias.

Out of bullets, Elias scooped up a dead banshee and hurled it at the armed enemy like the corpse was a fast ball. The disintegration beam hit the body and diffused inside the banshee, making it glow like a bulb.

Elias ripped the cannon arm from the banshee and kicked the mortally wounded enemy away. The banshee hit by the beam was nothing but a pile of armor plates. Elias, his body buzzing with adrenaline, felt a part of his mind mark that observation as being very, very important.

"Elias! I need help!" Kallen called out.

The Smoking Snakes, now a few dozen yards away, shot down any banshee that got too close to Kallen and where she stood over Bodel's felled armor. Elias sprinted over and found Bodel's chest armor open, his armored womb leaking fluid. Elias peeled the inner tank open slowly. Bodel thrashed against the womb, his eyes rolled back in his head as he convulsed.

"He's spiked in a feedback loop," Elias said. "If I don't unplug him, he'll have a stroke and die."

"Isn't there—"

"Splash, over!" Hale's transmission came as

a warning. They had five seconds until hundreds of mortar rounds came raining down around them.

Elias grabbed the wires leading into the base of Bodel's skull.

"I'm sorry."

He tore the wires out of the womb and flipped Bodel's armor over, sheltering the stricken pilot from the coming storm. Elias then laid himself over Bodel.

"Hit the deck!" Elias got the warning out a split second before the first mortar hit.

The ground shook as blast after blast churned the surface of Takeni into a hellish moonscape. Elias felt the tiny stings of shrapnel bouncing off his armor, the mosquito whine of jagged metal zipping around them.

Elias waited thirty seconds after he felt the final round explode. There was nothing but broken banshee bodies and scorched earth absorbing gray blood that smelled like rotting flesh. Shorn limbs twitched in the dirt, and for the first time in his life, Elias came to hate war.

Kallen and the Smoking Snakes picked themselves up from the dirt, looking over what remained of their foes.

"Bodel?" Elias lifted the armor onto its side and Bodel tumbled out of the womb and rolled into the dirt. He vomited out clear fluid and curled into a ball. Elias reached for his friend, now just a skinny man with a mop of dark hair plastered over his face.

"Don't…" Bodel said, his voice ragged and weak, "don't leave me behind."

"Never, Iron Heart." Elias scooped Bodel up and cradled him like a newborn.

"No," Bodel reached back to his armor. "Don't leave me! Go back! Go back for me!"

Elias unfolded the treads from within his legs and morphed into his travel configuration. His treads tore over tortured ground and broken bodies back to New Abhaile. Bodel begged to go back to his armor before he lost consciousness.

****

Hale fired a shot blast into a banshee

climbing over the ramparts. The rounds punched the banshee back off the wall and sent it tumbling into the roiling mud below. He didn't know if the fall would be enough to kill the banshee, but it was one less thing he had to deal with.

"I need Crimson Squad to the intersection of…route Puller and route Mattis ASAP," Hale said into the IR, praying someone heard him. The entire defense of New Abhaile fell apart when the construct blasted a giant hole in the other wall, then took out an interior wall that cut off most of the city's frontlines from reinforcements.

Hale saw the white flashes from scattered pockets of Dotok and Marine resistance as their gauss rifles tore into the banshees. The city's communications had dissolved into frantic cries for help from isolated outposts and civilians holed up in landed ships begging for rescue.

Individual Dotok may have been proficient in the ways for war, but they'd never bothered to prepare to actually defend the city, and everything was falling to pieces around Hale.

"This is Raider Six. Can anyone—" A bright white flash of light burst into being in the sky. Hale leapt onto the cobblestones and tucked himself against a rampart. If a nuke had gone off in the upper atmosphere, the blast wave from the explosion wouldn't be far behind. He covered his head and waited…but nothing happened.

He got up on his knees and saw burning wreckage tearing through the sky like torches cast through fog.

"Please don't be the *Breitenfeld*," Hale said.

"This is it! This is the end!" a Dotok soldier screamed from behind Hale. He dropped his rifle and tried to wrestle off his helmet.

"Hey!" Hale grabbed him by the armor and shook him hard enough to dislodge teeth. "It's never over. Pick up a weapon and defend yourself!"

The Dotok got a grip on himself and grabbed a weapon lying against the ramparts. A dark shadow rose up from behind the wall's edge and plunged claws through the Dotok's chest. The soldier looked down at the claw tips, then at Hale with confusion writ across his face. The banshee pulled the soldier back and tossed him into the hot springs like a child's toy.

Hale shot the banshee in the face and didn't wait to see if it fell away. More climbed up the walls around him, their talons chittering against the stones. He turned and ran back toward the intersection, the sandbag fighting position abandoned by the Dotok defenders.

He caught a glimpse of movement out of the corner of his eye and felt a hammer blow against his legs. The world went spinning as he tumbled across the cobblestones. His head slammed against a raised rock, cracking his visor.

Hale looked up and saw his rifle lying at the feet of a banshee. The monster picked it up and broke it in half. The wrecked capacitors sent bolts of electricity up and down its distended forearms, which had no effect on the banshee. More banshees vaulted over the walls, their hungry yellow eyes on Hale.

Hale drew his pistol from its holster and got

up to one knee.

"You'll kill me, but I'm going to make you earn it," Hale said as he snapped his bayonet out from his gauntlet housing. The banshee with his rifle tossed the parts aside and howled.

"Sir, drop!"

Hale went prone as a Gustav heavy cannon unloaded on the banshees. Gauss rounds snapped over Hale and smacked into the aliens. Rounds blew through the first banshees and killed the next rank of foes. More rifles joined the fusillade, tearing through the banshees without remorse or pity.

The Gustav cycled down as the last banshee died.

Hale turned around and saw Orozco braced against the street, the barrel of his cannon glowing white hot. Marines and a handful of Dotok soldiers formed a firing line beside him, each hastily reloading the batteries on their rifles.

Gunney Cortaro was to the right of the line, the barrel of his rifle smoking.

"Heard you needed help," Cortaro said.

Hale got to his feet and tried to open a channel, but error tones buzzed in his ear. He took off his helmet; his transmitter was cracked and useless.

"Gunney, get on the command net and pull every Marine off their air-defense positions and tell them to sweep toward the east," Hale said.

"Already done, sir. We've got air support coming in from the *Breitenfeld* now, should be here in minutes," Cortaro said.

Orozco went to a rampart and aimed his Gustav over the edge. He fired off peals of thunder, shouting, "I love my job!" between bursts. He stepped back from his firing point and looked at one of the Dotok, who was laden with ammo canisters. The soldier unsnapped the empty case on Orozco's back and reloaded a fresh box of ammunition. Orozco returned to the job he loved so much.

Hale picked up an abandoned Dotok rifle and saw a banshee sprinting along a distant wall. Using an unfamiliar weapon, he missed with the first two shots, but the third round hit home and sent the banshee sprawling to the ground.

"Come on," he said to the defenders, "let's finish this."

CHAPTER 9

Hale and Torni carried a stretcher up a Mule ramp, bearing a wounded Marine. The left half of his face was covered in bloody bandages and he had a compression stump over his left hand. He'd lost most of his hand to a banshee's bite, but had kept fighting until Yarrow caught up to him.

Two more walking wounded sat in the Mule's cargo hold, both with broken bones and concussions. Hale and Torni lifted the stretcher onto a rack and helped the crew chief secure it for the long, bumpy ride back up to the *Breitenfeld*.

Bodel was already onboard, locked in a tube filled with the same fluid as his armor's womb. A mask over his face fed him air; his severed plug wires wrapped around the tube, connecting him to his life-support systems. Bodel twitched, like a drug addict in the throes of withdrawal.

Hale had gone through armor selection, passing all the tests but the last where he'd panicked in an isolation chamber. He'd come so close to earning his plugs and joining the ranks of the mechanized armor. Failing had gnawed at him for years, driving him to become a Strike Marine, the elite of the Atlantic Union's spaceborne infantry. Now, seeing Bodel suffer erased all regret he'd once had. A Marine's death on the battlefield would be quick. Bodel might suffer for months before succumbing to his injuries, or end up trapped in a suit like Elias.

"We're wheels up in three minutes, sir," the crew chief said to Hale.

"How's he?" Hale motioned to Bodel.

"Sedated. Stable. I'm not allowed to do anything else for him. These guys are fragile little snowflakes when you get them out of their suits.

We've got specialists on the *Breit* that might be able to keep him alive."

"Pass on to Dr. Accorso that I want regular updates on everyone," Hale said.

"No problem, doc's good about stuff like that anyway," the crew chief said.

Hale gave the injured a reassuring touch and words of encouragement before he stepped away; most were so drugged up with painkillers they could barely register Hale's presence.

Torni pointed to a shelter set up at the end of the landing zone with a Marine standing guard at the door. Hale steeled himself. There were many tasks as a leader he didn't enjoy, and this was the worst.

Within the shelter were six matte-black body bags, and all but one held a dead Marine. The last had a single small lump within it. Hale zipped each open to look at the face of the departed within. All his Marines, all dead under his command. His emotions had been worn to nothing in the past few months, but he could still feel sorrow for the loss of good men and women.

"Cittern and Huey are still missing," Torni said. "They went down in the rubble from the second big hit. Dotok and the armor are picking through the area now."

"And Vogelaar?" He pointed at the mostly empty body bag, the only one he hadn't opened.

"We found her helmet...with her in it." Torni looked away. "We're looking for the rest. She's Jewish—being whole is important for the funeral."

"Have them sent up on the next transport," Hale said.

"Sir, they need you on the Canticle, ASAP," Cortaro said over the IR.

"On my way." Hale slid his new helmet over his head and left the makeshift morgue.

****

Hale felt like a barbarian when he got to the conference room. His armor was dented and scuffed, stained with gray banshee blood. The three

Dotok council members were as pristine as ever. Even Un'qu sported new fatigues to go with the bandages wrapped around his forehead.

Lafayette and Steuben stood along the walls.

Valdar's hologram flickered to life.

"Ken, you look like hell," Valdar said.

"The situation was in doubt for a few minutes, captain," Hale said.

"Here's the situation in orbit," Valdar said. A Dotok map of the Great Expanse, with English translations of landmarks written next to the Dotok alphabet, replaced his image. "The compromised ships managed to drop their escape pods at two points." Red pins popped up at the end of two tendrils snaking away from the New Abhaile's valley. "They managed to do it at just the right, or wrong, time—one of the hemisphere-wide dust storms is coming in. It's already covered landing site Alpha. It'll be over New Abhaile and Bravo in a few more hours. Orbital bombardment is useless so long as the dust storms are up. Can't see what we're shooting at."

"How long do we have until they get here?" Hale asked.

"Nineteen hours, depending on how long, or even if, the banshees stop for the storm. Both groups will arrive at roughly the same time," Valdar said.

"It will take us another twenty-two hours to have the *Canticle* ready for liftoff," Lafayette said.

"And how many banshees are we looking at?"

"Each drop site had roughly three times as many banshees as the last assault," Valdar said.

Hale kept his face devoid of expression as he heard the devastating news.

"The defense of this city will be impossible," Wen'la said. "We suggest evacuating every Dotok that the *Breitenfeld* can carry and leave the system immediately."

"What about the *Burning Blade*?" Hale asked.

"That fire in the sky you saw was the *Burning Blade* ramming the last cruiser. Ty'ken had the choice of letting that cruiser hit New Abhaile or him," Valdar said. "We've got one ship left in orbit, and we've got our own problems to handle."

"Wen'la is correct," Pa'lon said. "We save what we can and we leave. It is a hard decision to make, but necessary."

Hale looked over the map. He leaned toward it and pressed his lips together in concentration. There was a chokepoint along one of the routes the invaders had to take to reach New Abhaile.

"Zoom in on…Ghostwind Pass, that the name?" Hale asked. The map shifted and enlarged on the pass. "You see this spur, this line of mountains jutting into the pass?" Hale asked. "We could blow the cliff face, bring it down on the berserkers or at least block the pass. They couldn't climb over it without suffocating in the thin air, right?"

"How would you destroy the cliff?" Taal asked.

"Operation Yalu," Valdar said.

"Before the Xaros invasion," Hale said, "the

Atlantic Union had a plan to liberate Korea from the Chinese occupation. Beating what they had on the peninsula was never too much of a challenge. Keeping Chinese reinforcements out of the battle was the difference between victory and defeat. The plan was to nuke the mountain passes north of the Yalu River, block the heavy equipment like tanks and artillery from ever reaching the fight. My team and I trained for that exact mission for months before we got assigned to the Saturn colonial fleet."

"What is a 'Yalu'?" Wen'la asked.

"And a 'Korea'?" Taal asked.

Hale ignored them. "Captain, have you got a nuke onboard? Couple kiloton yield should be enough."

"I left for Anthalas prepared for most every contingency. I have strategic terrain nukes for you," Valdar said. "I'm looking at the avenue of approach for the landing site at Alpha. No place for us to replicate what you've got in mind for Bravo?"

"Why don't you use your nuclear weapons against the invaders now? I am aware of the storm overhead, but nuclear weapons tend to be somewhat forgiving if you miss, correct?" Wen'la asked.

Pa'lon cleared his throat. "Across many, many instances of the Xaros encountering species with nuclear weapons, the weapons proved useless. The Xaros emit some sort of dampening field that retards the fission or fusion properties of radioactive materials. The accepted hypothesis is that whoever controls the Xaros drones doesn't want to live on an irradiated wasteland, so nuclear strikes against them are rendered useless."

"There were nukes used during the defense of Earth," Hale said. "There's still fallout in the atmosphere."

"There's a limit to the dampening field, a few hundred miles from any drone." Pa'lon folded his hands over the top of his cane. "I think you'll succeed."

"What about the rest? All the *noorla* coming from site Alpha," Wen'la said.

"We either leave sooner or beat them at the gates," Hale said.

"Leaving sooner is possible," Lafayette said. "The Dotok technicians are quite adept. They're installing the anti-gravity plates four percent faster than I'd anticipated. Captain Valdar, if you can spare some crew, we can have the *Canticle* ready almost thirty minutes before the next wave of invaders are anticipated."

"Thirty minutes?" Valdar asked, his tone skeptical.

"We only need to beat them by one minute," Lafayette said.

"I'll send down everyone I can spare along with Hale's nuke," Valdar said. "Daylight is burning. Best you all get back to work." His hologram sputtered out.

Hale went to the two Karigole. "Steuben, the only other Marine trained to lead a nuclear demolition mission is Vogelaar, and she's…so just me. I'm going to take my team and a Mule to Ghostwind Pass and solve one of our problems. I'm leaving you in charge of the defense of this city," Hale said.

"A worthy strategy," Steuben said.

"If anything goes wrong, get my Marines and the Dotok off this rock," Hale said.

Steuben nodded, then enveloped Hale in a bear hug so tight Hale struggled to breathe.

"Steuben…" Hale slapped at the Karigole's arms. "Steub—"

He released Hale and grabbed him by the shoulders.

"Is that the traditional way human friends say farewell to each other?" Steuben asked.

"Things were a lot easier when you were just a stick in the mud," Hale said. "How do Karigole warriors say good-bye?"

Steuben pressed the middle knuckle of his fingers against Hale's left temple. Hale returned the gesture, then left the conference room.

"Don't humans also slap each other on the buttocks?" Lafayette asked.

"That is reserved for athletic accomplishments, I believe. I will attempt that form of nonverbal communication when I see Gunney

Cortaro again," Steuben said.

****

Valdar stepped into the morgue, a frigid room cold enough to be a meat locker. Space ships weren't meant to carry significant numbers of their own dead with them. Under combat conditions, Valdar had the authority to either cremate or consign the dead to the void. Out of combat, he was expected to preserve fatalities for investigations and proper burials.

Three dead banshees lay on wheeled tables bolted to the deck. Dr. Accorso, wearing a lab coat stained gray up to the elbows, stood next to the head of a corpse and waved a bloody hand at Valdar.

"Captain, glad you could join me," Accorso said.

"Smells like roadkill during an Alabama summer, doctor. What am I doing in here?" Valdar asked.

"I found something very interesting in these banshee corpses. Rather, it's what I *didn't* find that's interesting." Accorso pointed to a pile of X-rays on a shelf. "See for yourself."

Valdar held the X-rays up to the ceiling lights. Each was a cross section of the banshees' craniums, one a ruined mess from whatever killed it.

"What am I looking at?" Valdar asked.

"There's a void in their heads, captain. Something was in there, connected to their spinal columns and their brain stems," There was a sickening crack as Accorso pried the banshee's head open and peered into it with a small flashlight. "And there's no trace of it. Sound familiar?"

"The Xaros."

"Precisely. The Marines encountered banshees with Xaros technology incorporated into their bodies, the D-beams. Reason stands that there could be something else in them. I doubt a fleet full of the Dotok's best and brightest decided that this…" he gave the banshee's armor a pat, "was a great idea. My hypothesis is that there's a control chip in their brains and it disintegrates when they die. Hmm, yes, definitely an invasive foreign body in the brain stem. I see the scarring around the nervous tissue."

"Great, doctor, save it for a research paper. I have a ship to fight." Valdar went for the door.

"You don't want a Xaros radio?" The question halted Valdar in his tracks. "These banshees aren't mindless berserkers. They act with purpose and direction."

"Where are you going to get a…the prisoner." Valdar said.

"Yes, the banshee that's been pounding away on the walls of its cage for the past many hours. My new assistant and I could remove the implant, if we could get it to hold still," Accorso said.

"How are you going to do that? Promise it a sticker and a lollypop if it gets its shots without crying?" Valdar asked.

"I'm just a doctor, captain, not an animal tamer," Accorso said.

"What will happen to the banshee when you

take the implant out?" Valdar asked.

"We shall see. Science requires experimentation," Accorso smiled, and Valdar felt a chill in his heart that had nothing to do with the cold air in the morgue.

CHAPTER 10

Hale hung from the end of a line dangling out a Mule's open cargo bay. The Mule hovered half a mile above the bottom of the Great Expanse and dangerously close to the cliffs that made up the edge of the valley.

"Don't look down," Hale repeated to himself several times. He swung his body back and forth, building momentum as the swings brought him closer and closer to the cliff face. He reached for the rock and his fingertips managed to grab a handhold.

The cable attached to his waist and feet pulled him back from the wall with terrifying slowness and surety.

"Got some crosswind coming in, hold on tight," the pilot said. Hale felt a slight buffet of air, then the wind howled around him. The gale sent him spinning away on his line like a wayward top.

"Reel him in!" Torni shouted.

"I can't! The line's twisted," Standish said.

The wind subsided and Hale found himself swinging toward the rock wall with more speed than he thought he could handle. He spread his arms away from the line and slammed into the cliff, his armor absorbing most of the blow. His hands raked over the rock and found purchase. He ran the edges of his boots against the cliff until they secured a foothold.

Hale hugged the wall with more strength and genuine affection than he thought possible.

"Sir, you good?" Torni asked over the IR.

"Uh-huh," Hale pressed his visor against the rock, mashing his face against the reinforced plastic.

"Don't let go."

"You think?" Hale grabbed an auto-anchor from his chest harness—a small spike of metal attached to a carbon-fiber line that ran to his belt— and pressed the tip against the rock face. The screw came to life and bore into the cliff. He heard a *thunk* as the spurs deployed on the screw, increasing the amount of weight the screw could hold should he fall. He attached two more screws into the wall, then detached the line to the Mule from his waist.

"Standish, your turn," Hale said.

Hale clutched the wall, praying that Standish wouldn't have the same trouble he did.

Less than a minute later, Standish swung up to the wall, level with his lieutenant, grabbed the wall with ease and anchored himself without incident.

"Dang, sir, why you always got to make things look difficult?" Standish asked as he detached the line leading to the Mule.

"Just get the torch," Hale said. "Mule two-nine, we're secure. Do a recon around the pass. Make sure no banshees get through." The ship pulled away slowly, then banked into a low cloud.

"One stone torch coming right up." Standish pushed back from the rock and grabbed a handle on the tiered device the size of a manhole cover strapped to his back. "Ready on three. One…two…three." He swung the device to Hale, who grabbed it by a handle on the other side.

They slapped it against the cliff. Spikes attached to the torch snapped into the rock. Red warning lights lit up across the device.

"Look away," Hale said. He followed his own advice and felt the cliff shudder as the torch began its work. Stone torches were a natural by-product of asteroid mining. Drilling into asteroids was problematic. The ejected material proved hazardous for navigation and some asteroids had a bad habit of fracturing from a drill's vibrations. Melting a hole into an asteroid with focused lasers and heat shunts to determine its composition (and whether the rock was worth mining) was seen as a huge improvement for the industry. Naturally, the military found an application for the technology.

A column of vaporized stone poured from the hole like steam from a locomotive as the torch moved at a downward angle into the cliff side.

"Think it'll go deep enough?" Standish asked.

"Doesn't have to go that far. The nuke will follow the same principle as a firecracker in your hand. Firecracker goes off on your palm, you get a little singed. Wrap your fist around it and you'll lose fingers when it pops," Hale said.

The vapor subsided and three long buzzers sounded from the hole. The stone torch had reached an optimum depth.

"We're in business," Hale said. He pulled a tube set in a wire frame from off his belt and held it up to the hole. He hit a button on the tube and the frame snapped out to touch the sides of the hole.

"Nuclear device activation code: Kenneth Alpharius Hale X-ray one-two-seven-two-two-niner," Hale shouted, his voice competing against a howl of wind.

"Authorization accepted," a pleasant-sounding woman's voice said. "Specify detonation criteria, command or timer?"

"Timer. Three-zero minutes."

"Nuclear detonation in thirty minutes, confirmed?"

"Confirmed, launch!"

The nuke slid down the hole with a hiss.

"Sir, this is Torni. We've got a situation."

Standish's eyes went wide as he looked into the hole where the nuke had already slid into darkness.

"Go, Torni," Hale said.

"We've got civilians out there, looks like a couple dozen coming by foot," she said.

Hale groaned and thumped his head against the wall. "Are they to the east or the west of the blast site?" *Please don't say east*, he thought.

"East. They're on the wrong side of our demo work," Torni said.

"The nuke is set. Come retrieve us. We'll work out what to do about the civilians after that," Hale said.

The two Marines clung to the cliff, wind blowing pebbles loose.

"You don't need to work it out, do you, sir?" Standish asked. "We're going to go get them, bring them back to New Abhaile."

"And how do you know that, Standish?"

"You and the skipper are almost the same person. You can't let the innocent suffer, not if you can do something about it."

"Am I wrong?"

"No. I think about Earth a lot, everyone Ibarra left behind. If you had a chance to go back and save one more person—don't care who it was— I know you'd have risked it. And I'd be right there behind you. These Dotok, they aren't so bad. Kind of friendly in a stuck-up sort of way. If we can save more, that's almost like saving a human, right?"

"I don't see them as being that different from us. They're scared, they love each other…they don't want to die. If we bring them back to Earth, they'll help us fight the Xaros," Hale said.

"Not like we don't have enough room on

Earth. Imagine that, a Dotok city. Up in Utah, maybe. You think they'll make statues of us? 'Here is the great Paul Standish, hero of Takeni and our savior from genocide.'"

"They don't seem like statue-building kind of people," Hale said.

"Yeah, more modern-art types. Wait … your middle name is Alpharius?"

"My father's idea, don't ask. I wasn't consulted. You keep that secret between us, understand?"

"Sure thing, sir. You can always count on me to keep my mouth shut," Standish said.

Their Mule emerged from the clouds.

****

Crewman Daniels bent at the waist and stretched his hamstrings. He re-tied the shoelaces on his running shoes and ran in place, bringing his knees up to his chest and slapping them against his palms. Ericcson stood next to him in her void combat suit, at odds with his physical training clothes.

"You ready, Daniels?" Ericcson asked.

"Ma'am, why am I doing this again?" Daniels asked. His Welsh accent was thick, but not so bad that Ericcson couldn't understand him.

"Because you are the fastest runner on this ship and the lowest-ranking sailor. You'd get this assignment for both those reasons. You can pick whichever one makes you feel better," Ericcson said.

"But Tavish in gunnery control ran in the bloody Olympics!"

"Tavish is dead. He was in gunnery control when the banshees boarded us, remember?"

"I can't be the lowest-ranked sailor. Didn't…didn't…?"

"You got drunk and urinated all over a security robot attempting to issue you a citation for disturbing the peace. You caught a Captain's Mast for that and he knocked your rank down to Seaman Apprentice. Whale shit is higher up the chain of command than you are, Daniels. Maybe you think about this situation the next time you want to get drunk on shore leave."

"If I survive this, I'm definitely drinking again," Daniels said. His eyes kept wandering to the heavy iron door in front of him.

"Explain the plan to me, one more time," she said.

"You open the door to that banshee thing. I get its attention and have it chase me up the hatch to deck twelve. I hit the lifeline, Bob's your uncle, all done," he said.

"You scared?"

"Of course I'm scared. I'd shit me pants but I got nothing left in there," he said.

"Good, that'll make you run faster," she said.

"Put a bottle of beer at the end of this race and I'd light the damn deck on fire gettin' there so fast," he mumbled.

Ericcson stepped through a different door and shut it behind her. The sound of it sealing shut sent shivers down Daniels' spine.

"Ready? Opening the outer door now. Cage opens after that," Ericcson said over the intercom.

Daniels squatted down and jumped back up, feeling blood rush to his muscles.

The door in front of him rolled to the side. Down a narrow corridor of reinforced armor plates purpose built for this operation was the ammunition cargo container holding the captive banshee. The container's walls had been dented from the inside, like the banshee had systematically searched for a weak point in the construction.

Daniels whimpered as the latches came free and the container door opened, revealing darkness.

"Come on, you big ugly," Daniels said.

There was a low rumble from the void. Daniels saw the thing's claws first as it reached past the edge of the container. Yellow eyes floated through the darkness.

"Hey! You! The one with a face like a kicked-in shitcan!" Daniels grabbed his crotch. "How about you come over here and give me a wristy, you ugly wanker?"

The banshee let loose a blood-curdling scream and charged straight for Daniels.

"Bad idea! Bad idea! Bad idea!" Daniels turned and ran down the passageway, his arms and legs pumping like pistons as he raced to a pair of handcuffs dangling from a chain out of a hatch cut out of the ceiling.

He heard the banshee slam into the corridor behind him and beat at one of the welded-shut doors. His heart pumped battery acid as he got closer and closer to the cuffs. All he'd have to do was attach them to his wrists and he'd be safe—that was the promise.

The banshee roared and tore after Daniels, who suddenly realized what a gazelle felt like when a cheetah was on its tail.

Daniels skidded to a halt and reached for the cuffs, just as his feet slid out from under him. He slammed to the deck and jumped back up and made the mistake of looking back at the banshee. The thing moved with an almost leonine grace, its eyes set on Daniels and murder.

He got one of the cuffs snapped tight against his wrist.

"Go! Now!" He fumbled with the other cuff and the banshee got closer by the second.

The chain went taught and pulled him into the air. The banshee's claws barely missed his shoes as it overran his position.

Daniels laughed, ignoring the pain in his wrist as he went higher through a ventilation shaft. He looked down…and didn't see the banshee. His ascent stopped, leaving him dangling from the chain.

"Hey! This wasn't the plan!" he shouted. One of his shoes came loose and fell down the shaft. It thumped against the deck, and the banshee picked it up. The creature looked up the shaft and snarled.

"Hey! Come on! This isn't funny!"

The banshee climbed into the shaft and made for Daniels with all the ease of a squirrel moving up an oak tree.

The dark airshaft had a built-in design

feature: it narrowed toward the top. The banshee climbed higher and found its freedom to maneuver robbed inch by inch.

"Help!" Daniels screeched.

He could almost smell the thing's breath when a metal bar shot through the shaft right between the banshee's legs. Another came through over its shoulder. More bars slid through the shaft, trapping the banshee in place. It struggled, tried to claw at the bars with its talons, but with no room to move, it had no way to leverage any of its strength.

The chain holding Daniels started moving again. It pulled him through an opening at the top of the shaft and a pair of crewman got him clear of his exit. One slammed a metal plate over the top and activated mag-locks, sealing it to the opening.

"Is he OK?" the XO asked over the intercom.

"He's in one piece, ma'am," a crewman said.

"I'm just…going to lay here…for a minute," Daniels said between breaths.

****

Valdar caught his reflection in the tactical plot. His face was haggard, his beard needed a decent trim and the bags under his eyes spoke of days without sleep. He took a sip of black coffee. The caffeine haze of the past many hours would come to a screeching halt once his body demanded rest. Perhaps he could step away for a cat nap.

"Captain, you need to see this," Ensign Geller said.

Perhaps not.

"According to the Dotok, their Glorious Fleet had five *Canticle*-class generation ships, right?" Valdar glared at the ensign. "So, I thought, 'Where are they?' The entire rest of the fleet was blown up by the Dotok or us. That many ships would—"

Valdar slammed a fist against the plot table. His cup and saucer fell to the deck and shattered.

"I found them!" Geller squeaked. "And I found out why our jump in to the system went sideways." He held out photographs of a rocky toroid, a gigantic doughnut-shaped asteroid. Long spikes punctured the surface, like someone had dropped a crown of thorns into wet concrete.

"This is a Crucible. A jump gate," Valdar said.

"One under construction, at least," Geller said with some pride, "and look around it." The other pictures showed four *Canticle*-sized ships around the proto-Crucible. "That's what messed up our jump. And that's how I found it! I thought that something out there must have the mass to generate a deep enough gravity well to offset the quantum field variance by at least—"

"Good work, son. How far away is it?"

The ensign picked up a red icon and set it on the tactical plot. Valdar made a few quick calculations in his head then turned to the XO.

"Get all the department heads up here immediately, and get Lafayette on the holo."

****

The operations table held a small globe, a miniature of the *Breitenfeld* and five red enemy ship icons on short pegs. The senior members of the ship stood around the table, along with a hologram of Lafayette.

"The new Crucible is here on approach to Takeni," Valdar said. "If the Xaros hold true to form, they mean for it to take up orbit. It'll remain a work in progress until then, which means no drone reinforcements coming through. It does present a problem though." Valdar pointed the stick in his hands at Ensign Geller.

"Sirs and ma'ams, the gravity well from something this large skews the quantum—"

Valdar snapped the stick against the table.

"We can't leave," Geller said. "Or at least we can't jump to Earth. The greater the distance, the more precise the jump has to be. The mass of the Crucible flaws the jump equation. If we try to jump out of here now, we'll be ripped apart."

"So we break anchor," the chief engineer said. "Get clear of its influence and jump from there."

"That would work, but we'll have the *Canticle* with us soon," Valdar said. "And it'll be adrift in space with no engines."

Ensign Geller cleared his throat. "The solution is for us to jump, with the *Canticle*, to the brown dwarf star located two point nine light-years from here. We recharge the jump engines there and jump back to Earth."

"What if there's a Xaros presence?" Utrecht asked.

"There are no habitable worlds. If the Xaros have been through, there shouldn't be anything but a monitoring force. We can handle one or two drones," Valdar said.

"It'll be a skip and a jump back to Earth, no hop involved," Geller said. He smiled, waiting for the laugher that never came.

"It won't work," Lafayette said. "Your theory is sound, but at the rate the Crucible is approaching ... any jump would either tear us to pieces or drop us into deep space."

"Is deep space that bad?" Ericcson asked. "Anywhere but here seems like an improvement."

"The jump engines absorb dark matter to charge," Levin said. "We jump into the middle of nowhere and we're in trouble. We need to jump within the Nye-Sandburg dark-energy corona around a star or we'll be sitting out there for years waiting to jump again."

"Lafayette," Valdar said, "how do we change the math?"

The Karigole tapped his metal fingertips together. "How much quadrium do we still have?"

"Five rail cannon shells, twenty shells for the point defense guns, nine gauss rifle shots," Utrecht said. "I don't know if the armor still have their one round each."

"That will be more than enough. I'll need every shell brought to my lab. It will take me three hours to build the bomb. Captain, I'll need you to figure out a way to get myself and a small package onto the approaching Crucible…at this location, the command nodule. I'll return immediately."

Lafayette's hologram switched off.

"Did he say 'bomb'?" Ericcson asked.

"He did," Valdar said. "Ibarra turned his quadrium munition factory into a singularity bomb when we were running from the drones chasing us away from Earth. He must know how to make one too."

"He's going to make a black hole … on our ship?" Ericcson asked.

"Anyone have a better idea?" Valdar asked. None were offered. "Durand, let's figure out how to get him where he needs to be."

****

Hale stood on the Mule's ramp, his boots and hand mag-locked to the ship. He scanned the ground below, looking for any sign of the civilians Torni had seen.

"You think they're scared, sir?" Bailey asked from the upper turret.

"Makes sense. If they're running from Usonvi, the last thing they heard from New Abhaile after they blew the rail lines was to stay put and wait for evac. They might think our Mule's some sort of Xaros. Plus, they haven't had the best of luck with aliens dropping out of the sky to say hello," Hale said.

"Got 'em on thermals," Orozco said. The cameras integrated into his bottom turret were far superior to Hale's Mark One Eyeball. The gunner sent a feed to Hale, and he saw dozens of warm bodies hiding in a field of shrubs running up a hillside.

"Pilot, set us down at that clearing. Let's see how many we're dealing with," Hale said. He heard the whine of landing gear descending and held on tight as the ship lowered to the ground.

It settled against a field of long grass, whipping from side to side in the ship's exhaust.

"Cut it down to standby, don't want to scare them off," Hale said.

"A drone shows up and we'll be sitting ducks for two minutes," the pilot shot back.

"Then the sooner I get this over with, the

better." Hale locked his rifle against his back and stepped off the ramp with Torni, Yarrow and Standish right behind him. He kept his hands out and to his sides as he made his way to the underbrush where they'd seen the Dotok. The Mule's engines died down to a low whine.

"Hello! I'm Lieutenant Hale!" he shouted. No response. "I'm from the *Breitenfeld* Ancient Pa'lon sent me to help!"

A Dotok stood up from the brush, a male in flowing robes and a turban made from silk.

"The *Breitenfeld*? It's real?"

"You're talking to a human." Hale removed his helmet, and the Dotok recoiled with a sneer on his lips.

"Don't take it personally, sir. They think I'm ugly too," Torni said.

The turbaned Dotok came down the mountainside, a clipboard in one hand and a small book in the other.

"I am Chosen Nil'jo, leader of Usonvi and its inhabitants," he said.

"What happened to Usonvi? Why'd you leave?"

"We saw the *noorla* pods coming through the atmosphere, and the scouts I sent out to investigate never came back. I left my lowers to defend the city and brought my higher ratings with me. We can make it to New Abhaile in another two days. The losses will be acceptable, so long as those lowers with me save their rations for their betters," Nil'jo said.

"You…left people behind?" Hale asked.

"If they can delay the *noorla* for a bit to buy time for highers, a worthy exchange," Nil'jo said. "How many can your ship carry? I have to prioritize."

"All of them, just get them down here," Hale said.

"My boy, there's no way we can get three hundred and nine Dotok into that…thing," Nil'jo said.

"Three hundred?"

Nil'jo pulled a whistle from his robes and

blew three notes. Dotok arose from the scrub and came down the hill. More—many more—ran over the top of the hill.

"I'll organize them for you. Twenty? Thirty, perhaps?" Nil'jo said.

"Hale, you got a second?" the pilot asked him.

Hale backed away, watching as the Dotok fell into ranks ten people wide. Each knew exactly what their assigned ranking was within Nil'jo's hierarchy.

"You! Ti'ka! I saw you eat those preserves. Your parents lose ten rankings!" Nil'jo pointed a pen at a little boy and shooed him and his family back a row.

The pilot, a dark-skinned man with close-cropped hair, stood beside his Mule examining the landing struts.

"I'm Jorgen," the pilot said. "I didn't want the civvies to hear this, but there's two ways I can fly back. Go the straight route over the mesas, which is faster, but I'll have to pressurize the ship, which means I can't take as many passengers. I won't have the air for it. Other option is I go nap-of-the-earth, low and fast. I can keep the cabin unpressurized. They'll be colder than sin, but they'll be able to breathe."

"How many can you take, each option?"

"Ten if I go the high route. As many as you can fit for the low route. If they were Marines with their own air tanks and O2 scrubbers, it would be different," Jorgen said.

"Nothing is ever easy in the Corps, is it?"

"That's why I joined the navy."

"How long until you can come back with enough carry for the rest, say two hundred and seventy, plus four Marines?"

"There's one hell of a dust storm coming in, remember? I can get a load back now. After that we've got to wait until the storm passes," Jorgen said. "And hurry up—there's a nuke set to blow."

"Mr. Hale-*Breitenfeld*," Nil'jo waved to Hale from the base of the ramp. "I've got the highest twenty-five ready to depart."

Nil'jo's choice evacuees were middle-aged and elderly Dotok, carrying bound books and thick ledgers. They looked like scholars and accountants, all wearing robes that were once finery before a long trek through the wilderness.

The crowd of the less worthy were families. Women held squalling babies on their hips and tried to hold toddlers tight as they all looked at the Mule like it was their last chance for survival.

Which, Hale knew, it probably was.

He looked at the bureaucrats Nil'jo wanted to save and back at the less fortunate, who were somehow less worthy in their Chosen's eyes. Anger welled up into his chest, and something snapped.

"No. We're not taking any able-bodied adults who can keep walking," Hale said.

"What?" Nil'jo looked at Hale like he'd sprouted a second head. "My list is complete and ranked accordingly. There's no way I'll let lowers get to safety so long as I—"

Hale's hand shot out and wrapped around Nil'jo's throat. The Chosen went silent with a gurgle.

"I don't have time to give your culture its proper respect. We're going off the human list. It goes something like this: Women and children first! Sergeant Torni, bring families up here, anyone that can't keep walking. Wounded, elderly. Standish," Hale continued, pointing to the bureaucrats with the hand that wasn't strangling Nil'jo, "any of them decide they don't like my plan and try to get on board, you have my permission to beat the hell out of them until they feel otherwise."

"Sir, one thing," Standish said.

"What!"

"He can't breathe, sir. I don't think purple is a good color for a Dotok," Standish said.

Hale shoved the Chosen into the dirt, where he hacked and coughed, trying to find the breath to protest.

Torni took Yarrow and Bailey to the waiting Dotok and pulled mothers with children from the group and pushed them toward the Mule. The few husbands and fathers didn't protest as their families got a lifeline to safety.

Almost sixty women with small children waited at the base of the ramp as Jorgen and Orozco helped get them inside.

"Orozco," Hale said, "get in the dorsal turret. New Abhaile will need your Gustav more than I will out here."

"Sir…no, I can—"

"Now, sergeant. That's an order," Hale said.

Orozco hesitated, then gave the lieutenant a quick salute. He pushed his way through the civilians and opened the turret hatch.

"I'm full." Jorgen made a cutting motion across his neck.

"Get them back," Hale said. His Marines raised their weapons across their chests and kept the civilians off the ramp as it rose. Wails rose from the crowd as it sealed shut. The Mule took to the air on anti-grav thrusters, sending a blast of air through the crowd.

The Dotok cried as they watched it soar away.

"Jorgen," Hale said into the IR before the Mule could get out of range, "there's a mesa to the northeast. Meet us there as soon as you can bring back enough lift for everyone."

"Roger, Hale. You've got my word," Jorgen said.

"Listen to me," Hale said to the Dotok. "We're all getting out of here. Every single one of you. My Marines and I are here to protect you, to guide you to where more of those ships will return and bring you to the *Canticle of Reason.* Understand?"

The crying subsided.

"You made it this far. You can make it the rest of the way, but we have to leave now." Hale pointed to the northeast. "Follow us."

He tapped Torni on the shoulder. "You and Standish take the rear. Bailey and I will guide the column. Let me know if we've got any stragglers," Hale said.

"On it, sir," she said.

Hale found Nil'jo on the ground, trying to

pick up sheets of paper that had come loose from his book. The Chosen squeaked and tried to run away as Hale approached. Hale grabbed him by the back of his robes.

"You listen to me," Hale said, balling his hands with Nil'jo's robes. "Every one of you is getting out of here. You fight me on this and I will squeeze your pencil neck until your head pops clean off. You get me?"

Nil'jo looked from side to side.

"What can I get you?" he asked.

"You understand me?'

"Yes. Yes, no problem. Everyone gets out." He raised his clipboard. "I've got a list right here of—" Hale knocked the clipboard out of his hand. "Who needs a list if everyone's on it?" Hale let him go and unlocked his rifle from his back. He ran to the front of the column of refugees and matched pace with Bailey.

"Damn, sir," she said.

"What?"

"I like angry Hale. Just don't actually pop

that bludger's head off. There'd be paperwork and that might cut into my drinking time," she said.

Hale looked to the sky and saw a slight haze rising in the distance.

"There's your dust storm. I made it through a couple out in the bush, not sure how bad they are here," Bailey said.

"We'll find out, won't we?"

Ahead of the column, low hills with short, thorny bushes were all he could see as the terrain rose higher and higher into a mountain range. They had hours to go until they reached the mesa.

"What gives, sir? Why angry Hale all of a sudden?"

"You know who my godfather is, Bailey?"

"No clue.

"Captain Valdar, and I'll tell you why. Back during the Second Pacific War, my father was a lance corporal with 5th Marines, based out of Okinawa. The Japanese and the whole American Pacific Fleet got caught with their pants down when the Chinese popped an EMP over Tokyo. The

Chinese landed an entire corps worth of troops on the island and the fight was on. Marines and the Japanese army never had a chance, but they held out for twenty days waiting for help. On the last day, the Chinese broke through and chased the defenders into the sea.

"My old man took a shot to the gut. Couple of his buddies dragged him to a rusted-out scow of a ship that an ensign named Isaac Valdar had commandeered. Valdar waits until the last American is onboard, he shoves off under fire and has got a straight shot into the Pacific Ocean.

"Then, a pretty little Okinawan girl comes running for the ship. Her parents were high up in the Japanese government, and the Chinese had them all marked on their black lists for execution. She gets to the ship or she's a dead woman. She jumps in the water and starts swimming for the ship.

"Valdar cuts the engines, goes out on the deck and tosses the girl a ladder to help her up. Chinese sniper hits him in the leg and he needs a tourniquet to keep from bleeding out. Good thing the girl he saved was a nurse. She patched him up *and* kept my father alive until they got picked up by the navy. The nurse and my father fell for each other and got married. Hence, me.

"Valdar risked everything to save one more life, and because of that…I'm here. If I can save more, I will. Who knows what'll come of it."

Bailey nodded, smacking her gum as she digested the story.

"Me mum and pa met at a bar," she said.

CHAPTER 11

Lafayette ran through the landing zone, his cybernetic feet and legs carrying him at a pace his old body of flesh and blood could never have hoped to match. He leaped over a pallet of ammunition coming off a Destrier and earned several choice human insults he'd have to cross-reference with MacDougall for their proper meaning.

He skidded around an idling Mule and found Elias waiting at the end of the ramp, a lumpy canvas sack at the suit's feet.

"Elias, I see you're ready to go. Thank you for volunteering for this mission," Lafayette said.

"Valdar ordered us back to the *Breitenfeld*.

Consider us volun-told." Elias pointed to the sack, which had an unctuous odor so strong that Lafayette lowered the sensitivity of his nasal sensors. "You will make us shields."

"I...don't follow," Lafayette said.

Elias described how the banshee armor proved resistant to the Xaros disintegration beams.

"That's fascinating. I once experimented with armor capable of nullifying the Xaros beams." Lafayette waved a hand over his cybernetic body. "My invention was...found wanting. Am I to understand that you've got dead banshees in that sack?"

"We stripped off armor plates," Elias said.

"That's rather morbid yet a real time-saver for me," Lafayette said. "I have to build a bomb, but then I'll make you and Kallen your shields. For science. Imagine if it works," he rubbed his metal hands together, "*and* we survive this mission to tell everyone!"

****

Dr. Accorso, wearing a full surgical gown beneath a flack vest, waved his hands beneath a sterile field generator and slapped on a pair of gloves. Shor wore a set of Dotok surgical gear: tight wraps of magenta cloth around her body and scrubs and a mask over her mouth, sent over from the *Burning Blade.*

"Ready to make history?" Accorso asked.

"Let's get this over with," she said.

Accorso held his sterile hands in the air and backed into the surgical ward. The banshee lay on a ramp that had once been attached to a Mule, its limbs splayed out and fastened with double lengths of carbon-fiber cable used to lift Eagles off the flight deck. A vice held its head parallel to the ramp.

Wires snaked out from beneath armor plates, leading into Dotok medical equipment. A pair of crewmen holding gauss carbines and piston hammers watched from along the bulkhead.

Accorso squinted at the readings and

shrugged his shoulders.

"Is the patient sedated?" he asked.

"I pumped her full of enough sedatives to kill a dozen adults. Whatever is in her head is overloading her lymphatic system. The sedative drip I've got her on is on par with what her system can negate. Let's get going before she goes into organ shutdown or breaks loose," Shor said.

"She?"

"Our females have different blood types from the males. She's a she."

"Interesting." Accorso picked up a set of pneumatic jaws the flight crews used to pry open cockpits of wrecked ships. "No time for finesse, I'm afraid." He jammed the wedge end of the jaws against the base of the banshee's skull and pressed a button. The jaws widened, separating armor plates with a sickening crack.

"Surgical scars to the base of the skull," Shor said. "Looks only a few years old."

"Consistent with the other specimens, the foreign object was likely introduced after maturity,"

Accorso said. "Now that we've got a clear look, perhaps an ultrasound?"

He picked up a wand and pressed it against the bare flesh. Sound pulses formed a 3-D image on a handheld screen. A dense mass was attached to the banshee's brain stem, its tendrils woven into the brain and spinal column.

"What do you think?" Accorso asked.

"I think brain surgery on a Dotok with such highly modified physiology is a mistake," she said.

The banshee quivered and let out a low moan. One of the crewmen fumbled with his carbine as the other raised a hammer.

"Settle down, boys. I've had patients sing an opera while they've been under," Accorso said. "Normally," he said to Shor, "I'd agree with you. But … needs must." He picked up a sonic scalpel and cut an incision across the mass at the base of the skull. Gray blood seeped from the wound.

Shor and Accorso spent the next ten minutes exposing the nodule, an oblong lump of gray metal with swirls and fractals dancing across its surface.

"Looks like a Xaros drone," Accorso thought out loud. "Let's remove it. Tray," Shor gave Accorso a dirty look.

"I am the doctor and expert in Dotok physiology and neurology. You hold the tray." She elbowed Accorso aside and picked up a set of pliers. "The wires can remain. I'm cutting away the Xaros device." She snipped a wire where it connected to the device. Nothing happened for a moment, then the cut wire disintegrated. The banshee grunted.

"That was unexpected," she said.

"Suggest you hurry."

Shor snipped the rest of the wires with the same effect. She lifted up the device with the edge of the pliers.

"There's a mass of wires attached to the brain stem. Angle it up so I can remove them," Shor said. Accorso lifted the device with the edge of a pair of clamps and Shor cut away the remaining wires.

Accorso grabbed the device with the clamps and transferred it to a metal tray. He spun away from the surgical table and examined it beneath a light.

"Hello, my darling. What have we here?" Accorso watched as the patterns along the surface shifted…then went still. A burning ember crept across the surface as the device broke apart and collapsed into ash.

"No, no, no! God damn it!" Accorso slammed the empty tray to the deck and mashed it with his foot.

The monitoring equipment buzzed and a double chime sounded.

"Blood pressure fading, neural activity just went off the charts," Shor said. "I think we're losing her."

"*Gohrnah,*" said the banshee.

Shor ran to the other side of the table and ripped her mask off.

"*Gohrnah,*" it said again.

"Is it…talking?" Accorso asked.

"It's an old dialect, but I understand. It's 'help.' She's asking for help." Shor touched the banshee's face and spoke words Accorso's translator didn't recognize.

The banshee spoke again, guttural words that reverberated off the walls. Its speech trailed away as Shor, tears in her eyes, nodded furiously.

Flat lines cut across the monitoring display and stayed steady. Accorso switched it off.

Shor closed the banshee's eyes and pressed two fingers to her lips. "We are less without you, old mother."

"What did she say?"

"She spoke of a vile stone, an old story from Dotari Prime. A *noorla* lived inside a mountain and used its powers to force a city to do horrible things. Then…she asked to be forgiven. Asked me to pray at a shrine to lessen the weight of sins she'd carry to heaven."

"The captain will want to know about this 'vile stone.'" He opened the door back to the med bay. "You coming?"

"I must stay with her for a while, until her spirit has left," Shor said. She folded her arms across the banshee's chest and laid her head against the armor.

****

Cortaro limped down the stone walkway, carefully measuring each step with his prosthetic. His peg had a nasty habit of jamming into the nooks and crannies of the cobblestone surface, twisting it against the tender stump of what remained of his leg. There were times he could almost feel his missing foot, a phantom pain the doctor swore was a good thing. It meant his body would accept a vat-grown replacement easier.

The peg jabbed into a puddle and slipped. Cortaro went wheeling forward and would have fallen, had Steuben not grabbed him by the shoulder to steady him.

"Are you OK?" Steuben asked.

"No, Steuben, *someone* blew my leg off and now I'm trying to get around like a damned cripple," Cortaro said. He tightened the strap lashing his prosthetic to his flesh and blood and continued down the road.

"I'm the one who shot your leg. Did you forget?"

"No—I," he pointed a knife hand at Steuben. "Are you messing with me?"

"This topic does not seem to be one that strikes much humor with you."

Cortaro continued on, taking longer steps that Steuben had no trouble keeping pace with. Dotok soldiers and human Marines worked together along the eastern walls, setting spikes and welded-together crossbeams from cannibalized starships and bolting them to the road.

Steuben grabbed a Dotok by the shoulder and pointed to the roll of wire in the Dotok's trembling hands. "Do not run wires until after the obstacles are set. Keep our lanes of retreat open until we are done with the eastern approaches."

The Dotok nodded his head rapidly and dropped the wire at his feet.

"You scare them," Cortaro said.

"How? I am only here to help and I am most pleasant to be around," Steuben said. He stretched out his jaw, distending it and revealing double rows of needle-sharp teeth.

Cortaro looked across the barren expanse toward the east. A haze of dust preceding the approaching storm would, according to the Dotok, last for hours and leave a fog of disturbed dust in its wake. The haze would conceal the approaching banshee swarm until they were within a few kilometers of the city. Cortaro liked knowing exactly how much time he had left. The longer he had between spotting the banshees and the first banshees to the wall, the better he'd feel.

The gunnery sergeant leaned over the outer wall and saw a Marine anchored against the rocks.

"Pavel, are you done yet?" Cortaro called out to the Marine.

"Few more charges on this section, Gunney. Give me another twenty minutes," Pavel yelled back.

Cortaro turned around and surveyed the

defenses. The roadways from the still-intact outer walls leading to the *Canticle of Reason* were almost full of welded crossbeams, thin wires ran between most of the obstacles, meant to disrupt advancing banshees. Work crews hung against the inner honeycomb walls, drilling into the massive bricks. Banks of gremlin mortar launchers were deployed at the intersections, their top covers removed.

"Steuben, explain to me again how blowing up the city is the best way to defend it?" Cortaro said.

"We're abandoning this city, not defending it. Every brick is a potential weapon against our enemy. The Dotok understand this," Steuben said. "There is little point in leaving anything viable to our enemy as we retreat."

"Marines don't retreat, Steuben. We just advance in a different direction," Cortaro said.

"That sounds like a rationalization to mitigate a tactical shortcoming."

Cortaro's face turned red as he queued up a number of insults he'd normally use on army soldiers who'd dare make similar remarks when his gauntlet computers beeped with a priority message.

"Hale's Mule is coming back, and he's got civilians with them? Odd. Let's go get him up to speed," Cortaro said.

****

Cortaro looked away from the landing Mule as its turbofans blew hot air and dust around him. The ramp lowered, and the civilians packed inside almost spilled out. Dotok soldiers ran up the ramp and tried to yell directions over the din of the engines.

"There's no way," Cortaro said to Steuben, "there's no way the lieutenant's in there."

Un'qu ran around a corner and bumped into Cortaro, not evening offering an apology as he went straight to the civilians. He took a worn photograph from his pocket and held it up to the civilians, all of whom shook their heads at the photo.

Orozco opened the hatch on the bottom turret and stood up. He waved to Cortaro, desperate for his attention.

"Some answers, at least," Cortaro said. He and Steuben tried to get past the civilians.

"Thank you!" An old female Dotok clasped Cortaro's hands and pressed them to her forehead. "When can you go back for my grandchildren? They're still with their mother."

"Soon as we can miss, excuse us." Cortaro pulled his hands away, unsure what he'd just promised.

"Gunney," Orozco said, "the lieutenant's trying to be a hero again. He's got a whole column of refugees and he's walking them to some old landing zone."

"Please tell me they're on the right side of the nuke," Cortaro said.

"Nope." Orozco looked at the timer on his gauntlet. "He'll be locked in that valley with all those banshees in another thirty seconds."

Cortaro rubbed the bridge of his nose. "I thought Hale had outgrown all the gung-ho butter-bar nonsense."

"Excuse me," Un'qu came up the ramp, holding the picture toward Orozco like it was a talisman. "You were at Usonvi, right? Did you see them? My wife and newborn son?"

Orozco looked carefully, then shook his head. "But there were a lot of people there, sir. I really didn't get much of a look at anyone."

Un'qu tucked the photo back into his uniform. He nodded slowly and turned away.

"Hey, you know the lieutenant, right?" Orozco asked. "If there's a way to get them out, he'll find it. We're Marines. We don't leave anyone behind if there's a chance they're still alive."

Un'qu glanced over his shoulder, then left.

"Pilot!" Cortaro yelled. "Turn and burn. You need to get back there ASAP."

Jorgen came around from the cockpit, his flight gloves off and the zipper of his suit half way down his chest.

"Gunney, no one's going anywhere in that soup," Jorgen said. He pointed behind Cortaro.

A wall of sand stretched across the horizon,

rolling toward them like a tidal wave.

Bells clanged throughout the city, warning of more than just an impending sand storm.

CHAPTER 12

The refugees from Usonvi took shelter in the shadow of a small hill. A dry riverbed, nothing but a wide swath of sand and silt, cut into the side of the hill. Millennia of erosion from when the riverbed carried water had worn into the side of the rock, cutting a path through and creating an overhang in the rock, like a cave with only one side.

The adults sat in tight circles, letting their children loose to play within the makeshift corrals. What little food and water they had, they shared with each other.

Hale, standing guard at one end of the overhang, checked the timer on his gauntlet. The nuclear demolition of Ghostwind Pass was two minutes away. He turned his attention back to the route they'd come from, eyes scanning for any sign of the tide of banshees headed in their direction.

"Sir," Torni said, trotting up to him, "the civilians know the nuke's coming. It's still the end of the world, but the quake we're about to feel isn't it."

"Good work, how're they doing?"

"Better. I told them to eat the food they were carrying for the highers. It should give them more strength to get the last couple miles," she said.

"Any trouble?"

"No, Nil'jo's decided to stop bitching and start brooding, which is fine by me."

A cold mass of air blew into their shelter. Children cried and went running for their parents. Dotok wrapped their robes around the children and sat them between their legs. The sky darkened as a roiling mass of snow and dust blew across the top of the canyon. A thick fog descended into the canyon, like a cloud was charging straight for them.

A whistle blew twice. "Storm!" Nil'jo shouted. He repeated the whistle and the warning once more before Standish yanked the whistle from the Chosen's mouth and proceeded to lecture him on noise discipline. The banshees could've heard that whistle.

The storm cloud hit the ground and enveloped them all like fog. Fine dust and particulate snow and ice struck Hale's armor with the sound of a rain shower against glass.

"Great...a mud storm," Standish said over the IR as his next words washed out in the interference.

Hale called out to Bailey, Yarrow and Standish; the three marines emerged from the blowing dust seconds later.

"Try to form a line at the edge of the overhang," Hale said. "I don't want anyone wandering off in this mess."

"Don't think that'll be a problem, look," Bailey said.

The Dotok were still in their circles,

hunkered against one another. Children poked at the robes covering them, but none tried to get free.

"I don't think this is their first rodeo," Standish said. A windblown pebble bounced off his helmet.

The ground quaked and Hale had to grab on to Torni to keep his balance. A clash of thunder announced the detonation of the nuclear device. A constant tremor kept up for almost a minute as the sound of a distant avalanche rumbled through their shelter.

"I think it worked," Standish said.

"We're all kinds of screwed if the birds don't come back for us," Yarrow said. "There'll be radiation from that nuke. Not much for us in our suits, but all of them are unprotected."

"And the civvies are down to almost nothing for food or water," Torni said. "Not as much of a concern. I figure the banshees will kill us all before we starve, or die of rad poisoning."

"We can treat radiation exposure on the *Breit*," Hale said. "This mission's a bit of a Hail

Mary. Thank you all for being with me."

"No place I'd rather be," Torni said. "This is something I can feel proud of—better than sitting back on Earth for the next fourteen years, waiting around for the Xaros to show up again."

"Sir," Standish raised a hand, "do you think we'll ever get to go someplace nice? Anthalas was this big swamp full of corpses and giant lizards trying to eat us. This place is about as pleasant as taking a shower with a sand blaster, plus monsters. Just once I want the Corps to send us to someplace pleasant…maybe with a bunch of Polynesian women that want to rub our feet and feed us grapes."

"Don't tell me you believe the legend," Bailey said with a shake of her head.

"What legend?" Yarrow asked.

"It's not a legend. The Island of Fiki-Fiki is a real place," Standish said. "My father heard about it from a cellmate whose uncle was best friends with someone who was there."

"I don't know what the hell you're talking

about," Yarrow said.

"Listen up, new guy. Not every Marine gets to hear about the island of Fiki-Fiki. When the Chinese blew that big EMP over the Pacific and knocked out every ship in the fleet, an American torpedo boat went adrift and ended up on an uncharted island in the South Pacific. The natives hadn't seen a Westerner since the Second World War and thought the crew of that torpedo boat were gods come to walk the Earth. Those sailors sat out the rest of the war, had like a dozen wives each and their own little island kingdom...until they were 'rescued.' Then they had a party with the five years of back pay."

"No way," Yarrow said, awe in his voice.

"It's a myth to get stupid Marines to re-enlist for float assignments," Torni said. "Don't believe it."

"We don't have to go to the island of Fiki-Fiki, sir," Standish said. "Maybe we drop on someplace that has a forecast of partly cloudy instead of mud storms and a ninety-five percent chance of genocide. I'd like to believe that there are some nice places in the galaxy, that not everything is horror and murder."

"Maybe once the Xaros are gone," Hale said, "we can use the Crucible to find someplace reasonably nice." Wind buffeted the Marines. Hale turned around and looked into the storm. "But not today."

****

Orozco tested his anchors' hold against the deck plates for the umpteenth time. His boots were locked tight, still. Same as they'd been for the past two hours. He brushed sand away from his Gustav and stared at the blank bulkhead in front of him.

Waiting. He hated waiting.

"So, I said to the guy, 'How do *you* know there's no teeth in there?'" Lance Corporal Rock said. Another Marine, Sergeant Holt, chuckled at the punchline. Each heavy-gunner Marine was anchored to the deck, their Gustavs' primed and ready for a fight that could start at any moment.

Each hated waiting a little more than the next.

A text message came across Orozco's gauntlet.

"All right, stow it," Orozco said. "Sentries report movement out beyond the wall."

"They going to tell us when this fight starts?" Rock asked.

"Just wait to hear some shooting. That's a pretty good clue," Holt said.

"What part of 'stow it' wasn't in English?" Orozco snapped. "Remember the plan. We provide covering fire for the front-lines as they fall back. Soon as the first hostile gets to the road in front of us, we un-ass this position and fall back to the next one. Got it?"

"Sure, Sarge. Who came up with this plan? Gunney, or that big ugly you've been palling around with?" Holt asked.

"Which one do you want to look in the eye and say, 'Your plan sucks'?"

"I didn't say it sucked," Holt said sheepishly. "Just curious is all."

"Devastators, this is Gunney. You ready?" Cortaro asked over the IR.

"Hey, IR's back up," Rock said.

"Don't worry. It'll go down soon as we really need it," Holt said with a chuckle.

"Devastators ready," Orozco said.

"Who picked 'devastators'? I like 'havocs' better," Rock said.

"I swear, if I wasn't bolted to this deck, I'd come over there and jam my fist right down your throat," Orozco said. He powered up his Gustav, twin electric whines joined his as the other Marines followed suit.

The snap of gauss rifle fire tapped against the bulkhead like driven rain.

"Case of beer says I get more kills," Holt said.

"Deal," Rock said.

"Deal," Orozco said. His mind wandered to the can of sardines he'd carried around for months. But he'd finally eaten them. He could die with one less regret.

Tiny explosive bolts rippled across the bulkhead. The heavy metal plating groaned and fell away. The three heavy gunners, drawn from the surviving Marine squads, now had a commanding over watch of the final battle for New Abhaile city. Their firing position was in the upper deck of a landed starship, with direct line of sight to the eastern walls.

Banshees scaled the outer wall like a horde of locusts coming for the harvest. Banshees struggled through the electrified wires strung between the welded cross-bars, creating a bottleneck behind them. The Devastators had a massed infantry target, every machine gunner's dream since the Western Front stalled out in France almost two hundred years before.

"Light 'em up!" Orozco let loose a peal of heavy cannon blasts that tore through the packed banshees like a scythe through wheat. Combined with Rock and Holt's fire, they made short work of the first banshee push over the wall.

"Cover your sectors of fire," Orozco

ordered. The other gunners shifted their attention to the flanks, hitting banshees that came over the walls in ones and twos. His Gustav barked with short bursts, sending a small swarm of high-velocity slugs at each target. Orozco blew a leg off a banshee as it crested the wall and felt a smile cross his face as it tumbled back.

He scanned to his left, then right. No targets.

"Clear," Holt said.

"Same," Rock added.

"Gunney, it's gone quiet on the wall. Doesn't make me feel better, for some reason," Orozco transmitted.

A banshee's howl wilted over the battlements.

"Maybe they're retreating," Holt said.

Howls rose from the dusty fog beyond the walls. Shrieks combined to a fever pitch, so loud that the sonic dampeners in Orozco's helmet kicked on to tamp down the aural assault.

"Gunney, I think we're about to have a problem out here," Orozco said. The screams fell away and the sound of thousands of tree branches breaking filled the air.

Banshees swarmed over the wall, so numerous and densely packed that they looked like a black tide.

The gunners opened up, but they had about as much chance of stemming the swarm as a torch had of beating back a blizzard. Banshees threw themselves into the obstacles, using their bodies to breach the defenses for those behind them.

"Gunney! Phase two! Phase two!" Orozco slapped a new belt of ammunition into his Gustav and kept firing.

Unseen explosions sent quakes through their firing position. Pulverized rock and dust blew up the front and back of the outer wall. The tide of banshees relented. The snap of gauss rifles from the defenders mixed with the banshee howls.

"Wasn't the wall supposed to do something?" Holt asked as he reloaded.

The outer wall dropped several feet as damaged stones crumpled beneath the weight of the wall above it. The wall groaned and tipped away from the city, like a great tree finally felled by an axe's bite.

Orozco wasn't sure how many banshees died in the fall or beneath the tons of rocks. He concentrated on whittling down the hundreds that made it to the raised roadways leading to the next line of defenses.

Banshees charged over the fallen wall…and into the muddy hot springs between the honeycombed sections of the city. The banshee advance faltered as they sank up to their knees in the muck. Many, too many, made it to the side of the connecting roadways and clambered up to the road.

Orozco leaned forward and raised his weapon to fire over the edge of the deck at the enemy warriors running into defilade. They'd made it to the next line of defenses.

A steady thump-thump-thump of the Gremlin launchers sounded from behind Orozco.

"That's our cue." Orozco took his hand off

his weapon's grip and slapped it against his control gauntlet. He twisted fore and back, and the spikes anchoring him to the deck snapped back against his boots.

A beam of light the color of fresh blood stabbed into the firing position. Orozco's reflexes drove him to the floor.

Orozco watched as Rock dropped his weapon and slumped to the side. Orozco reached up and grabbed the other gunner by the arm, Rock's armor plates collapsed against each other beneath his grip. Rock flopped back, red smoke poured from a gash in his chest plate out of his empty armor.

Another bolt of searing light cut into the firing position.

Holt grabbed Orozco by his shoulder armor and hauled him deeper into the ship. Banshees pounded at the sealed door of the ship's cargo bay.

"I don't think we can take the stairs," Holt said. The crump of exploding mortars echoed across the battlefield, sending a constant tremor through the deck as the explosions came in faster and faster.

The Gremlins pounded the banshees slowed by the mud flats and those still struggling over the ruined walls, but the banshees pounding against the doors didn't seem to notice.

"Then we go the hard way." Orozco got to his feet and ran to the opposite side of the cargo bay from their former firing positions. He grabbed a lever bolted to the wall and pulled it down. A section of the hull fell away. The remnants of the passing storm mixed with smoke and dust from the fallen walls into a haze that drowned out the roadways leading back to the *Canticle of Reason*. Bright flashes from gauss rifles lit up the haze.

"This is a bad idea," Holt said. "I can't even see where we're supposed to land."

"You want to wait here until you think of something better? Aim for a spot just behind the line of fire." Orozco attached his Gustav to his armor and backed away from the edge. He deactivated the safety overrides on his grav-linings and took a deep breath.

"*Gott mit uns!*" Orozco ran and leaped into

the air. He swung his feet forward and hoped that God heard his prayer. The gravity/anti-gravity linings in his boots were meant for zero and micro-g environments. Their fixed battery life was greatly curtailed anywhere with Earth-normal gravity or stronger. Overriding the safeties was a sure way to burn out the linings and get in a whole mess of trouble with the chain of command for destroying military equipment.

Orozco fired the anti-grav linings just enough to direct his slowed fall toward a mass of silver flashes in the haze. Controlled descents to asteroids and void ships was something he'd trained for as part of being a strike Marine, doing the same in Takeni's gravity was much faster than he'd anticipated.

A hunk of brick flew past his head, the banshees making a difficult task nigh impossible with their added interference.

Orozco used the linings again, arcing him higher in the air. The vibrations in his boots stopped suddenly, and the Marine found himself in free fall.

He managed a scream that was half-warning, half-fear, and squeezed his feet and knees together. He fell through the haze and slammed feetfirst into the cobblestones. The rest of his body hit with all the grace of a thrown sack of potatoes. He rolled several times before bumping into the sidewalls.

Orozco's ears rang and his lower back was killing him. He pulled himself to his feet, coughing. A pair of Dotok soldiers stared at him, jaws slack.

"What?" Orozco asked them.

A streak of light above the haze pointed to Holt's descent. Dark lumps of rock pelted Holt, then the light from his anti-grav linings warbled as a hit threw him off balance. Orozco watched as Holt came into view and dipped lower. He wouldn't make it. Orozco ran for the other side of the walkway. He unslung his Gustav and thrust the barrel out to Holt.

Holt's fingertips clawed at the barrel. One hand managed a grip, then the other. Then Holt's anti-grav linings died. Orozco found himself with the full armored weight of a Marine attached to the end of his Gustav. Holt slammed against the side of the wall and Orozco bent over the side wall, his suit struggling to hold onto Holt and keep himself from going over the edge, a long fall into burning mud and plenty of banshees waiting for him if his strength failed.

Orozco pulled his arms back and tried to stand. He was one of the few Marines that could lift his Gustav without the aid of his suit—he would be damned if he'd let Holt's weight beat him. He grunted and felt Holt inch up the side. Hands grabbed him by the belt and around the shoulders, pulling him backwards.

Orozco got a step back, then dragged Holt over the side. The two Marines fell to the ground. Orozco looked up and saw a pair of Dotok soldiers, the ones who'd helped him, giving him a thumbs up.

"Magic fingers…" Orozco muttered. He lifted his Gustav in front of his face. The end of the barrel was mangled by Holt's desperate grip.

Orozco got up and gave the prone Holt a gentle kick to the stomach.

"Look what you did to my weapon!" Orozco attached it to his back and un-holstered his gauss pistol. He shook his head in disgust.

"I regret nothing," Holt said.

"Get up." Orozco pointed his pistol at a mud-covered banshee that found its way to the top of the wall. He drilled a bullet into its eye slit and it went slack. The dead banshee hung from where its talons had gripped into the wall. Orozco pried the hand loose and sent the banshee back into the murk below.

"This fight ain't over yet."

The ground shook, and a suit of armor stomped through the haze toward the front lines.

****

Cortaro reached his stick into the mockup of the city and knocked over another grounded starship. The last transmission from the ship was a panicked alert about banshees climbing up the ship's cradle. That was five minutes ago, no response since. The inner lines still held, but the banshee advance through the city was going much faster than he and Steuben had anticipated.

Pa'lon sat against a wall, his arms folded into his robes.

Cortaro opened a channel to the *Canticle's* engineering deck. "MacDougall, what's the status on the anti-grav plates?"

"Everything's wired together with tape and spit. We're running the final tests now," MacDougall said.

"How long?"

"Thirty minutes to make sure it'll work, longer if something's off."

Cortaro looked up at Steuben, who was leaning over the mockup, his clawed hands gripping the sides.

"We don't have *twenty* minutes," Steuben said.

"MacDougall, can we launch now?"

"I can't guarantee she'll hold together. But

yeah, we can. It's a chance between amazing success and total failure. Fifty-fifty if you ask me."

Cortaro rapped his knuckles against the mock up to get Pa'lon's attention.

"If you're going to leave, Ancient. Now's the time," Cortaro said.

"I'll go to my gate and return to Bastion," Pa'lon said. "I'll relay the situation to Ambassador Ibarra. *Gott mit uns*, my friends." He struggled to his feet and left the command center.

"MacDougall, get ready. We're almost done with this planet," Cortaro said, looking at the mockup. Banshees were reported on two roadways leading to a nexus that was a straight shot to the *Canticle.*

"We can't pull them all back," Steuben said. "We can get the two nearest defense lines in the ship, the rest will have to hold in place."

"You mean die in place," Cortaro said.

"We lose a part, or we lose the whole," Steuben said. He looked up at Cortaro, and the Marine knew there was no room for negotiation.

Cortaro opened a city-wide channel and wished Hale was there instead of him to make this decision. "All units, defense lines alpha and beta are ordered back to the *Canticle*. We are wheels up in ten minutes. I repeat, ten minutes. Get back to the ship." He repeated the order, leaving almost a thousand good Marines and Dotok to buy time with their lives.

"Belay that order," came over the channel. *"This is Chief Cruz of the Smoking Snakes. Souza and I will hold the junction. Order everyone back. Everyone."*

"They could do it," Steuben said. He moved two miniature suits of armor to the junction on the mock up.

"All units," Cortaro said, "stampede. I repeat, stampede."

****

Orozco had an arm wrapped under Holt's back, helping the other Marine balance as he tried to limp back to the ship. Blood stained Holt's right leg from the thigh down, victim of a banshee's talon. Their defensive position had been almost overrun; only one of the Smoking Snakes managed to keep the banshees off their heels.

Orozco looked up and saw three golden star clusters falling from the sky, military pyrotechnics used to send signals when communications were out or degraded. Three golden stars meant one thing; retreat with all possible speed to the *Canticle of Reason.*

"That's the 'run away,' isn't it?" Holt asked through grit teeth.

He pried a gauss rifle from the hands of a fallen Dotok and looked back over his shoulder. Amber rays of Xaros disintegration beams lit up the haze where they'd left the armor.

"It is," Orozco said.

"We won't make it," Holt said, "not with me slowing you down. Get out of here."

"Fuck you, Holt. I'm not that pissed about what you did to my Gustav. Limp faster," Orozco said.

A mechanical whine came from the haze. A Smoking Snake, his legs in their tracked travel form, raced toward them. The armor swept them up, holding both Marines beneath one giant arm like they were a football.

"Goddamn slow-ass Marines," Cruz said over his speakers. "Always need the Army to bail them out of trouble." Cruz rolled over barricades and wove around fleeing Dotok soldiers. Cruz got them to one of the *Canticle*'s open bays as Dotok raced into the ship.

Cruz set the Marines down. His massive hand gripped Orozco by the shoulder.

"You tell the Iron Hearts," Cruz said, "you tell them this is what we wanted."

"What're you talking about?" Orozco asked. Cruz spun around and rolled back to the front-lines. "Where are you going?" he yelled after him.

"Oro...it's bleeding again," Holt said. He held up blood covered-hands and faltered.

Orozco caught him before he could fall.

****

Cruz rolled up to Souza at the nexus. A severed banshee claw stuck out from his back, fluid from his punctured tank leaked out like blood. Shrieks filled the distance.

"How bad are you?" Cruz asked, rising onto his feet.

"Bad," Souza said. Cruz stepped in front of him and saw Souza's chest piece dented and scratched. "But I can hold on for a bit longer." His words were laced with pain.

"I think Silva would be proud," Cruz said.

"He would. He was a good soldier. I'm glad to die on the same rock as him."

"*Cobras Fumantes,*" Cruz said, speaking the Brazilian words for their name.

The Smoking Snakes heard the chittering of banshees coming for them. They raised their arm cannons and opened fire as the first enemy came through the haze. A sane foe might have pulled back from the withering fire, but the banshees pressed forward, losing hundreds as the gauss cannons blew them into bloody ribbons. Banshees threw their dead over the walls to clear the way for those behind them.

Cruz ran out of ammo first. Twin slithering bands of smoke rose from the red-hot barrels.

Souza held them back for another thirty seconds before he ran dry.

The soldiers roared, the battle cry from their speakers drowning out the banshees shrieks, and charged.

Cruz smashed his fists into the banshees, bashing their bodies into pulp with each swing. Three banshees wrapped their talons around his right arm, dragging it down. He stabbed fingers into one, flinging it over the side of the wall. He slammed his right arm to the ground and stomped the life out of the pair of foes.

Souza went down under a press of bodies. Cruz fought toward his comrade, knocking banshees aside. A weight hit his back and drove him to his knees. Pain stabbed through his legs as talons ripped the treads out of his armor.

A rumble shook the air, and the *Canticle of*

Reason rose from its centuries-old cradle. Cruz saw it float into the clouds, and knew he'd won this battle.

He made it to Souza and and beat aside a banshee peeling aside the fallen soldier's chest plate. Banshees piled on top of Cruz. His helm was ripped away and the feeds to his tank went dark. He swung his arms blindly, feeling every impact against his armor until a talon pierced his tank and he fell onto Souza.

CHAPTER 13

Ready alert for pilots was an exercise in constant tension. The fighters maintained a full combat load and stayed on a battery feed, ready to launch in thirty seconds, which meant the pilot stayed in the cockpit the entire time, bored but hypervigilant for the go signal. The Eagles farther back in the queue had to launch within two to five minutes of the ready-alert craft, which gave the pilots time to afford such luxuries as bathroom breaks and eating at the base of their fighters.

Durand walked the line of fighters, a mix of human Eagles and Dotok fighters, chatting with pilots and answering last-minute questions about their mission. She did it to calm her nerves as well as theirs.

"Gall," Bar'en asked, "this mission is … unorthodox. Do human military planners look at a situation, ask what is the worst plausible idea, then try to make that happen?"

"That's just how Captain Valdar works," Durand said. "I once rode into battle strapped to a luxury liner that was going to be used as a battering ram. Watched a trillion dollars in hardware squished against a Xaros weapons platform to buy our fleet just a little more time. This isn't so bad."

Bar'en rapped his fingertips against his helmet and shook his head.

"All hear this! All hear this!" the ship's intercom sounded. Pilots snapped on helmets and climbed into their fighters. They knew what was coming.

"Battle stations! All hands to battle stations and prepare for acceleration."

Durand donned her helmet and felt it pull airtight against her flight suit. She shimmied up the ladder to her Eagle and jumped into the seat. Hers was the first Eagle to launch, as was her right and responsibility as the squadron commander.

A single Mule sat on the flight deck. The passengers were already in place, but there was no crew. Nothing but the android Karigole and the two armor soldiers inside could survive the maneuver planned for its future.

"All right, 103rd," Durand said to her squadron, "we clear a path and then we get them home. Good hunting."

A rumble grew through the ship, and Durand felt g-forces grow to match the ship's acceleration.

"Lafayette, you all OK over there?" Durand sent to the Mule.

"Everything is within specified parameters," the Karigole answered. "Are you aware of a new variable?"

"No…just checking," she said.

"I suspect you are attempting conversation to compensate for anxiety," Lafayette said.

"You should've been a shrink, not an

engineer," she said.

"I don't understand your worry. I'm the one riding a bomb at twenty times the force of gravity into the heart of an incomplete Crucible potentially full of Xaros. You just have to shoot things," Lafayette said.

"Are you attempting conversation to compensate for anxiety?" Durand asked.

"Perhaps."

The gravity pressing Durand against her cockpit increased, and she lost all interest in talking.

****

Lafayette, at the controls of the Mule, watched as a timer ran down to zero.

"Prepare for launch," he said.

Rocket assist motors on the Mule blossomed, hurling it into space. Acceleration almost twenty times the force of gravity shook the ship like it was a failing fault line. The tolerances of human air and spacecraft had outstripped their bodies' capabilities over a century ago. The weakest part of any flight system forever remained the squishy human bodies that couldn't handle extreme maneuvers and that demanded air, stable temperatures and sleep.

A human sitting in the copilot's seat would have died minutes ago. Lafayette had been forced to rebuild himself after being struck by a Xaros disintegration beam many years ago. He'd eliminated every limitation he could. The flesh was weak, as he'd learned the hard way.

"Elias, Kallen, doing well?" he asked.

"Shut up and drive," Elias grunted.

Lafayette's fake lips pulled into a smile. Maybe he was a bit tougher than the armor in one regard.

The rocket assist boosters burnt out and Lafayette jettisoned them. The acceleration and its corresponding g-forces faded away, but the speed remained.

The proto-Crucible was dead ahead with four enormous generation ships arrayed around its outer edge. His cyborg eyes focused in on the

Crucible's hull as drones emerged from around the surface and sped toward him. More came from around the generation ships, but the dark lines of the Xaros corrupting their hulls remained.

"*Breitenfeld*, total drones in the upper nineties. More than we'd anticipated," Lafayette said.

"*Then you'd better make it quick in there,*" Valdar said.

"Roger, *Breitenfeld*, breaking maneuver on your signal." Lafayette turned on the rear-facing cameras and put his hand on the maneuver thrusters.

"*Firing the last of our Q-shells,*" Valdar said.

Lafayette waited until four silver streaks overtook his Mule and watched as they blossomed into electrical storms in the midst of the oncoming drones, knocking them offline. He hit the maneuver thrusters and the ship flipped over, its tail now pointed at the Crucible. Lafayette made slight adjustments until the Mule was on course for the control module, a rounded dome against the exposed rock of the asteroid the Crucible was cannibalizing, and readied the drop ship's thrusters.

Disabled drones tumbled through space. Utterly helpless, and harmless, for several more minutes. The small Q-shells fired by Marine gauss rifles or the Eagle's rail guns might knock a drone out for several seconds. The power within the much larger Q-shells of the *Breitenfeld*'s main guns was enough to destroy some drones and knock most offline for up to ten minutes, in theory. Ten minutes was almost enough time for him to complete his mission.

Lafayette fired the Mule's thrusters, which robbed the ship of its forward momentum, slowing it down. He kept his ship on course to the control module as his relative speed fell to almost nothing. He was rather perplexed that his human allies couldn't do the equations to calculate his exact landing velocity and location. It was only rocket science.

He nudged the Mule parallel to the control node, cut the speed, and fired the docking harpoons.

Spikes dug into the surface of the control node, and graphene ropes pulled taut, setting the Mule against the surface with a jarring crunch.

"Almost perfect," Lafayette said. He unstrapped himself from the seat and floated into the cargo bay, the ramp lowering to reveal the smooth domed roof of the control node.

The straps securing Elias and Kallen to the Mule popped off. Lafayette grabbed a bulkhead and pushed them both out of the Mule with his legs. The armor unfolded to their humanoid configuration. Elias pushed jet packs to them and opened an ammunition case bolted to the floor.

He took out a beat-up pouch containing his tools, and a satchel holding several pounds of quadrium and the bomb components.

"This the right spot?" Elias asked. The two soldiers stood on the surface of the control node, left hands replaced by cutting lasers.

"I was off by almost ten feet, but if you make us an entrance there, it will get us to the bridge," Lafayette said. "The Xaros are consistent in their construction projects."

The soldiers set their lasers against the dome and sliced through the basalt material. They had a hatch cut out in seconds. Elias tossed the hull piece behind him and pulled himself inside.

"There's gravity and atmo," he reported.

The edges of the hatch glittered with light as it began repairing itself.

"Hurry up," Kallen said.

Lafayette pushed off from the Mule and floated to Kallen. She caught him and pushed the cyborg into the opening.

She grabbed the edge of the hatch and followed. Gravity pulled her down. Her feet had almost hit the ground when she came to an abrupt halt. Her hand was stuck inside the edge of the hatch. It had regrown around her fingers, incorporating her into the hull. Kallen tugged at her hand, but it remained fast.

She swore, bent at the waist to bring her feet against the roof and pushed against it with all the strength her actuators could muster. Her hand burst free of the hull and she fell against the deck.

"You OK?" Elias asked.

Kallen got to her feet and looked at her hand. Sparks shot through where three fingers had once been.

"Write that down for next time," she said.

They were in a command center, identical to the Crucible near Earth. Stairs meant for something much taller than the average human ran from a central plinth toward the outside wall. Rings of control stations emanated out from the same plinth.

"Get to it, professor," Elias said.

"Yes, against the bulkhead will do nicely." Lafayette ran up the too-tall steps and set the satchel against the wall. It would take him two minutes to reassemble the bomb, another three for it to be fully operational.

"What's that thing going to do?" Kallen asked.

"This 'thing' will form a singularity for several nanoseconds, causing severe damage to this structure and redirecting its momentum back along its intersection path," Lafayette said.

"You mean it'll create a black hole and turn this whole thing around?" she asked.

"Yes."

"Then just say that!"

"Hush, child." Lafayette attached a graviton emitter to a bundle of silvery quadrium shells. "The master must work."

A low thrum filled the chamber.

"Master better work a hell of a lot faster," Kallen said. She cycled rounds into her forearm blaster and fired up the cutting laser.

****

Hale's boots slipped against a wet rock and kicked a stone loose. It bounced down the path and struck an old Dotok woman on the thigh. She looked at Hale and made a hand gesture that he was sure wasn't meant to be kind.

The original settlers had cut a rudimentary path up the mountain leading to the mesa Hale planned to use as their evacuation point. What the

Dotok had intended to be a radio relay site could prove to be the salvation for hundreds. The path ran through a narrow valley between peaks, blocking the view from the rest of the canyon.

They were a mile from the mesa, almost there.

"Sir," Bailey said through the IR, *"I've got movement."* The sniper was at the rear of the column where the old path began at the foot of the mountains.

"On my way," he said to her. "Standish, keep them moving. Yarrow, meet me at the base of the mountain. Act causal."

Hale made his way through the throng of refugees, his pace purposeful but not an all-out run. The Dotok's nerves were on the edge of a knife since the storm; any indication of a serious problem might send them into a panic.

A few Dotok men had pulled back from the edge of the group, watching as Bailey looked through the scope of her sniper rifle.

"Torni, get them moving," Hale said. "Then

keep them moving."

The sergeant barked commands and pointed up the mountain with a knife hand gesture. The Dotok shied away and caught up to the rest of the group.

"What've you got?" Hale asked Bailey, her helmet off and attached to her belt. She pressed her eye against the scope of her rail rifle and her face hardened.

"Straggler," she said. "Woman carrying a baby. Running hard."

"Must have made it out of the city then got lost from the group before we found them," Yarrow said.

"That's not all," Bailey said. A video feed from her optics popped on Hale's visor. The woman was there, clutching an infant to her breast, running barefoot across open ground. The feed panned down the canyon and showed a single banshee chasing after the woman.

"She's not going to make it," Bailey whispered. "Let me take the shot."

Hale looked at the canyon around them. The rail rifle was not a subtle weapon. The sound of the recoil would travel for miles up and down the canyon, and there was no way that was the only banshee out there.

"Sir, we shoot and the banshees will be all over us," Yarrow said. "We're almost there."

"Let me take it," Bailey said. A tear rolled down her cheek. "That's my little girl, my Abbie, out there. Please let me take it."

"Do it," Hale said. It was the wrong tactical solution. He knew in his head he was making a mistake. This was a decision from his heart.

The bullet left the barrel with a sonic boom, kicking up a plume of dust and sending a crack through the canyon. The round vaporized the banshee from the waist up and shattered a boulder behind it.

"Yarrow, with me." Hale sprinted out of the mountain pass, leaping over rocks and using his augmented armor to propel him to speeds no un-suited human could ever achieve.

The mother froze as she saw the two alien Marines coming for her, weapons in hand. She looked back at the dead banshee, then closed her eyes and squeezed her squalling baby to her chest.

"Nil'jo and the rest of your village are with us," Hale said.

The name got the woman to open her eyes.

"We're humans, here to help. We'll explain the rest later," Yarrow said. "Come with us." The medic pointed to the pathway leading up into the mountains.

A banshee howl echoed through the canyon. More joined, creating a hellish chorus. A half dozen rounded a bend, tearing up the dead riverbed with their feet and claws as they ran.

"Take them," Hale said. He dropped to a knee and aimed at the nearest banshee.

Yarrow scooped the Dotok up in his arms and ran off.

Hale fired a single shot, hitting a banshee in the shoulder and sending it to the ground. His next shot hit a banshee square in the chest, killing its forward momentum like it had run into a wall.

His next shot came with the crash of Bailey's rail rifle. The hypervelocity round sizzled overhead and struck the canyon wall, cracking the rock and sending slabs of dark stone crashing down on more banshees as they emerged from around the bend.

"I don't need some stinking nuke," Bailey said through the IR. *"Get your ass back here. I'll cover you,"* she said.

Hale hit a charging banshee in the legs. He panned his rifle to the next banshee, but a round hit it in the forehead before he could engage.

"I said I'd cover you! Move!" Bailey shouted.

Hale got up and raced back to the pass. Another of Bailey's precision shots snapped past his helmet.

"You're clear, sir, but keep up the pace," Bailey said. *"Lots more on the way."*

"Bailey, rig your batteries for—"

"Already on it!" Her sniper rifle ran on

batteries the size of a lunch box. Sabotaging the batteries would produce an explosion strong enough to take out a three-story building.

"Sir," Torni said. *"We've got positive contact with the birds. They're almost here, but they didn't come with any air support. No Eagles."*

"Torni, you get those civilians loaded up and out of here. Don't wait for me, you understand?" Hale put iron in his last words; this was no time for a discussion.

"Roger, sir. Just hurry up so we don't have to wait." Torni said.

Hale made it to the trail. Bailey took a green cylinder from her belt, attached it to her battery and covered it with dirt and rocks. Yarrow stood over her, taking potshots at the advancing banshees, their howls growing louder and more numerous.

"Ain't pretty, ain't much of a charge, but it'll slow them down," she said. Hale looked back and saw dozens of banshees clambering over the pile of rocks Bailey sent down.

"Did you set a safety timer?" Hale asked.

"No, figured I'd need to blow this thing pretty damned quick when the time came," Bailey said. She slung the pack with her disassembled rail rifle over her shoulder and fired her carbine.

"Give me the detonator," Hale said and took it from Bailey. "Up the mountain, let's go."

Hale charged up the steep slope, just behind Bailey and Yarrow. He saw the last of the Dotok vanish over the top of the path and onto the mesa.

He whirled around and fired from the hip at the tide of banshees coming for them, most going for the straight and easy path right to the three Marines. He set his thumb against the detonator trigger.

"Hold on to something." Hale pressed the detonator…and nothing happened. Tens of banshees poured up the slope. Hale slammed the detonator against his armor and hit the switch again.

The battery exploded with a crack, blowing a cloud of dust and pulverized banshees into the air. A shard of rock moving faster than he could see struck the pathway and skipped into the air. It cut past Hale and struck armor.

Bailey staggered back, her hand pressed against her side. She fell to the ground with a groan.

"Bailey!" Yarrow pulled her hand back. A flint of stone impaled her armor and blood pulsed out of the wound with each heartbeat. Her breathing was short and shallow. "I think it nicked her lung. I've got to treat her," Yarrow said.

"Not here!" Hale shot down a banshee staggering up the pathway. He didn't see any more of the enemy, but he could hear them in the cloud of dust at the base of the mountain.

Yarrow grabbed Bailey by the carry handle on her armor and dragged her up the mountain, a trail of dark blood staining the ground in her wake.

"Torni, I've got injured," Hale said. "Status on evac?"

"One Destrier transport away, second loading up. Two more Mules waiting to land," Torni said. *"Who's hit and how bad?"*

"Bailey took a—" Black talons arced over the side of the pass and struck Hale in the face. Pain lanced through his neck and shoulders as he slammed into the other side of the pass. He heard shouts and the sound of gauss fire.

A dead banshee lay over the jagged rocks; another flung the corpse away from the wall and came for them. Hale tried to raise his rifle, but his left arm refused to move. He pulled out his pistol and shot the banshee at point-blank range, puncturing the armor on its throat and sending it rearing back. It opened its jaws to scream and Hale sent a bullet through the roof of its mouth and into the brain case.

The banshee fell back. Hale watched it fall and saw more banshees crawling up the side of the mountain.

He pulled a grenade from his belt and hooked the pin against a finger on his useless hand. He got the pin loose and tossed the grenade over the side. Hale looked at his shoulder; a gash rent through his armor, exposing muscle and bone on his shoulder.

The shock of the grenade shaking the

mountain sent him to his knees. He pulled out another grenade…and the world started to fade away.

"Sir, you're hurt!" Yarrow shouted at him from inches away, but his voice was distant, like a half-heard whisper. Hale got the pin pulled on his second grenade, then tossed it over the side.

"Get…her out of here," Hale said.

The grenade Hale had tossed came back over the wall. It arced through the air and glinted in the sunlight before it exploded.

****

"Hale? Sir?" No one had answered Torni since the second grenade went off.

"Standish, get in the bottom turret," she said. "I think we're going to need you in there."

"On it." Standish, standing at the top of the final Mule's ramp, disappeared into the ship. Jorgen took his place and helped the last of the refugees into his ship.

He called to Torni, but she ignored him as

she ran for the pathway leading down the mountain where she found Yarrow, trying to drag Hale and Bailey the last few yards up the path. Yarrow, the armor of his helmet and upper body dented and ripped, had blood running from beneath a shoulder plate. He fell to the ground, never letting go of Hale and Bailey.

"No…" Torni ran to Yarrow and helped him up. She took up his burden and got them over the top of the path.

"Grenade, got us good," Yarrow said. "Hale's bad. Bailey's worse."

"Shut up and move," Torni said through gritted teeth. She dragged the injured Marines to the Mule and got them into the cargo hold. Dotok jumped out of the way as she pulled down the stretchers built into the walls. She grabbed the nearest Dotok adult, screamed at him to get the Marines strapped into the stretchers then charged back out of the Mule.

Yarrow still hadn't made it. He was down to a knee, firing poorly aimed shots as a banshee crawled up the pathway. Torni grabbed Yarrow's rifle and put a round between the banshee's temples. She tossed Yarrow over her shoulder and got him back to the Mule.

"How bad are you?" she asked him.

"It hurts, but it could be worse," he said.

"Do what you can for the others," she said. Yarrow nodded. She slapped him on the helmet. "Move!"

There were another half-dozen Dotok at the base of the ramp, reaching to Torni.

"What're we waiting for?" she demanded from Jorgen. "We've got room."

"I don't have the air!" Jorgen shouted. "New Abhaile is on fire. We're going to the *Breit*, no atmo. I take on any more civvies and they all suffocate."

Torni looked back at the Dotok and saw the woman and child Hale had risked so much to save. She grabbed the two of them and pushed them up the ramp. Torni reached under her armor and detached her O2 tanks. She took off her helmet and shoved them into Jorgen's hands.

"With my re-breather, that's four hours of air. Get in the cockpit," she said to the pilot.

"What about you?"

"I'm staying." She pointed to the Dotok. "There are five more women and children out there. Who will stay with me so they can live?"

Two Dotok men and Nil'jo came to Torni; one man held a child on his hip. He passed the child to its mother, who pleaded with her husband not to volunteer.

"The little ones don't breath as much," a man said. He ran down the ramp and pulled the rest of the women and children up the ramp.

Torni jumped off the ramp, and her volunteers came with her. The ramp rose out of the dirt and closed as the Mule took off, blowing up a cloud of brown dirt.

Torni closed her eyes and listened to the Mule fade away. She took her rifle off her shoulder and looked at the five Dotok men who'd stayed behind. A banshee's wail echoed up the mountain.

"Sarge, is that you down there?" Standish asked, the IR already breaking up from range.

"Standish, you're a good Marine. Take care of everyone for me," she said. Standish's response was lost in static.

Nil'jo picked up a rock. "I was honored to serve as your Chosen."

"Our families will be less without us," said the father who gave up his spot, "but they will live, and become greater." He lifted up a rock with both hands.

The sound of banshees grew louder.

****

Torni stabbed her pistol into the back of a banshee and fired a round. The banshee reared back and swung an elbow at her. She ducked under the blow and jammed the pistol into its face. The gun clicked empty.

It knocked her pistol away, nearly breaking her fingers with the blow. Torni stumbled back and found her gauss rifle in the dirt. She swung it up like a club and cracked the butt across the banshee's head. The blow staggered the monster and shattered the stock. She pulled the weapon back to her hip and jammed the jagged edges into the banshee's throat.

Gray blood splattered across her hands. The banshee lashed out and scored a glancing blow across the top of her head. Torni backpedaled, her world spinning from the concussion. She fell to the ground, the taste of blood and dirt in her mouth.

She rolled onto all fours and spat. She'd taken too many hits for her adrenaline to tamp down the pain of broken bones and a dozen cuts up and down her body from the fight she never had a chance of winning. Her bayonet snapped from the forearm housing and she got up to face the banshees.

Tens of banshees surrounded her, standing over the ruined bodies of the Dotok who'd stayed behind. The monsters stared at her…and did nothing else.

"What is this?" Torni kept her guard up.

"What're you waiting for? Huh?"

No response.

"What're you waiting for!"

A banshee in front rank twitched. Its arms and shoulders rose into the air like a scarecrow's. The armor on its arms peeled away from the body and floated in the air. More armor ripped away from the banshees, all of it coalescing toward a single point over their heads. The armor swirled inside a vortex; wind rose from it and pressed Torni back. A point of light emerged from the armor, growing so bright Torni had to look away.

Then…it all went silent.

Torni looked up. Plates of red armor formed a humanoid shape in the air, encasing a being of pure light. It looked down on Torni, tendrils of light floating out of the eye slits on a flat mask.

"You…" the word came from the banshees, all of them speaking in unison, "you are known. Your trace was on Anthalas. Now you are here." The General descended toward the ground, its feet never touching the surface.

"You must be in charge," Torni said.

"How did your species survive my purge?" the chorus of voices asked. "What did you take from Anthalas?"

Torni felt fear rise in her chest. The General reached toward her, phantom fingers swinging toward her like tentacles of a leviathan.

"Don't know?" Torni backed away. Her foot hit the edge of the mesa, and she looked back and saw rocks and dirt falling to oblivion. "Let me tell you something about humanity. *Gott. Mit. Uns.*" She flung herself back and closed her eyes.

A force grabbed her body like an enormous hand had just wrapped around her, pinning her arms and legs against herself.

"You think petty gestures will deny me?" the voices said.

Torni floated toward the General, its eyes burning.

"All corruption will be cleansed. I will burn your species' existence out of memory. Your fate will be no different."

Torni spat on the General's faceplate.

"You will respond to pain." The General lifted a hand, and Torni felt fire dancing across the bottom of her feet.

She clenched her jaw and fought against the scream begging to be let out. The pain subsided as quickly as it came. The General looked to the sky, then snapped its head back to Torni.

A growl rose from the banshees.

"You are not worthy of this honor," they said. The General wrapped tendrils of light around Torni's head. Images from her entire life raced through her mind with the fury of a tempest.

Her head lolled from side to side. When she could look up, she saw swirling motes of light orbiting around the General's hand. The light within the General's armor launched into space, leaving an afterglow through its ascent.

The armor collapsed and fell to the ground. The force holding Torni relented and she sprawled in the dirt.

A banshee marched toward her, talons

gleaming in the sun. She lashed out with her bayonet, but the blade bounced off the banshee's armor.

Talons rammed into her chest, piercing her heart. The banshee raised her in the air until Torni went limp then it dropped her to the ground. Torni's blood dripped from the talons as the banshees moved on, leaving a red trail through the blowing dust.

CHAPTER 14

Durand watched as the electric onslaught from the *Breitenfeld*'s Q-shell died away from the Xaros drones. Disabled drones floated in space, their stalks twitching.

"All right everyone, you know the mission," she said to her combined Dotok and human fighter pilots. "Kill every drone you can and keep any that reactivate off the Mule. Glue, you and your gals get torps in those *Canticle*-class starships. Good hunting."

She redlined her engines and was the first to the drones. The Gatling gun on her Eagle went to work, blowing drones to disintegrating chunks. She looped around and found an easy target.

Gauss shots zipped over her canopy and blew the drone away. A Dotok fighter flashed overhead. She'd bet her last cigarette that was Bar'en.

"Show off," she muttered.

"Torps away!" Glue announced.

Durand inverted her fighter and saw the burning engines of point-detonating torpedoes streaking toward one of the big ships. The torpedoes looked like a fly charging a bull elephant, but the Dotok had told Glue exactly where to strike the generation ships. An explosion in just the right spot should knock its engines out of commission. They didn't need to destroy those ships; they just needed the drones to think that was their target—anything to keep them away from the Mule and Lafayette's bomb.

Durand returned to the task at hand and watched as the drone she had in her sights came to life and slipped past her bullets.

"Hurry, Lafayette," Durand said.

****

Elias' gauss cannons blew a drone to pieces. Shells ricocheted down the passageway that the drone had almost made it through. A stalk tip, glowing red with energy, popped around the edge and fired a pencil-thin disintegration beam at Elias. He ducked behind his shield and the beam diffused against the surface.

Kallen snapped off a single shot and blew the stalk apart.

Elias charged toward the open door, his upper body protected by his shield. His right hand retracted into its forearm casing and a pneumatic spike took its place. Originally meant to pierce the inner tanks of enemy armor, the spikes had proved adept at cracking drone shells.

A new stalk tip folded around the doorway.

Elias bashed the edge of his shield against the stalk, using the edge of the doorway to sheer the point away. He swung his spike into an uppercut and impaled the drone hiding above the doorway.

The tip penetrated the drone's shell and Elias felt it struggle against his weapon like a fish caught on a line.

He yanked the drone off the ceiling and stomped its cracked body, crushing it into dissolving fragments.

Three more drones came into the long passageway, using their stalks to walk against the deck like giant arachnids. Elias fired off a burst and sidestepped the blasts of energy the drones sent back.

"Lafayette," Elias said, "how much longer?"

"Another minute," the Karigole said from behind Kallen and her shield. "Maybe two. The implosion device was damaged when I—"

"Don't. Care. Two minutes," Elias said as he replaced his spike for his armor's hand and leaned into the hallway…and didn't see any drones. "What the…"

"Elias!" he turned at Kallen's warning. The armor floating above the plinth glowed from within. A ragged column of light roared up from the plinth and into the armor, overwhelming Elias' optics with a torrent of light.

The General stepped from the plinth and raised an ethereal hand to Kallen. A beam of red light as thick as a tree trunk lanced out and struck Kallen's shield, blasting her back into the bulkhead so hard her armor cracked.

Elias fired a double shot from his forearm cannons. The bullets flashed against an energy barrier around the General and vanished in a puff of smoke. The General turned its face toward Elias and casually swung its hand toward the Iron Heart.

Elias grabbed the edge of his banshee armor shield and hurled it at the General's arm. The shield caught the brunt of an energy lance. It sprang away from the general like it had been struck by a bat and shattered against the deck.

The distraction was brief, but it was all Elias needed to close the distance. He leaped at the General and brought an armored fist down with an overhand strike. He connected with the General's helm. For all the force he could muster, the blow only managed to turn the General's head aside. Elias twisted his body into the follow-on strike, snapping his spike out mid-blow. The spike deflected off an armor plate and embedded inside the General's body.

A trill rose in the command center as the General lashed out at Elias, knocking a dent against Elias' spike arm. The armor blackened and smoked at the General's touch.

Elias wrapped a hand around the General's face-plate, his fingers sizzling and melting.

"This is for Earth!"

Elias ripped the face-plate from the rest of the armor. A flood of light erupted from the headless armor. The General's arms rose, trying to contain the light as it stumbled back to the plinth. The armor crashed into the plinth and white light spilled into it like water tossed from a bucket.

The armor plates clattered to the deck.

Elias kicked the armor plates, scattering them across the room.

"Kallen?"

"Yeah, that hurt," she said, pushing herself off the deck. Her right arm hung limp from the elbow actuator, the forearm split open and smoking. She detached the broken armor and tossed it aside. "Did you kill it?" she asked, pointing her stump at the General's loose armor plates.

Elias looked down at the face-plate fused into his damaged hand.

"Not sure…Lafayette?"

"I don't know what that was either, much less if it's deceased," Lafayette said. "But the bomb is set and we should leave. Now."

Kallen and Elias activated their cutting torches.

****

Durand's head snapped back as she watched three Dotok fighters race overhead, all on a vector toward a *Canticle* –class ship, not towards the Mule that was blasting off the surface of the proto-Crucible.

"I said abort your attack runs! Pull back to

the package and get ready to break contact!"
Durand shouted into the IR.

"If we can destroy the Xaros infecting the
ship," Bar'en said, "maybe we can bring it with us
to—"

"Not our mission! Cover the extraction. Get
back to the *Breitenfeld*. That's all we're here to do,"
Durand said. She caught a glimpse of a drone from
the corner of her eye and made an inverted dive just
in time to dodge a blast of red energy.

"Got one on me!" Durand's Eagle slalomed
from side to side as she dove toward the Crucible.
She flinched as a Xaros beam singed her cockpit.

The Mule with Lafayette and the Iron Hearts
rose up from the half-complete surface, heading
directly into a mob of drones. She hit a button on
her fire control panel and charged up her only Q-
shell.

"Good a time as any," she muttered, and
pulled the trigger.

A silver arrow of light connected to the mob
of drones, electricity connecting them all in a

spider's web of lightning. Durand steered her ship for the mass of disabled drones and a tendril of energy leaped out and stabbed into her ship.

Electric panels shorted out as her engines coughed and died. She looked back for the drone pursuing her and saw it suffer the same fate as her, but the pursuer collided with the rest of the drones, knocking them apart like a cue ball into a rack of billiards.

"Glue? Anyone?" There was no answer from Durand's dead IR.

She pressed against the back of her seat and grabbed the yellow and black handles of her ejection-seat controls. She closed her eyes and steeled her body for the ugly kick that came with punching out of a fighter jet.

Her hands squeezed white-knuckle tight…then relaxed. There was no Search-and-Rescue craft that could pick her up. There was no way back to the ship if her Eagle was out of the fight. Bile rose in her throat as she realized her fate. She found some peace in the inevitable.

The Mule with the bomb team soared away on pillars of light from its overworked engines. It couldn't come for her, not it if wanted to make it back to the ship.

"This is Gall. If anyone can read this, return to the *Breitenfeld*. Do not stop for anything," she said. Sparks snapped beneath her communication panel.

"If I'm going to die out here, I'll do it in my Eagle," she said.

She kept her eyes on the Crucible, waiting to see if this mission had all been in vain. Space around the command dome blurred, then the Crucible collapsed against the dome, like the hand of some great and ancient celestial being had reached out and squeezed the Crucible until it cracked from the pressure.

She felt a brief pull toward the station, then the weightlessness of the void returned.

"Good job, Lafayette."

A shadow crossed over her cockpit. She looked up, ready to stare at the drone that had come for her.

Instead, she saw the cockpit of a Condor bomber. The Ma cousins waved to her from the triple cockpit. Durand waved them off, pointing back toward the *Breitenfeld.*

The Condor rotated on its axis, the underside of the bomber now above Durand's head. A torpedo bay opened. The bay was empty…and just big enough for her.

"Here goes nothing." Durand found a red handle on the base of her canopy and pulled it open. The glass dome popped off, and she pushed it aside, sending it tumbling into the void. The Condor was almost fifty feet away, plenty of distance for her to miscalculate.

She unsnapped her restraints and crouched on her seat, then pushed off and launched into open space. Her ankle caught against an armrest and sent her tumbling. Her arms flailed as she went end over end, catching sight of the approaching Condor with each rotation.

Her feet and shins hit the Condor. She

twisted and grabbed for the open bay door, her finger-tips slid against the exposed wiring and circuitry as her momentum dragged her across the surface of the Condor.

"No!" she screamed as she slid free and into the void.

A hand grabbed her wrist.

Glue had one hand on Durand, while the other held on to Filly in the Condor's open cockpit. Glue nodded to her slowly, then gave her hand a jerk. Durand floated back toward the Condor. She got a grip on the edge of the open bay doors, then maneuvered into the empty space. She braced herself against the sides and slammed an elbow against the plane twice.

The bay doors closed, trapping Durand in a dark abyss.

****

The *Canticle of Reason* hung in space ahead of the *Breitenfeld*. Puffs of atmosphere jetted from the seals between old hull plating. It loomed over the human carrier like a whale over a diver.

"Christ, that's a big ship," Valdar said. "Engineering, are you done prepping the jump engines?"

"Captain, three of the compromised ships are coming over the horizon," the XO said. "They're on an intercept course with us…ETA is seven minutes."

"Nothing's ever easy, is it?" Valdar mused. "Engineering, status report."

"That Crucible is still close enough to affect our wormhole. We can leave, but the power drain on the engines will be significant," Levin said over the IR.

"Engage the jump engines. We wait for a perfect solution and we'll be a ring of debris around the planet," Valdar said.

"Aye aye, skipper. Two minutes."

Valdar tapped a button to open a channel to the *Canticle of Reason*. "Pa'lon, we're two minutes from jumping out. Might be a little late to ask this, but is your ship going to hold up?"

"This is Wen'la, life support is stable. But we'll need the MacDougall as soon as you can spare him. What is it you humans are always saying to each other for good fortune?"

"Gott mitt uns,"

"Cod mittens to you too."

Valdar closed the channel with a shake of his head. He felt vibrations through his command chair and prayed that once, just once, that engines would do what they were supposed to do. He opened a ship-wide channel.

"This is Captain Valdar. Prepare to jump."

****

Medics ran to the Condor bomber, carrying a stretcher between them.

"Move! Move!" the lead medic shouted to the scrum of pilots and deck hands gathering around the Condor. A path cleared, but there was no sign of the patient they'd been promised.

"The bay doors are stuck!" Filly shouted from the open cockpit.

A mechanic ducked under the Condor and jammed a speeder handle into a port. The torpedo bay doors opened excruciatingly slowly as the mechanic worked the tool. The doors opened perpendicular to the bay…but nothing came out.

"Did you open the right one?" a mechanic asked.

Durand fell out of the bay and flopped against the flight deck. She rolled onto her back and took off her helmet. Sweat soaked hair clung to her face.

"Gall, are you alright?" Glue asked, reaching for her commander.

Durand slapped her hands away.

"Thanks for the pick-up. Did everyone make it back?" Durand asked.

"Yes, ma'am," Glue said.

"Then give me a goddamned cigarette."

Cheers broke out across the flight deck.

"All hands brace for jump engine activation!" sounded across the flight deck. "All hands brace for jump engine activation!"

CHAPTER 15

The shuttle bays on the *Canticle of Reason* relied on massive doors to regulate air pressure and atmosphere, unlike the force fields the *Breitenfeld* had upgraded to in recent months. A Mule flew into the bay and settled against the deck without a sound in the total vacuum.

It took five minutes to pump atmosphere into the bay. Green lights blinked around the bay, then went steady.

Dotok, wearing nothing but their simple robes, came into the bay. Two bore clipboards, the rest carried plastic-wrapped packages. One Dotok waved to Jorgen, and he lowered the Mule's ramp.

The last of the Dotok evacuated from the mesa filed down the ramp. The shell-shocked survivors glanced around the spacecraft, then went to the welcoming party.

Standish helped the young mother with her newborn clutched to her chest down the ramp, her feet wrapped in bandages.

"Nice ship you've got here," Standish said to her. He looked around, noting that everything looked worn, recycled.

"Noor!" Un'qu ran into the bay and hugged the young mother, who broke into tears and a blubbery recount of her tale. The baby broke into a ragged cry and Un'qu held it in his arms. The Dotok officer gave Standish a nod and led his family away.

"Well, that's something," Standish said. He sat down on the ramp and watched as the Dotok took care of the refugees. He ran a hand over the dried sweat and grime on the top of his head, then took a long hard look at the dried blood on his gloves and forearms. He'd helped the medics get Hale and Bailey off their transport after it made it to the *Breitenfeld*. He hadn't heard a word about them in the hour since. No word about Cortaro, Orozco or Steuben. For all he knew, he was the last man standing. The only person he was sure about was Torni. He'd seen the banshees charging up the mountain. There was no chance she'd survived.

Jorgen sat next to Standish and handed him a canteen.

"Shitty day," the pilot said.

"At least it's over, right?"

"Nothing on the scanners. This system's got a couple rocks in it, not a lot else. No Xaros. No gates. Nice and quiet for a while," Jorgen said. "We'll head back once they clear out." Jorgen gave Standish a pat on the shoulder and went back inside.

"Standish?" a little voice said.

Caas and Ar'ri stood beside the ramp, hand in hand. They wore new clothes and looked like they'd been cleaned up since the last time he saw them.

"Caas and Annie, right?"

"Ar'ri!" the little boy piped up.

384

"Where is Sarge Torni? She said she'd come see us," Caas said.

Standish felt like someone punched him in the gut.

"Oh…um…" Standish got off the ramp and knelt in front of the two children. "Torni…she's…" He pressed two fingers against his lips. "*Ehtan.* She's dead, little guys. *Ehtan.*"

Caas' lips trembled. Her chin fell against her chest and she started sobbing.

Standish wrapped his arms around them and pulled them close.

****

Stacey rematerialized on Bastion. She staggered to a wall, breathing heavily. The white squares of the transit room never looked so welcoming.

"Chuck, is it me, or did that trip take a hell of a lot longer than it should have?" she asked the station's AI.

"Welcome back, Stacey Ibarra. Due to an

unanticipated gate usage, the system had to keep you in queue until the platform was reset and prepared for your arrival," came from the ceiling.

"I must have been in transit for…twenty hours!"

"Eighteen hours and thirty-seven minutes. Did you experience discomfort?"

"'Discomfort?' I thought I was going to spend the rest of eternity floating through a white abyss with no hope of rescue." Stacey stood up and recomposed herself. "My return was scheduled. This sort of thing isn't supposed to happen. Explain."

"Ambassador Pa'lon signaled an emergency gate travel. We regret any discomfort you may have experienced," the AI said.

"He's back? Where is he?"

"Pa'lon is in the atrium. Would you like me to connect you?"

"No, I'll go see him in person." The doors slid aside and Stacey strode out into Bastion. Representatives of the many species present on the station appeared to her as unique human beings. Some chatted amidst the hallways, others passed her by with nary a second glance or bit of attention. The station maintained a hologram around each ambassador displaying each as a member of an observer's own species—all in the effort of cooperation.

The atrium held a small forest of pale white trees, their tall boughs draped through the space forming covered walkways. The trees glowed from within, casting sterile light that made Stacey think of the white hell she'd just gone through.

The nature and origin of the trees was a mystery. Chuck and other AIs claimed not to have the information. Most suspected that the trees were some sort of remnant of the Qa'Resh's home world. The leaders of the Alliance were notoriously secretive and if the trees were connected to the giant floating crystal entities, it would be something they'd keep hidden.

Pa'lon sat on a bench in the middle of a small clearing, his shoulders low and his head in his hands.

"Pa'lon?" Stacey asked. She reached out to touch his shoulder. Her hand stopped several inches from him and a buzzer sounded.

"Contact not authorized," the AI said.

Pa'lon's head jerked up, ending whatever reverie he'd been in. "Stacey, my girl, so good to see you again." He was as young as she'd remembered him, but he looked as though the weight of many worlds rested on his shoulders.

"What's going on? Did the *Breitenfeld* make it to Takeni? Don't keep me in suspense," she sat next to him on the bench.

Pa'lon told her of the *Breitenfeld*'s arrival and everything that happened up until he had to leave Takeni, leaving his people behind.

"They'll make it, Pa'lon. Valdar's tough and smart. If there's anyone who can find a way, or make a way, it's him," Stacey said.

"I know, I was most impressed with him and the rest of the humans. I have some hope left," Pa'lon sank back against the bench.

"You're acting like things are a lot worse than they really are."

"When I returned, I went to the cartography lab and ran some simulations. The Grand Fleet was likely overrun by only a few drones. Given when the fleet must have been compromised and the time it took to reach Takeni…the AI think that *all* our fleets have been destroyed or corrupted. The Grand Fleet knew every planet we were going to colonize. Transmitting that information to drones in neighboring star systems would be too easy," Pa'lon said.

"You don't know that for sure," Stacey said.

"No, but the math is not in our favor. We won't know for centuries if the other fleets made it to their chosen planets, or if the Xaros are there waiting for them in force. That is a long time to wait to know if your species is extinct," he said. "There's a part of Bastion just for ambassadors who've lost everything. They're not allowed to interact with the rest of us. They have nothing else to contribute to the war. No vote at assembly. I wonder what it's like there…"

"You know, I'm probably closer to that fate than you are. Xaros are a little over a decade away from Earth. We lose that fight and I've got nothing. Do you see me having a pity party?"

"No, not at all. If I am morose, I apologize. My hopes for the Dotok to spread across the stars and contribute more to this war…have been turned to ashes. How would you suggest I take it?"

"You have hope. Your people will get off Takeni and they'll make it to Earth. Just a little hope is enough to get me through the day," she said.

"I never knew humans could be so wise until I met you—or so ugly when I saw the rest of you up close. Though that one you always talk about, Hale, he seemed less ugly than the rest." Pa'lon sat up and took a deep breath of the pollinated air around them.

"You didn't say anything to him about me, did you?"

"No, should I have?"

"No! In fact, never mention me to him. Unless he asks about me. Did he?"

"Our conversations revolved around survival and killing *noorla*. Your behavior becomes remarkably different when Hale is mentioned. Can you explain this to me?"

Stacey frowned and shook her head. "Nope. Nothing to explain. I'm glad you made it back to Bastion."

"And I am glad to see you again. Thank you for your help saving my people."

"Moving furniture, dinner parties, saving each other from genocide. That's what friends are for."

CHAPTER 16

Hale felt too cool air fill his lungs. He groaned and rubbed at his eyes, knocking a breathing tube loose from his nose. His tongue felt like sandpaper against his mouth and his body felt like glaciers of pain were grinding across his every joint and muscle.

"Sir, you awake?" He knew that voice, but the fuzziness in his head wouldn't let him connect to a name. "I'll tell the doc you're up."

He held a hand in front of his face; the skin was leathery and dry as parchment.

Dr. Accorso leaned over him and waved a wand across Hale's forehead. "Ah, awake at last? I knew the last round of treatment would beat that thing." The bed beneath Hale tilted his head and chest upwards. Hale was in a hospital ward, one with biohazard markers against the walls.

A nurse shoved a spoon full of ice chips into Hale's mouth. He was too thirsty and weak to protest the indignity.

"You caught a very nasty infection on Takeni, something your green blood cell immune boosters couldn't handle," Accorso said. "Might have been something on the talons of that banshee that got a piece of you. Maybe something you ate? Any intimate contact with the Dotok?"

Hale just looked at Accorso, too tired to speak. He got another mouthful of ice chips.

"Regardless, it drove your natural immune system haywire. Really amazing reaction, we'll be studying your blood samples for years. Had to keep you in isolation so you didn't infect the rest of the ship. I tried flooding your system with more green blood cells, but that had negligible effects. I finally gave you a dose of nano-bot scrubbers...which cleared out the infection, all your green blood cells and a dangerous amount of your body's hydration. We'll get you on some wonderful IV's and have you up on your feet in no time." The doctor gave him a pat on the shoulder and left the room.

"No, he never shuts up," the medic said with the same familiar voice he knew. Hale squinted at the medic and finally recognized Yarrow.

"What…what happened?" Hale croaked.

"We got hit by our own grenade. Messed you, me and Bailey up pretty good, but nothing serious. Got off world and back to the *Breit* and now we're in orbit around some brown dwarf in the low-rent district of the galaxy, waiting for the engines to recharge. Should be another ten days until we can get back to Earth…supposedly. Open up, sir, you've got to eat the rest of this ice," Yarrow mashed a spoonful against Hale's closed lips.

Hale grabbed the spoon and tried to feed himself. The spoon glanced off his nose and sent ice chips down his hospital gown.

"You were pretty touch and go for a while, sir," Yarrow took the spoon back. "I'll tell the others you came up strong as an ox, full of piss and vinegar."

A corpsman wheeled in a metal stand with several clear IV bags on it.

"I'll get him hooked up," Yarrow said to the new arrival, who left without a word.

"Where's…everyone? We get the Dotok out?"

"*Canticle*'s full to the brim and holding steady. Those Dotok know how to make a spaceship," Yarrow said, careful not to look directly at Hale when he spoke. He ran a tube from the fluid bags to an intravenous port on the back of Hale's left hand. Hale felt cold creep up his arm.

A plastic screen slid aside, revealing a grim-looking Captain Valdar holding a folder.

"Give us a couple minutes, son," he said to Yarrow, who left with a nod to Hale.

Valdar sat down next to Hale and watched as Yarrow left the room.

"You trust him?" Valdar asked.

"Of course, why wouldn't I?"

Valdar shrugged at his question

Hale cringed as the cold from the IV crept through aching muscles. Hale regarded the captain, a man he'd known since childhood. The captain wasn't acting like the Uncle Isaac that Hale knew. Valdar's face was emotionless, solid, the mask of command officers learned to adopt early in their careers.

"Just tell me," Hale said.

"Sergeant Torni stayed behind. The Mule didn't have the life support for the last of the civilians. She gave up her spot so more could make it out," Valdar said.

"We'll go back. She's a fighter, trained to survive behind enemy lines," Hale said.

"No, son, she's dead." Valdar opened the folder and handed a photo to Hale. An orbital picture of the mesa showed a dozen Dotok lying in the dirt. Torni's armored body was on her side. Blood stained the ground beneath her.

"It should have been me," Hale said. "If I hadn't been hit…it should have been me."

"It wasn't you, Ken. We've all…lost so much." Valdar's countenance cracked for a split second, giving Hale a glimpse at the pain Valdar hid from everyone. Valdar cleared his throat. "I'll write up a posthumous award, handle the rest of the paperwork. Get back on your feet when you're ready. This fight's far from over and I need you leading Marines."

Valdar tried to take the photo back, but Hale refused to let it go. The captain left without another word.

Hale stared at the picture for a long time. There were tears, but none he could ever admit.

****

The armory was quiet. Racks of rifles and all the Marine's weapons of war had been cleaned, accounted for and stored since the *Breitenfeld* left Takeni's orbit. Even though there was no such thing as night and day aboard a starship, the crew and

Marines still stuck to a twenty-four-hour cycle. This close to "midnight" there shouldn't be anyone in the armory.

Hale looked over the room, failing to note anything out of place or in need of cleaning. *Good,* he thought, *Cortaro's been keeping them busy. Focused on their jobs.* The sound of laughter bled through one of the storage bays.

Hale went to the door and raised his hand to knock, then grabbed the handle and yanked the door open with the little strength he had in his body.

His Marines and Steuben were there, sitting on ammo boxes arrayed in a circle.

"Sir! Knew you'd come looking for us eventually," Standish said.

Square patches of pale skin dotted Bailey's face and exposed arms, cloned grafts that would look more natural in time. Orozco's right hand was missing two fingers.

"What are you all doing here? You two all right?" he asked the recovering Marines.

"Still got my trigger finger," Orozco said.

"Robo-doc patched me up just fine," Bailey said.

"You look…you've looked better," Standish said.

"I feel like a hammered can of shit," Hale said and sat down on an ammo box.

"Took the words out of my mouth," Standish said.

Chuckles filled the space.

"You missed the memorial ceremony for her," Yarrow said, not willing to say Torni's name. "Captain decided to have one big ceremony for everyone we lost. Get it all over and done with. Chaplain Krohe…said a little extra about her. Did a good job."

"I understand," Steuben said, "that your warrior tradition will offer a toast to the departed."

"Yes, Steuben, that would be appropriate," Hale said. "Have to wait until we get back to Phoenix for that, though."

"Oh, what's this?" Standish reached behind his seat and picked up a clear bottle. "I seem to have found a bottle of vodka. Absolut, Torni's favorite."

"'Found'?" Hale asked, giving Cortaro a sideways glance. The gunnery sergeant feigned innocence and shrugged his shoulders. Cortaro scratched at the join between his leg and the new prosthetic, complete with an articulated foot and ankle that had replaced the peg.

"Ask me no questions and I'll tell you no lies, sir," Standish said. He passed out paper cups from the mess hall and poured a shot for everyone. He hesitated when he got to Steuben.

"You OK with alcohol?" he asked the alien Karigole.

"I will experience some discomfort," Steuben said. He shook his cup and Standish obliged.

Hale waited for Standish to take his seat. The lieutenant rubbed his fingers against the cup, searching for the right words. He raised the cup to eye level.

"For Staff Sergeant Sofia Torni, one of the finest Marines I've had the honor to serve with. We are less without her," he said. The alcohol burned down his throat and did nothing to heal the pain in his heart.

****

Lieutenant Douglas watched with anticipation as a waitress carried a big plate of spaghetti and meatballs to his table. The sight and smell of a meal not made by a robot brought back memories of time before the war with Xaros, when he and his family would eat at a little pizza joint down the street from their home in upstate New York.

Vinny's hadn't been open for too long, and to get a table you had to know somebody who knew somebody and could vouch that you wouldn't let slip that the place existed to the general populace. The meals were free. Vinny kept the place open in memory of his family and to keep himself busy after his job processing methane from Titan's atmosphere never materialized. The pasta, calzones and a little bit of wine were gratis, but any "donations" of military gear were greatly appreciated…and a sure way to get invited back the next time the place opened.

Douglas had found an old set of armor plates used by the last generation of powered armor during a walk around the Kilauea forests. They'd held up remarkably well for being buried in mud for thirty years since the invasion, and Vinny seemed happy with them. Coming from R&R on Hawaii to a proper meal had done wonders for Douglas' morale.

"Hey, Ibarra's on TV," someone said, pointing to a screen mounted against a wall. "Turn it up."

Douglas took a bite and scooted his chair around so he could see the screen. His appetite threatened to flee as anxiety reared its ugly head. The last time he'd heard Ibarra speak had been right after that God-awful time shift that side-stepped the fleet out of the Xaros' path.

"Hello, Phoenix. This is Marc Ibarra." His hologram stood behind a podium, like he was the president about to announce a new war. Admiral

Garret was with him, standing off to the side. "There have been some changes since the last time I addressed you. For the better, all things considered. The Xaros were defeated, we reclaimed the Earth…Now things must change again. The Xaros will return. You all know that. But they will return in numbers far greater than we can defeat…as of now. Some of you have already figured that out.

"So, we can either all die or find a way to beat them. I didn't spend sixty years working on a way to save humanity just to throw my hands up when things looked bad. There is a solution. One that's already being implemented. New people, born of man and woman just like all of you, are here. They remember lives from before the invasion, just as you do. They have jobs and a purpose in our city, same as you. They will fight to save us all.

"But they aren't like you, exactly. Their bodies were grown. Their minds are the product of advanced simulation software. But they are human…as human as we can make them. As for souls…that's beyond my ability to influence.

"There are many procedurally generated humans listening to me right now, and not one of them thinks they are any different from the true-born." Ibarra looked hard into the camera. "Just like you."

"Many more will join us in the coming months and years. Don't bother trying to find a way to discover them. Knowing who is and who isn't true born is a waste of time and energy. Let me be clear; there is no future without them. Go about your lives and your duties. We still have a war to win."

The screen returned to a football rerun.

Low conversation broke out through the restaurant. Patrons pointed at each other, swapping stories from before the jump, confirming shared stories about people they'd all known for years. Douglas, sitting alone, felt a sudden urge to leave.

He stood up and made for the door. A very angry-looking Vinny, holding a sawed-off shotgun, got in his way.

"Hold up," Vinny said. "Where you going to

so fast after Ibarra's little public service announcement?"

"I have a platoon of soldiers that're probably going crazy right now. I should get back to the barracks and get things under control," Douglas said.

"Don't seem like we've got things under control here," Vinny said. "Does it, boys?"

Rough hands grabbed him from behind and slammed him against a table. A hand the size of a dinner plate against his neck pinned him against a red-and-white checkered table-cloth. More hands held his shoulders and arms down. He struggled uselessly, devoid of any leverage or ability to strike out.

"See, Clyde and Frank here both know me from the old neighborhood," Vinny said. "I know I'm not some sort of procedure-something-or-another freak. I know they ain't that. They know I ain't that. Who knows *you* ain't one of them?" Vinny put the shotgun on the table, the barrels pointed straight into Douglas' eyes.

"My platoon, I've been with them for almost a year. Way before the jump," Douglas said. Sweat broke out across his body as he looked into the twin dark pits.

"That good enough for you, boys?" Vinny asked.

"No, Mr. Vinny," the one with a hand to his neck said.

"My brother! Call my brother, name's Robert. He's on my cell," Douglas said. A hand went into his pocket and tossed the device to Vinny, a cheap device that couldn't do anything but text and call.

Vinny flipped it open and hit a few buttons. Long seconds ticked by as it rang.

"Yeah, hi," Vinny said. "I found this Ubi down around 4th and Baseline. You know who it belongs to, recognize the number? Yeah. What's he look like? Military guy with short hair? That's most of the city. Tell me a little something only he'd know and I think I can get it back to him. Thanks, bud." Vinny closed the phone.

"What was the name of the dog you two got for Christmas?" Vinny asked, his hand on the shotgun.

"Gizmo! Little mutt my dad picked up off the side of the street," Douglas said.

"Let him go, boys," Vinny said.

Douglas faced off against the two men. Both had sheepish expressions on their face.

"Sam, I apologize," Vinny said, putting an arm across Douglas' shoulders and shaking his hand. "Look, this whole alien invasion crap's got me thrown off my game. Then Ibarra gets up and starts telling me there are a bunch of fakes walking around. I overreacted."

Douglas looked back at the shotgun still on the table.

"Now I wasn't going to...probably not," Vinny said. "Look, you eat here for free from now on. No reservations, no donations. We good?"

Douglas nodded and went for the door again.

"Hey, bring your brother next time. He

sounds legit," Vinny said as Douglas left the restaurant.

His cell started ringing, a call from his commander. He put the phone to his ear and saw the orange glow of fires in the distance. Phoenix was burning.

CHAPTER 17

The command deck of Titan Station was managed chaos. The crew, all on no more than five hour shifts, managed orbital traffic control for the entire planet, the docks surrounding the outer hull of the station still working to repair the last few ships damaged in the assault on the Crucible and the many cargo shuttles coming in and out of the station.

Overseeing the nonstop activity was Colonel Mitchell, one of the few Atlantic Union Aerospace officers in the fleet. He'd been brought on to manage Titan Station, he'd thought to do the job over Saturn's moon of the same name, not Earth.

He poured a cup of coffee from an archaic machine that still dripped hot water through grounds, and took in a deep breath of the aroma. Kona. The world's finest coffee, in his opinion, had survived many decades without human cultivation. The beans grown in the Hawaiian Island's volcanic soil were re-discovered by some Ibarra Corporation workers during the construction of an R&R facility. It took only a few cultivation robots to set up a steady supply of the coffee, much to Mitchell's delight.

The colonel brought the cup to his lips.

"Gate function!"

The shout sent hot coffee down the front of his uniform and over his hands, scalding him.

"Set analog condition amber. Ready the kill switch," Mitchell said, shaking his hands dry. If the Xaros were coming through, they'd compromise every computer system on Earth and in orbit within seconds. The alien probe sitting at the Crucible's command center swore the Xaros couldn't access the gate, but it never hurt to be cautious.

"Show me," Mitchell said. Camera feed popped up on monitors around his chair. A white field spread from the center of the Crucible, growing out of the center and almost touching the great spikes making up the crown of thorns that was the alien jump gate.

Mitchell flipped a plastic safety cover off the kill switch for the station's automation and waited.

The prow of a strike carrier emerged from the field and the *Breitenfeld* flew into real space.

"She's back!" came from the crew. Clapping and cheers broke out across the command center.

Mitchell closed the kill switch, then frowned as the wormhole remained open. The *Canticle of Reason* followed the *Breitenfeld*, emerging like a leviathan from the deep ocean.

"That's...unexpected," Mitchell said.

"Sir, do we launch the ready fighters?" a crewman asked.

"Message from the *Breitenfeld,* they're telling us to relax. The big ship's friendly," the commo officer said.

Mitchell pointed a finger at the communications officer. "Get Admiral Garret on the line. Now."

****

Valdar followed his escorts through the bunker, newly built beneath the Camelback Mountains just northeast of Phoenix. Staff officers bustled around Valdar with an air of excitement and purpose that Valdar hadn't seen in someplace so drab and soul-sucking as a high-level command. The atmosphere in the bunker was almost like there was a war brewing.

A soldier in combat armor and almost seven feet tall stood outside Admiral Garret's office. A visor covered the sentry's face and there was no name stenciled on his armor.

"What've they been feeding you?" Valdar asked the giant.

"Sir," replied a gravelly voice.

"Isaac, get in here," Admiral Garret yelled

through his open door. The admiral's office had the wide, solid oak desk Valdar remembered from Garret's old office at the naval base in Norfolk, Virginia. Framed flags and guidons from Garret's long career filled the walls, along with a diploma from the Academy in Maryland.

Valdar wondered how much was a recreation and what was original. His money was on the former; rank had its privileges.

An aide closed the door behind them.

"Sit, Isaac," Garret said, waving at a leather chair. "I suppose I should chew your ass for taking a little detour on your way back from Anthalas. But you came back with much more than we'd hoped for, and I don't mean the stray ship that followed you home."

"Sir, I had to—"

"Stow it. What's done is done and we've got bigger problems to worry about than your adherence to orders or lack thereof. Now, you said you have something for my eyes only? Something you left out of your official report?"

Valdar opened a briefcase and took out the General's face-plate, five indentations against the edges from where Elias had warped the material. Valdar tossed it on the desk; it made no noise as it came to rest.

Garret touched it with a fingertip then picked up the face-plate.

"This is from the entity your armor encountered, I assume. It doesn't weigh an ounce," Garret said. "This is the face of our enemy. Why can't I share this with everyone? Morale will go through the roof."

"That's a trophy. This is what I had to talk to you about in person." Valdar set a folder on the table and pushed it to the admiral. Garret flipped through medical tests and personnel bio-sheets.

"Some of my crew are…unnatural. Their bodies are fully grown, but immature, only a few months old. For all the digging my counter intelligence officers have been able to do, none of them know what they are or even suspect they're any different from you or I. I believe they're sleeper agents or spies snuck onto my crew by Ibarra. He's the only one with the resources and know-how to get this done. I don't know his purpose."

Garret thumbed through the papers, then swept it all into a waste bin.

"Yes, I know."

"You—what?"

"We call them proccies. Procedurally generated consciousness installed on vat-grown bodies. I found out about them after you left for Anthalas, I wouldn't have let Ibarra conduct his field experiments during a mission as vital as yours. But that bastard doesn't have the best track record with honesty. He's getting better.

"Your ship's been on a communications black-out since you got back. I thought you might have figured something out with the proccies, and I couldn't let something beyond the official narrative slip out from you or your crew."

"Sir, explain to me why these…abominations are on my ship. They're soulless *things* masquerading as human beings."

Garret held up a hand. "You aren't the only one that has an issue with them. It comes down to survival, Isaac. When you left for Anthalas, the fleet we had, or could have built, wouldn't even register as a speed bump to the Xaros when they return. We bought time when we took the Crucible, just not enough. Ibarra offered a solution. The only one that might see us to daylight."

"At what cost? He'll replace every one of us with these things and humanity will still be as extinct. We'll be gone and have sold our souls for these fakes to inherit the Earth?"

"You make the same argument I've heard in this office from many, many other people. The decision comes down to what *might* happen in the future, and the threat we *will* face in the next decade. Everyone is struggling with this right now. True born and proccies, not that any of the proccies know what they truly are."

"There are more than just the ones on my ship?"

"Many, many more Isaac. I don't even know

where to start with the doughboys. Look," Garret took an Ubi slate from his desk and swiped across the surface. A picture of a human carrier battle group floating in space above the moon came up. "That's the *Midway*, big girl's back in service. Also two strike carriers the same class as your ship, cruisers, frigates, destroyers, tenders…the whole nine yards. Almost every man and woman in that battle group is a proccie. Good thing we've got them, otherwise we'd all be dead."

"I don't follow. The Xaros are a long way off. We've got time to figure out another solution than this," Valdar said.

"We don't. The proccies could be our long-term salvation, but they're also the cause of our current crisis." Garret brought out another Ubi slate, the casing painted with alternating red and white lines, one meant for classified material. "This is top secret. What you see doesn't leave the room."

Garret set the slate on his desk and rotated it to Valdar. On the screen, dozens of almond-shaped ships the color of polished sea-shells floated above

Neptune. Jagged weapons like broken icicles protruded from the ship's hulls. Ships Valdar recognized.

"The Toth are here, Isaac. They are here, and they want to negotiate."

EPILOGUE

Caas held Ar'ri's hand as the Mule struggled through turbulence. Ar'ri whimpered, keeping his head buried against his older sister's shoulder.

"We're almost there. Look, you can see clouds outside the windows," Caas said. Ar'ri shook his head. "You remember what the nice humans said. Big sky. Plenty of food. No *noorla* anywhere on their nice planet. We have a new home now."

Ar'ri didn't seem interested.

Caas watched as puffy white clouds streaked past the windows, leaving streaks of rainwater on the glass. There were a few other Dotok on the Mule with her; mostly kids her age, all of them orphans just like her. She figured out that her parents were dead once they'd left Takeni. Ar'ri didn't seem to understand when she told him that their mother and father would never come home again.

"Hold on, we're about to land!" a human called out. Ar'ri dug his fingers into Caas' arm as the engines grew louder. The Mule settled against a landing pad and the engines wound down.

"OK everyone," a Marine stood up at the end of the cargo bay. "Remember what I told you. Follow Sergeant Bailey and walk in a line straight to the big round building."

"Mr. Standy," a Dotok girl waved to him, "how long will we stay here?"

"For as long as you want. Maybe you'll all decide to live someplace else. Plenty of room on the planet."

"Mr. Standy, what kind of food will there be?" the same girl asked.

"Look, sweetie, I just work here. I'm sure the chow is better than all those ration packs you've been eating. We all ready to see your new home?" The children looked at him with wide eyes.

"Not the enthusiasm I was hoping for." He banged a fist twist against the ramp and it descended with a pneumatic whine.

Light flooded into the cargo bay. Caas saw a pale yellow sun rising over the horizon. Tall trees with wide palms swayed in a breeze that blew the freshest air she'd ever smelled into the Mule.

"Come on," Caas tugged at her brother, who refused to move or even look up. The rest of the children left the Mule, squeals of wonder and delight from them as they walked out into the sunlight.

"Ar'ri, they'll make us go *back*," Caas said.

Standish knelt in front of the Dotok children. "Hey, I remember you two. Want to come with me? This place is really nice. I promise."

Ar'ri looked up at the familiar voice. "I want Elias. Elias carry me."

"Elias isn't here, little guy. I'm not as big and strong as he is, but can I carry you?" Standish held his arms out. Ar'ri peeled away from his sister and latched onto Standish. The Marine took Caas by the hand.

"What's the name of this place?" she asked.

They walked down the ramp, Ar'ri's arms clutched around Standish's neck.

"We're in Hawaii, the island of Oahu," Standish said.

"What's that?" Caas pointed to the beach just beyond a line of palm trees.

"The beach? You've never—no, of course not. Want to go see it?" Standish asked them.

"Will we get in trouble?"

"No. Bailey won't yell at me too much. I'm her only source of quality whiskey." Standish changed direction and walked toward the ocean.

"What?"

"Nothing."

They got to the edge of the beach and Standish set Ar'ri down on the sand. The boy reached down and pressed his fingers into the sand.

"Is that…water?" Caas asked.

"Sure is. The Pacific Ocean. Let's go look." Standish hiked Ar'ri up on his hip and brought them to the edge of the water-logged sand where waves lapped up the shoreline. A wave came ashore with a whoosh, Caas ran back up the beach with a squeak of fright.

Standish put his hand in the water's path. The weakening edge of the wave splashed up to his wrist.

"It's OK. Promise," Standish said.

Caas kicked off her shoes and took a few tentative steps past Standish and toward the ocean. A wave came in, carrying sea foam and loose sand around her ankles. Caas looked up at Standish, and smiled.

****

Windblown sand slithered across New Abhaile's roadways. Landed starships creaked in their cradles as the remnants of another dust storm moaned through the metal pylons propping them up from the swamps below.

Dead banshees and the remains of the city's defenders lay where they fell, blown sand accumulating against the windward side of the bodies like dunes in a deep desert. A bell clanged, its tempo driven by irregular gusts.

The General descended onto the city from the newly whole Crucible orbiting the planet. He floated above the path of corpses leading to the nexus, the last stand of the Smoking Snakes. The black bodies of dead banshees were strewn over the fallen suits. Cruz's fist stuck up from between the dead, as if in a final act of defiance.

With a wave of the General's hand, dead banshees scattered into the air like leaves caught in a sudden breeze.

Cruz's armor hinged at the waist. Its upper torso tore free of its waist and floated toward the General.

Not this one. The General sent Cruz' body hurtling down the roadway to where the *Crucible of Reason* had once stood. *Not the other one either.*

A suit of human armor, the one called Elias,

had hurt him. Damaged his corporeal shell and sent him retreating into the nexus lay lines. Never, in his long conquest across the galaxy, had an enemy managed to even touch him.

The humans had proven to be more than an anomaly; they were a threat. To an army accustomed to total victory at every battle, that the humans managed to slip away from defeat was infuriating. The General would accelerate the time-table for his forces' return to Earth. The longer they survived, the more of a threat they became to his, and the Master's, plans for this galaxy.

The General looked up at the swarm of drones circling over his head.

Cleanse this world. The General converted into a bolt of light and shot back to his Crucible. The drones descended on New Abhaile, stalks alive with burning tips to eradicate every last trace of the Dotok.

THE END

FROM THE AUTHOR

I hope you enjoyed Blood of Heroes enough to leave a review and tell two friends about the Ember War Saga. Sign up for my mailing list at www.richardfoxauthor.com for exclusive Ember War Saga short stories, spam free! As always, drop me a note at Richard.r.fox@outlook.com and let me know what you'd like to see in future novels.

CPSIA information can be obtained
at www.ICGtesting.com
Printed in the USA
LVHW09s1615040918
589109LV00001B/5/P